Twister

a novel

by

John Lantigua

SIMON & SCHUSTER

NEW YORK   LONDON   TORONTO

SYDNEY   TOKYO   SINGAPORE

SIMON & SCHUSTER
Simon & Schuster Building
Rockefeller Center
1230 Avenue of the Americas
New York, New York 10020

Designed by Marc Strang
Manufactured in the United States of America

10   9   8   7   6   5   4   3   2   1

Library of Congress Cataloging-in-Publication Data

Lantigua, John.
*   Twister : a novel / by John Lantigua.*
*   p.   cm.*
*   I. Title.*
* PS3562.A57T8   1992*
* 813'.54—dc20*

91-37189
CIP

ISBN: 0-671-73722-8

During the writing of this book there came a moment when the author needed a favor and, characteristically, Douglas Landon Tweedale was there to help. He died suddenly just a few months later, at the age of thirty-two. He was a friend, and this work is for him.

Chapter 1

*I*t was just 8 A.M. when attorney Sam Houston Cain, seventy-six years old, eased his silver Cadillac into the carport at his law offices in the town of Paradise. The sun was well up over the stunted skyline, a white blister, and gravel popped under his tires like hot oil in a skillet. It was heading for ninety already, and the rest of the day would be hell.

Cain tucked the car into its shaded space, grabbed his cowhide briefcase, got out, and locked the car door behind him. There had been a time when you didn't need to do that in the town, lock doors; a time when the municipality, although one of the rowdiest places on earth, had in that respect been safe. People had looked to get rich by plundering what was under the ground, namely oil. Others exploited their skills at the poker table, or, in the case of some "ladies," exercised their talents on cots in the back rooms of saloons. Drillers and roughnecks were no angels, that was for sure; there were brawls in the barrooms, shoot-outs in the streets, sin everywhere.

But this was to be expected. After all, Sodom and Go-morrah were oil towns. When the Bible talked about "pitch pits" near those places, that's what it meant: oil. Petroleum and sin went together and had, all through history. Still, locally, there had always been limits. People hadn't preyed on each other's private property, or on each other, as they did now. Not in Paradise, Texas. In that regard it had been innocent.

Sam Cain squinted at the deserted, sun-flooded streets. As for himself, he had never been innocent, which was why he had done so well.

Cain put down his briefcase, hitched his pants, adjusted his pearl-white Stetson hat and touched the string tie at his throat. He was a short, narrow-faced man, with dark eyes extremely small behind wire-rimmed glasses. He told folks God had given him those small peepers in order to read the miniature print on oil-exploration contracts. He'd been doing just that since the late nineteen thirties, when petroleum was first discovered in the county, not far from where he stood right then. Wildcatters had come, as if following a voice in the desert, and begun drilling holes in the local cattle ranches. From one day to the next, oil gushed out of the ground in geysers. Men stood and watched with their mouths open and their eyes shining, the oil raining on them. It was those first gushers, and the glow in men's eyes they had produced, that led to the naming of the town: Paradise. It was a form of idolatry, as some people said. That was true. But oil was no false idol. It had made a number of those men filthy rich. Along the way, Attorney Sam Cain, who looked after their inter-ests, both in negotiations with the oil companies and in the political backrooms of Paradise, had done very well him-self.

But now the old lawyer squinted at the town and scowled. Those boom times were over.

"Paradise is gone ta hell," he mumbled.

Cain went to the curb, picked up a folded copy of the local newspaper, straightened up slowly, and looked down the street. The town seemed dusty and abandoned as if it were in the path of an encroaching desert. Businesses were boarded up and windows whitewashed. It was like the Dust Bowl days. There had been busts before, plunges in the price of oil, but not this bad. Over the past few years, people had left town as if they were escaping the plagues. They had suffered not only unemployment, foreclosure, bankruptcy, but family strife, crime, and violence. Any day the locusts would descend and the streets would run with blood.

Cain's scowl deepened as he read the small print of the town's decline. All these troubles had occurred to a degree during busts in the past, but now there was a new ingredient added to the stew: drugs being dropped from smuggling planes out over the prairie. Heroin, cocaine, marijuana. Like manna from heaven, at least for the smugglers. Now that the oil business had dried up, that was the new get-rich-quick scheme in Paradise. It was contaminating the town, just as if someone had poisoned the well water. Robberies and break-ins were up, and gunplay too. Jack Eames, the county attorney, was investigating the local connections, and Sam Cain might have something to tell him. He knew more about it than he'd been willing to say, in public at least, but if it went on, he would, no matter who it damaged. That was for sure.

"The place is gone ta hell," Cain mumbled again.

He picked up his briefcase, went to the side door, jiggled a key in the lock, and let himself in. For a moment he thought he heard a noise inside. He stopped and listened, but now the place was dead quiet. His secretary wasn't due in until nine. He hung his Stetson on the hatrack, shuffled past her desk, past the old framed WANTED poster hanging on the wall of a scowling, grizzly-faced murderer who had never been caught, and into his own office. There sat a big wooden desk and on it the sun-bleached, polished skull of a jackass. It had been a gift, representing his political affiliation, and was also there to warn against fools.

Cain put down his briefcase and opened the copy of the Paradise *Chronicle* he had picked up. Across the front page was a big six-column headline:

High School Teacher Accused of Immorality
Church Group Demands Her Dismissal

He snorted in disgust. That was the other curse driving a once-healthy town into the ground: a large and growing group of citizens who claimed to be "the chosen people," "God's elect." They had made a financial downturn into an Apocalypse. Their leaders had an explanation for the bust; they said the Lord was punishing Paradise because it harbored sinners; with no mention of the fact that the town had been founded by sinners and built by them too. Now they were trying to drive this poor teacher out of the high school. They said she was an immoral woman, a Jezebel. They were attacking her professionally and tearing at her personal life, hurling fire and brimstone at her. It was as if they were getting geared up for a lynching.

He threw the paper down and then he heard a noise. He went to the door and looked out. There was nothing there, just the empty office. Cain was getting old, too old—hearing things.

He went into the small bathroom next to the office and looked into the mirror. His small eyes were old and rheumy, but they still had some horse sense in them. The teacher, Margaret Masters, had come to Cain asking him to represent her in her fight with the school board. Cain had considered it. The movement against her involved censorship issues. It was probably unconstitutional, a blow against freedom of expression. A violation of both church and state. It was certainly demagoguery, aimed at the innocent and the ignorant.

Cain had let his cronies in town know his feelings about the case, but in the end he had declined the teacher's request. Given the ideological climate in Paradise these days, defending Maragaret Masters would be political suicide. And even at his age, Sam Houston Cain was not a man to dig his own grave, politically or otherwise. He had wished her luck, but declined.

He took off his glasses and dashed water on his old, lined face. When he looked up, he saw the hazy reflection of another person in the mirror, standing behind him.

"Hello," he said. Without the glasses, he couldn't see who it was. But it had to be a client, or someone who had come to talk to him because of his inside knowledge of the local political situation, the way people had in the old days.

"Ah'll be right with ya," he said, putting on the glasses.

But then the person moved toward him, a hand came up, and in the mirror he saw the head of the jackass. It was grinning at him with its long row of bleached white teeth, with those hollow eye sockets that spoke only of death. He looked at the person in the mirror, recognized the face, and suddenly understood. "Good Lord," he said. Then the jawbone of the ass came down on his skull.

Chapter 2

*I*t was 7 P.M., Friday, when Edward Thomas, journalist, spotted the town of Paradise balanced on the otherwise empty horizon.

It appeared suddenly, far across the Texas prairie, beyond the mesquite bushes, cattle fences, windmills, and oil pump jacks that flew by him on either side. He'd come six hours west from Dallas in his rental car, watching the landscape go from rolling green hills; to planted fields; to plains where the vegetation grew sparser and the land flatter, drier, and emptier; until you believed in a few miles it would end altogether and you would fly right off the edge of the earth into nothingness. Or whatever there was out there.

"In the beginning there was West Texas," Thomas had said to himself.

He reached down now and turned off the radio. He had been listening to a Roy Orbison retrospective—"Pretty woman, don't walk away"—and frequent tornado warnings. It was May and, according to the meteorologists, it was the season. Thomas, a greenhorn from New York, had kept a careful eye on the horizon. Just short of Odessa, he had seen a small dust devil, like a miniature tornado, kick up on the shoulder of the interstate. Thomas watched it warily as it picked up a handful of dust, swirled it in the air, careened out onto the tarmac, danced erratically across his path, and then dipped into the adjacent dry field. He tracked its whirling funnel until, just as quickly as it had materialized, it had disappeared into thin air without a trace. Thomas had been staring uneasily at the prairie ever since.

On the passenger seat next to him rode the tools of his trade: a stack of notebooks, pens, a tape recorder, a portable word processor, a camera and files, including the telephone number of Daniel Oates, the owner and editor of the Paradise *Chronicle,* whom he was on his way to see. It was in that newspaper the story had first been reported and a day later a four-paragraph UPI blurb appeared in the national section of *The New York Times.* Thomas, who had not written a word in two months, had sat staring at the article as if it were a sign in the heavens.

Prominent Texas Attorney
Severely Injured in Attack

PARADISE, Tex. (UPI)—Sam H. Cain, a leading attorney and local political figure, was in critical condition Thursday after an unknown assailant entered his law offices and viciously bludgeoned him with "the jawbone of an ass," sheriff officials said.

Cain, 76, was found unconscious by a secretary at 9 A.M. The weapon, the skull of a donkey, which had been part of the office decor, was found stained with blood lying next to the body. A Paradise Hospital spokesman said the attorney, who suffered a fractured skull, had not regained consciousness.

The town has recently been embroiled in a dispute between the school board and a conservative church group over the dismissal of a high school teacher. Although Cain was not a principal in the case, authorities were investigating the possibility that the attack was related to that conflict. They cited the biblical passage, from the Book of Judges, in which Samson slew 1,000 Philistines with the jawbone of a donkey.

Sheriff James West said there were as yet no suspects. "Nobody can believe this happened," he said. "No one can understand it."

Thomas had a clip of the story in his files on the passenger seat. Next to those articles lay several recent issues of *Epoch* magazine, the publication based in New York that had given him the assignment.

Thomas was a magazine writer. For almost twenty years he'd covered the biggest stories the world had to offer, traveling from the backrooms of Watergate to the boardrooms of Wall Street, from the wadis of the Middle East to the jungles of Central America. In between, he'd profiled starlets and oil sheiks, gurus, and mafiosi. Thomas knew no other life but that of a journalist. Month after month, he crossed the U.S. and foreign borders the way most people crossed streets. The currents of the late twentieth century, dislocation and violence on the one hand, high living and hedonism on the other, had carried him to the top of his profession. There were few human beings, he could say, who had his firsthand knowledge of the modern world, especially its excesses.

Then just two months ago had come Thomas's own "international crisis," as he called it. This was how he thought of it now, as if it were an event, a breaking news story, that had happened to someone else. It hadn't.

It had involved not the balance of powers but his own balance. While on assignment in an unstable Latin American country, covering the resultant violence, Thomas had gone haywire. Only rumors reached New York, but they involved a bout of heavy drinking, increasing surliness with his colleagues, and finally one night, during a political discussion with another correspondent at a hotel lounge, a sudden explosion of violence. The incident left the bar extensively damaged, his antagonist mildly injured in a hospital emergency room, and Thomas himself covered with bruises and glass cuts, sitting in a local jail and suffering from his own brand of shell shock. As one onlooker put it, the normally level-headed correspondent had "gone off like a bomb."

No one but Thomas knew at the time what had touched it off and he told no one. He had been escorted back to New York by a fellow journalist who had served him as both nursemaid and warder, and on the insistence of that friend he had allowed a psychiatrist acquaintance to see him. After a couple of visits, the shrink had reached a preliminary conclusion: in effect, Thomas's life had been mined.

"What made you think you could go from human tragedy to human tragedy all over the globe, year after year, and not have it get inside you?" What indeed.

Thomas had spent more than a month at home in New York recovering. His long, high-cheekboned face which had been pale as newsprint right after "the incident" had slowly regained most of its ruddy color. There was maybe a bit more gray in his straight black hair. But his dark, almost black eyes, filled with shock and confusion at first, had grown steadier. He had gone on the wagon and they were clearer. He was almost forty but looked a good five years younger, despite the binge.

His friends and colleagues, almost all journalists, grad-

ually had stopped treating him like a basket case. He told
them it had been nothing more than a question of too
much work and too much play. But the psychiatrist wasn't
satisfied with that analysis. He tried to get out of Thomas
what it was that drew him to other people's wars, exploring
what he called Thomas's shattered defenses, and counsel-
ing him on how to build new ones. The doctor asked
him about his personal life and Thomas told him his
only marriage had ended in divorce years back, and con-
stant, farflung assignments ever since had made a serious
relationship impossible. The psychiatrist also had asked
him if he had any religious belief and Thomas had said
no. Reporters dealt with what could be interviewed, recorded, photographed, not the unknowable. That was his
world.

The shrink had nodded sagely. "But life isn't just the
news, is it?" he had asked. "There are other stories behind
the scenes."

Thomas had thought about that, but not for long. He
had gone almost two months without writing, and his fi-
nances dictated that he get back to work. Two days ago he
had seen the blurb out of Paradise in *The New York Times*
and smelled a good story in it. Just why, he didn't ask
himself. He not only needed the money, he was restless,
itchy to work and to get out of the quagmire of his own
life.

Within the hour, he had called Texas, tracked down
Daniel Oates, and dug up background on the story. Then
he had gone straight to Marshall Mundy of *Epoch* magazine, at his offices in a midtown skyscraper.

Mundy was about forty-five, with silvering hair, gray
eyes, a modishly slim physique, and the pulsing style of a
man plugged in all over the globe. He was a creature of
the publishing business, a budding communications mag-
nate, with interests in cable networks, satellites, computer
newspapers, and more. Still, he insisted on keeping hands-
on control of *Epoch*, the oldest of his journalistic properties.

Thomas had written a number of articles for him over the years. The magazine was thin and slick, like its owner, and primarily a catalogue for upscale urban living. But it made an occasional stab at world and national affairs, and when it did, it paid well.

Thomas found Mundy sitting in his glass-walled office, surrounded by several computer and television screens, fax machines, telephones, and a long row of bottles holding vitamins and other vital additives. Mundy, attired in a stylish exercise outfit, squinted warily as Thomas entered, shook hands without standing up, and then evinced all the delicacy and diplomacy for which the profession was known.

"Are you back on line?" he asked. "I heard you had a meltdown."

Thomas winced. "There've been some rocky days, but now I want to do a piece."

He put the clip from the *Times* on Mundy's desk. "God and the Devil are wrestling for the American soul out in West Texas," he said, in the kind of language Mundy might use in the pages of the magazine. "They're reliving the Old Testament. It's the best story around and nobody's covering it."

Mundy picked up the clip and read it with eyes that moved quickly, like a laser printer. Thomas saw interest light up there, but then the gaze narrowed with obligatory editorial skepticism.

"It's a good story if you can get an interview with one or both of them, God or Satan, that is." He rocked back in his swivel chair. "Of course, it'll be tough. The Lord hasn't given a really long interview since Moses."

Then he smiled, cleverly showing beautiful white caps. Thomas didn't return the grin and Mundy swiveled back toward him.

"We don't write about religion, Edward. You know that," he said, dropping the clip on the desk. "Our product is decidedly secular."

"*You* know it's a political story," Thomas countered. "Religious overtones, biblical dressing, but it's still politics in modern-day America. Southern blacklash. The resurrection of fundamentalism, challenges to freedom of thought and expression. Constitutional issues. A progressive magazine should be sensitive to these phenomena, Marshall." He put a little spin on the word "progressive."

Mundy recoiled at the low blow, and Thomas took advantage of the opening to fill him in on the background he'd gotten from Oates. He told him all he knew about the town, its economic and political situation, and the latest events, the apparent persecution of a spinster English teacher who dared to teach modern literature, and the attack on the old lawyer.

"This is an assault on modernity itself," Thomas said.

Mundy ingested it all, frowning. He reached to the desk, opened a vial and popped a pill. Then he gazed out the window for a while, thinking.

"These are people digging in their heels against the New Age," Thomas told him.

Mundy nodded slowly. "Old Testament zealots roaming the Texas plains in the late twentieth century," he said finally, as if trying the idea on for size. "An attempt to turn back the clock religiously and politically. An attack on modernity itself, as you say, resulting in repression and even bloodletting." Mundy fixed on him. "And you need the money," he added cynically.

Thomas said nothing.

"I hate to bring up your personal back files," Mundy said, "but are you in shape to do this? Your recent troubles didn't induce this new interest in religious subject matter? You aren't still in the dark night of the soul?"

Thomas shook his head.

"And you can collect the data you need out there within seven days and get back here?"

"Yes."

Mundy's face went through a cybernetic reaction, a series

of squints and frowns as if he were computing what he'd heard. He stared into Thomas's eyes and finally nodded.

"Okay, Edward. I have faith in you. Just don't put any false gods before me. Abide by my deadline."

They had settled on a fee, a kill fee, and a travel advance. As Thomas was heading out the door, Mundy had a last word for him.

"Be careful out there, Edward. Their God is an angry God."

Thomas said he would. He had gone home to make the necessary arrangements and to pack. He called Daniel Oates and made an appointment to see him the next evening in Paradise. That same night he got on a plane for Texas, leaving the glass skyscrapers of Manhattan and Marshall Mundy far behind.

Now, two thousand miles away, he was reaching the first outbuildings of the town: an old wooden ranch house, a barn, corrals, and all around them the countless three-legged oil pumpjacks with their heads bowed grazing on the endless prairie. Few of them were pumping. According to Daniel Oates, Paradise was a town with a gaudy history. This was cattle country, turned rich oil country, but now it was oil country gone bust.

On the seat next to him also lay the fax Oates had sent him the day before, an earlier article on the school dispute. It quoted the Reverend Samuel Dash, the leader of what Oates had called "a radical apocalyptic religious cult." The reverend had an explanation for the bust.

"We're in the time of the plagues, just like Egypt five thousand years ago," he said. "We're reaping God's retribution for our sinfulness and corruption. And there'll be more of it. Vengeance is mine, sayeth the Lord." The Reverend Dash said the plagues would continue until all sinners had been driven out of town for good.

Thomas, a sinner, entered the city limits at 7 P.M.

A green and white road sign said:

Welcome to Paradise
Population 9,880

but someone had chalked through the number and written in a "0," as if the place were now a ghost town. Beyond the sign there was a billboard bearing the plaques of the town's fraternal organizations: Lions, Rotary, Kiwanis, Optimists. All of them were rusty and dusty.

Thomas slowed down as he reached the outskirts and began to see the real signs of the bust, the indications of flight and abandonment left by economic collapse. There wasn't a soul in sight on that strip and the first buildings he saw were all boarded up. The Paradise Cafe, a red brick establishment, sported a sign offering "Good Hot Lunch," although the food must have been very cold by this time judging by the layer of dust that coated the building and its general air of desolation. Tumbleweeds had blown up against the walls, the only customers trying to get in. The Cloud Nine Bar and the Pearly Gates Lounge looked as though they had at one time been quite lively. But a time long gone. Now they sat surrounded by empty parking lots of bleached dust and were as quiet as the dead. The Paradise Mobile Home Park, next door, was nothing more than a sign. There wasn't a trailer anywhere in sight. Its long row of mailboxes stood on the side of the road gaping emptily, except for one that appeared to be occupied by a bird's nest. An abandoned car sat in front of it, just off the blacktop, with its hood up, pointing forlornly out of town.

Then came a string of oil-related companies with dusty corrugated roofs, all of them closed down. They had optimistic names—Fortune Drilling, Bonanza Petroleum—names that sounded hollow now given their surroundings. Thomas saw old, yellowed signs in the windows: "No Job Applications Accepted," notices that had probably been there more than five years, since the bust had begun. Almost every building was missing pieces—a door, a window frame, roofing shingles, as if Paradise had been scavenged for parts to rebuild another town somewhere else.

On the buildings and on the otherwise empty advertising billboards were graffiti, all in bright red paint. The same two messages appeared over and over again: "The End Is Near" and "Jesus Is Coming." To Thomas it appeared the first had already come true for Paradise, while the second hadn't. If Jesus did come, He would be alone here. All that was left, anywhere along that strip leading into town, was that bleached dust and an eerie silence.

Thomas stopped for the blinking light. Across the intersection stood the Range Motel, where Oates had advised him to stay. It was a run-down one-story stucco place and the rooms had faded red doors. A big "For Sale" sign sat perched on the roof. Another sign out front advertised "Weekly & M nth y Rates—E.Z. Terms." It appeared no one was taking them up on the offer. Outside each room was a steel hitching post, but there was neither a horse nor a car tied up to even one of them. Thomas crossed the road and pulled in.

There was no one in the musty, wood-paneled office, but Thomas could hear television noise coming from a back room behind a beaded curtain. He palmed the metal bell on the Formica counter and looked around. A calendar advertising a drilling company and picturing a healthy gusher was dated 1986. A bit of nostalgia, given the state of business. Next to it on the wall was a sign: "This Motel American Owned and Operated." Thomas had seen such announcements before, especially in parts of the United States where nonwhite immigrant families had made inroads into the business. The sign was another bit of nostalgia.

Then a fat, red-faced, middle-aged man in a yellowed white shirt parted the curtain. He had mustard in the corner of his mouth, as if Thomas had interrupted his dinner. His gray eyes had the steady gaze of someone who watched a lot of television, or maybe it was that he hadn't seen a customer in a long while.

"I'd like a room, please," Thomas said.

The clerk drank that in slowly, and licked the mustard from his lip.

"Fourteen dollars per night or seventy dollars the week," he said in a thick Texas accent.

"One night, for now."

The man squinted, still untrusting. He had the disoriented but dutiful attitude of a soldier who had been assigned to a post long ago and had never been relieved after the war ended. He shuffled over and registered Thomas and then frowned at the registration card.

"Journalist, huh?"

"That's right."

He didn't like that either. Journalists only showed up in a place if there was some kind of trouble. Thomas had found that to be a common superstition. But the clerk couldn't afford to be choosy. He rummaged through a drawer, produced a key, and stared at it as if he'd just picked a lottery winner, or a loser, given his look.

"Number five, down on your right," he said, handing it over and collecting Thomas's money.

"What time is check-out tomorrow?"

The other man frowned and shook his head. There was apparently something Thomas just didn't understand about the motel, or about Paradise in general.

"Whenever the spirit moves ya, friend." Then he shuffled back through the beaded curtain to his television.

Thomas unloaded his suitcase and equipment quickly from the car and headed for number five. As he did, he saw the door to number three open and a man step out. So he wasn't alone in the place after all.

The man was Latin. He was dark and had a mustache that arched down on either side of his mouth. He wore a white guayabera shirt and jeans, and appeared to be in his late twenties. Short, but broad-shouldered and big-armed, he looked as if he'd done some hard work in his day. Those arms were folded across his chest now and Thomas made out a tattoo on his bicep: an eagle with a snake writhing in its talons, the symbol of the Mexican flag. He was staring out at the road, grim-faced, as if he were waiting for somebody who was late. Thomas nodded to him as he passed, but the man didn't respond.

Thomas's room wasn't exactly a suite at the Plaza, but it would do. It was vintage oil town. The wooden door had a ding in it about the size of a boot heel, a vestige of rowdier times. The bed was extra long, to accommodate some of the large men who worked in the industry, and the furniture was solid, nothing fragile. Hanging on the back of the door were the old rates: thirty-five dollars per day. The clerk had charged him fourteen. Yes, there was trouble in Paradise.

Thomas dumped his equipment on the bed, shaved for the second time that day, changed his shirt, and headed out again. As he did, he saw a car had pulled up outside number three. A tall, white, balding man in a checked shirt was standing next to it, talking earnestly to the Mexican.

As Thomas approached, the balding man looked up and stopped speaking. He watched Thomas as he passed. Then, as Thomas climbed into the car, the man took the Mexican by the elbow, led him into the room, and closed the door behind them.

Chapter 3

*F*ive minutes later, Thomas pulled up to the place where he was to meet Daniel Oates, a church on the outskirts of town called Paradise Revelation Temple.

He had reached it following the directions Oates had given him earlier in the day over the phone. They had taken him east of the motel, across a set of railroad tracks, and into a residential section. It was a treeless neighborhood lined with small, dilapidated wooden bungalows, the paint blistered by the Texas sun, the shingles curling. Again there was almost no one in sight and again he saw the red paint everywhere: "The End is Coming." Given the looks of the neighborhood, it sounded more like a hope than a warning.

He found the Temple on a parched, weedy lot at the edge of Paradise, on a dirt road packed with cars. It was a one-story hexagon made of white cinderblock, like a cement tent. A corrugated metal roof glowed red with the light of the setting sun. He could hear singing coming from inside.

Daniel Oates was waiting for him near the door. If Thomas didn't get another story in Paradise, he knew he had at least one: the editor of the Paradise *Chronicle* had to be the largest journalist on earth. Thomas, who had met his colleagues all over the globe, had never seen one bigger. Daniel Oates stood at least six ten in his low-heeled cowboy boots, new jeans, and red-and-green plaid cowboy shirt. His shoulders were wide and muscular as if he were wearing football pads, which he probably had at one time. His hips were unnaturally slim and he had just the beginnings of a paunch. In his mid-forties, Thomas figured, he was light-haired with a square chin and dark, watchful eyes behind horn-rimmed glasses. He wore a lot of pens in the pocket of his shirt and had the look of a man who had been keeping a careful eye on life in Paradise for a long time from that height of his and taking notes. It had left him with a fixed look that was both somber and wary.

They shook hands. "We better go in now and talk later," Oates said in a deep voice. "Don't want the Reverend Sam Dash to get riled at us." He didn't smile when he said it.

Over the years Thomas had covered the funerals of the rich and famous. Apart from those occasions, he had not been in a church since he was child, when his mother had made him go with her to mass. Now he followed Oates through a pair of thick wooden doors, which the moment they were opened let loose a flood of singing voices. They had to squeeze just inside the doorway, because the low-ceilinged space before them was packed with souls wall to wall. If there was no one on the street, it was because everyone was in church. Once the door closed behind him, Thomas was enveloped by the heat and the echo of the

singing. The sound bounced off the corrugated roofing
and resonated all around, as if the space were defined not
by the walls but by that din.

There were no windows. The lighting came from flu-
orescent tubes above that cast a glare on the congregation
and buzzed with heat. Thomas had already started to
sweat. He stood on tiptoe and saw rows of heads extending
to a stage up front, and on the back wall of the church
hung a large crimson neon cross, at least six feet high. The
red neon made the space feel even hotter than it was, if
that was possible. On one side of the cross was an organ
and other instruments, all with high black speakers that
Thomas associated with decidedly ungodly rock concerts.
The musicians who played them, wearing black robes,
pumped out a lively rhythm and made sure it was loud.

The pulpit, a simple lectern, was at center stage. On
either side stood two middle-aged men also in black robes
and bathed in the red light of the neon cross. One was
dark-complected and tall. The other had a badly scarred
face, the kind of disfigurement that might have been
caused by a fire or maybe acid. One side of his face was
smooth, white, hairless. The two men led the singing.
Thomas wondered which one was the Reverend Samuel
Dash.

Thomas looked about him and his attention was caught
by the murals on the hexagonal walls. He didn't remember
having seen anything like them in his churchgoing days.
They were brightly colored, rudimentary paintings, not
unlike illustrations in textbooks for very young school-
children, except that the figures were of human size and
some were of subject matter not seen in such books. There
were representations of Jesus Christ and of his angels, but
others were scenes of destruction, of horror. He made out
one in which the earth, with blue seas and green continents,
was splitting open and black, horned, demonlike figures
escaped its core. The next showed what appeared to be a
lake made of red and yellow flames, with people trapped
in it, screaming. They were also being rained on by a red

substance that had to be blood. In yet another of the paintings, human beings covered with soil and without eyes emerged from graves, looking like zombies. There were other such tableaux painted all around the church. Apparently scenes of the end of the world, the end that was coming soon and that was advertised all over town.

Thomas was the only one present who seemed impressed by the murals. He took his notebook out of his pocket and scribbled cramped notes describing them. The other worshipers were singing zestfully. It was an unusual population for a church, at least in his experience. As many men as women in that mass of souls, and many of them big, oilfield size. They were all white, or they had been. The faces of the men, in particular, were now mostly red, partly from the heat in the church, but also, Thomas figured, from the daily burning glare of the Texas sun. The number and size of the men gave the singing a tone that was at the bass end of the scale. Thomas listened closely and made out the refrain, "Bathed in the blood of the Lord." A macabre lyric, set, strangely, to that lively rhythm. They sang it with unexpected gusto. Some people raised their hands in the air, swaying them and shaking them, so that they moved like flames dancing in a breeze. Their faces appeared gripped by a mixture of agony and rapture. Next to Thomas, a small, white-haired man in overalls sang with his hands lifted, swaying, his washed-out blue eyes fixed excitedly on some point above, as if he were staring into the sun and in the process of going blind.

Then the musicians led the congregation into a last rousing chorus, wound it down, and the hymn ended. Someone yelled "Hallelujah," and the robed man with the dark complexion stepped to the pulpit.

"Praise the Lord," he said in a thick Texas accent, and, in unison, the crowd echoed him. "Praise the Lord."

"Can you feel the Lord right here in church with us tonight?"

From the crowd, a strained older voice rang out, "Thank ya, Jesus."

"Yes, indeed," said the swarthy man. "And isn't it good to be surrounded by the Lord's people, folks doin' the Lord's work, and makin' this a town where the Devil can't lift his head. Where Satan and his people are on the run."

"Praise Jesus."

"Yes, indeed. Well, tonight the Reverend Sam Dash, who knows a thing or two about the Devil, has a word for us straight from the Lord. So let's give a listen."

The tall man moved back from the lectern and Thomas looked to the man with the scarred face, expecting him to step to the microphone. But he didn't. Instead a younger, red-haired man who had been playing the electric guitar in the group of musicians, removed the instrument, propped it against a speaker, adjusted the black robe on his shoulders, flashed a broad, beguiling smile to the other musicians, and then stepped forward to the pulpit.

"That's Sam Dash," Oates whispered.

Thomas craned to see him. The Reverend Sam Dash was about six feet, narrow-shouldered, and thin. His thick, wavy, reddish-blond hair was combed straight back off his broad brow in a pompadour reminiscent of the 1950s. From a distance, he looked not much older than thirty. His face was unwrinkled, a sun-burnished red color, now heightened by the heat in the church and the neon light. His smile was bright white, but it was the look in his dark, lustrous eyes that most caught Thomas's attention. It was both wired and devilish. He was the picture of mischief and more than that, of intense pleasure, of glee. Thomas flashed back to his distant memories of church and didn't remember a priest ever looking like that.

As Dash stepped to the pulpit, he appeared to be laughing at some private joke told by someone right next to him whom no one else could see. He ran his tongue slowly across his lips, leaned toward the microphone, and said in a husky, seductive, whisper.

"I think this here service is fixin' to begin."

"Hallelujah," came the response from the crowd. "Thank ya, Jesus."

Dash's face lit up. "Is everybody high on the Lord to-night?"

"Praise the Lord."

The faithful clapped their hands, yelled invocations, and let out whoops of anticipation. The young Reverend Dash nodded and beamed to one side of the hall and then the other, like a performer or a candidate. He waved at one person and winked at someone else. It took a minute before the hullaballoo died down. Then he licked his lips and suddenly swallowed his smile, lowering his head. He stayed that way for some ten seconds, during which a stillness fell over the congregation, the way a courtroom becomes still before a verdict. He looked back up, solemn.

"I'm on a mission tonight, brothers and sisters. A serious mission in enemy territory." The voice was young and had the twangy tenor of an electric guitar. He stretched the notes out so that they resonated through the sound system. His eyes began to slowly scan the crowd.

"Because that's where we are, ain't we? Behind the lines. Past no-man's-land. In Satan's territory. For years you were people in captivity in this town, folks in bondage. Yes, you were. That was during the so-called boom years when sin was the rule in Paradise and the Devil called the tune. When we lived in the midst of drunkenness and whore-dom, avarice and abominations."

"Praise Jesus."

He nodded and his voice rose. "But we've broken those chains, haven't we, brothers and sisters? The tune is changin' in Paradise. We got Satan and his forces on the run. Don't we? Deliverance is here. Yes, it is."

"Hallelujah! Praise the Lord."

Dash smiled fiercely and waited for the cries to die down. Then he cocked his head to one side, and his voice filled with feigned incredulity.

"Now, brethren, there's people in this town sayin' we're dead wrong. That the Devil and his legions ain't in command in Paradise. That he don't trespass our streets and live in our barrooms. That he hasn't been runnin' our government and our schools for years. In fact, these here folks'll probably tell ya there ain't no such creature as the Devil, and there ain't no battle on for the souls of your children."

He stood stock-still and let those words sink in. Then he took the microphone from its stand, held the long wire behind him as if he were a rock star about to break into dance, and began to prowl the stage in a tense, agitated way.

"Well, I'm here to testify that there *is* a war goin' on in this town. Yes, there is. A war between those folks that's made a covenant with the Lord and those who serve Satan. And I'm here tonight to report from the front, brothers and sisters."

"Praise Jesus."

"Yes, I am. Me, the Reverend Sam Dash, up here on this stage, I'm volunteering for duty. And I'm the one to do it, brethren. Because I already been ta hell and back. I've beheld the Devil himself, face-to-face. Yes, I have."

He stopped abruptly, his finger touching his heart, both accuser and accused. His young, mischievous eyes panned the crowd slowly, histrionically, looking for someone who might challenge him. There was no one. Dash had them captivated. He had the almost spastic style of one of the wilder rockers, although when he spoke again, his voice was low and serious, but still rhythmic, as if he were shifting momentarily into the blues.

"Some of you know from your own experience that I'm tellin' the truth. Yes, ya do. Those who knew me back when before I hearkened to the word of the Lord. Ya'll know that I was raised in sin, that I was a child o' Satan. Yes, I was. You know that by the time he was of age, Sam Dash broke every law of man and God. I had an abidin' need ta sin." He began to stalk the stage again. "You name anything the Devil had to offer in this town and I had a taste for it. I did alcohol. Drugs. Women. I did moonshine, red eye, cocaine, meta-ampheta-mines. I fornicated with prostitutes and I stole my neighbor's wife ta boot. Couldn't get enough o' sin. No, I couldn't."

He reached the end of the stage and whirled around in the other direction, gaining momentum.

"But there wasn't enough sin for me in Paradise. It couldn't hold me. In fact, there wasn't enough evil for my thirsty young soul in all Texas. So I went lookin' for it all over the U.S.A. I crossed and recrossed this country. From New York to Loze Angelees, from the Rio Grande to the frozen North. Until I couldn't go no farther, brethren. Ya' understand? Until I ran outa land and outa evil. So what'd I do?" He stopped at the end of the stage, full of his own story, high on his own wickedness. He waved a finger into the distance. "I got on a ship, brothers and sisters. That's what I did. I went lookin' for evil all over the world. Africa. China. Tim-buk-tu. You name it, I been there and sinned there. Yes, I have. With the Devil at my side all the way."

He gestured at the empty space next to him. The small man next to Thomas was staring wide-eyed at the stage, as if he could actually see the Devil standing there. Others in the congregation seemed possessed of the same vision. Reverend Dash had the fascination of the sinner-saint. Of the man who had seen it all and returned to tell about it, like a traveler who had brought back shrunken heads from the Congo. It wasn't that he knew more about God but more about evil than this congregation did, or ever would. That was his fascination, his power, at least part of it, Thomas thought. That and a sensuality that came with it.

He swaggered back across the stage. "Talk about evil, I done it all. Stealin', assaultin', break and entry, sale o' narcotics. I been a pimp and a procurer, a robber with a gun." Then he stopped suddenly, as if someone had asked him a question. He scanned the crowd, his gaze slowing and stopping as he got to Oates, who stood a half head taller than the others around him. His eyes narrowed and he shook his head slowly. "No, I've never murdered anybody or tried to. It was about the only transgression and abom-

ination I never committed. Although God knows I might
have. Satan was standin' right next to me ready to give me
the order, but the chance didn't come."

Oates didn't react, but Thomas wondered if Dash might
be referring to the attack on the old attorney, Sam Houston
Cain. Now the preacher bowed his head and broke into
that same broad smile.

"That's why it kills me that some folks in this mun-i-ci-
pal-ity say I can't recognize Satan when I see 'im. That I
can't recognize those legions workin' for the Devil in this
town and just what they do around here." His sly smile
returned. "You can't con a con man, brethren, especially
one who's found the Lord."

Thomas felt the crowd begin to stir. A voice called out,
"Praise the Lord," and Dash began to strut the stage again
with that frantic, spastic energy, his voice rising.

"I seen Satan on the streets and in the alleyways of Paradise. I know he's in the bars and the motels, in the drug
dens, because I done business with him there in the past.
Yes, I have. In fact, he's all over this town. Because there
ain't no laws or ordinances to stop 'im. There ain't no
defenses to keep him out. That's because for years he's
been helpin' write our laws and he's been helpin' teach
your children. Yes, he has."

"Praise Jesus."

"It's in the schools that they mock the good book, brethren. They tell yer children the Bible is all wrong, that the
world came from nothin' and men came from monkeys.
It's in the schools they say it's wrong ta pray. Instead they
have 'em read about the so-called modern world and teach
'em filth. And that's because it's the Devil's mistress teachin'
in those schools. The Harlot of Babylon, brothers and sisters. I know 'er and I recognize 'er."

He yelled that. Then he jumped to the edge of the stage,
hunkered down and yelled it again at the top of his lungs.

"I know 'er and I recognize 'er."

Dash stayed balanced on the lip of the stage as his voice
echoed in that concrete tent. His face was a deep red, his

eyes moved over the crowd slowly, bleakly, and his voice dropped.

"That's why the Lord has sent these plagues on us. That's why you don't have work, why you lose yer homes, why you suffer sickness and yer children are diseased with drugs. And that's why the plagues'll continue. The Lord'll strike Paradise with even more tribulations until we drive the Harlot o' Babylon and all the rest of Satan's legions outa Paradise." His words became slow, deliberate, ominous. "The end is comin', brethren, and we have to get this town ready for the Lord. We have to drive those sinners out with our prayers, our voices, our votes. Any way we can. And if the town officials won't do what they should, we have to get rid of them too. Yes, we do."

"Praise Jesus." "Hallelujah." "Thank ya, Jesus."

Dash stayed perched on the edge of the stage, breathing deeply until slowly he straightened up and seemed to come out of a trance.

"Right now, let's each of us make contact with the Lord for individual guidance. Let's each of us get high on the Lord."

Dash closed his eyes and raised his hands to the sky and the members of his congregation did the same. The man next to Thomas stood swaying, his hands raised, his face transported. He prayed, but in a moaning, whining, unintelligible langauge. It was a sound that seemed to come from deep inside him, from some intense yearning, or pain. Thomas realized the man was speaking in tongues. Many of the people were, as if they all spoke their own individual language intelligible only to one's self and to one's God. Some of those languages were low and intense and rumbling, others were filled with sighs and shrieks. Thomas watched the man next to him and wondered what he was saying to his God and what the Lord was saying to the man, what he might be telling him to do and not do.

Then he felt a tug at his elbow and Oates was going out the door. Thomas took a last look at the mad, ecstatic face of the man next to him and backed out, closing the door on the horrifying murals and the arm-waving, transported crowd.

"The service will go on for some time," Oates said. Thomas blinked into the setting sun and nodded. He was still in a daze. Through the door he could hear the continuing cacophony.

They turned to go to the car, but then the man in the black robes with the scarred face appeared. Thomas hadn't noticed him leave the stage, but he came from around the corner of the building and cut them off.

"Good evening, Dan."

Oates stopped, surprised and not particularly pleased.

"Good evening, Lloyd." The man came up to them and Oates introduced Thomas. "This is Lloyd Haynes, a deacon of the church," Oates said.

"Chief deacon," the small man said to Thomas.

He was a strange-looking man, small and thin, with just enough skin on his skull to cover a severe hatchet face. His black hair was thick and flew back from his cadaverous brow as if he were walking through a windstorm. The eyes were dark and intense. And then there was the scar that made up the whole left side of his face. It was just smooth skin, white, without wrinkle and a bit shiny. Haynes held his head so that Thomas had to look at it.

"Leaving early, Dan?" Haynes asked. "It's a shame. We haven't seen you here before at the Revelation Temple."

His cordial words had a suspicious edge to them. Without asking, he wanted to know what they were doing there. Oates obliged him.

"I'm just showing Mr. Thomas around town. He's a visiting journalist from New York."

Haynes nodded slowly, knowingly. "Did you enjoy Sam Dash's preaching, Mr. Thomas?"

"Quite lively."

"Sam's a firebrand, all right. He'll split the heavens one of these nights." His dark eyes filled with a brooding intensity. "And he's right about what's happening here in Paradise, Mr. Thomas. About the plagues the Lord has sent on us and why. Make no mistake. And there'll be more of them. Yes, there will." His voice dropped to a trembling, ominous register. "Because we're getting to those last days the Good Book talks about in Revelation, Mr. Thomas, when the world is inside out. When evil masquerades as good, and darkness is light. When chaos rules. The Lord will come back to end it all then and the only ones who'll be saved, like Sam says, are the ones workin' for the Lord. Anyone not doin' the Lord's work is workin' for the Devil and they'll die and suffer forever in hell. Dontcha bet against it."

He kept staring, as if he could see these terrible events coming to pass on the screen of Thomas's face. Thomas tried to meet the fiery gaze in the other man's eyes, but it was unmeetable. The deacon looked to Oates and then back to Thomas.

"I know you journalists don't believe all this, but it's my duty to warn ya before it's too late."

"Thank you," Thomas said.

Haynes nodded. "Good evening to you, then." He started to turn away but then looked back.

"Dan, how's Sam Cain doin? Have ya heard?"

"He's the same. Still unconscious."

Haynes nodded. "We've been prayin' for 'im." Then he turned and disappeared into the church.

Oates and Thomas walked toward the cars. The sun was just setting and the western horizon was flooded in red.

"So what did you think of the Reverend Sam Dash?" Oates asked.

Thomas shook his head. "He's a firebrand all right. And a demagogue who's priming his parishioners for a witch-hunt. I assume he was referring to that high school teacher when he talked about the Harlot of Babylon who had to be run out of Paradise."

"Margaret Masters is the teacher's name," Oates said. "We're going to see her now."

They both got into Oates's car, a red Bronco, and headed crosstown toward the teacher's house. Their route took them through another desolate neighborhood, this one full of mobile homes, some of which appeared to have taken root and had rooms added on to them made of aluminum siding, wood, or even brick. It was a style of architecture, Thomas thought, that reflected the history of Paradise and other oil towns. They had been inhabited by transients, many of whom had come to Paradise looking to make a quick bundle. Of course, for most of them it hadn't happened that way. Overnight wealth had escaped them. Instead, they had found jobs and turned into residents, but the kind who were always ready to move again if things went bad. Many had apparently done just that with the latest bust. There were abandoned lots everywhere, some with dilapidated extra rooms standing there incongruously alone. Next to many of the structures were broken-down, abandoned cars that had been cannibalized for parts and left to rot. They were like the small separate dwellings Thomas had seen outside residences in Asia and that supposedly housed friendly spirits. Except that in the United States they housed the spirit of the road. The people he did see, a mixture of whites and Latins, tracked his car closely as it passed, just in case it was heading someplace where there was a better life.

Thomas turned to Oates. "What happened to this man Haynes, his face?"

Oates's eyes narrowed in a wince. "Lloyd was a policeman for years on the local force. One night he was chasing a stolen car, lost control of the cruiser; it rolled over and caught fire and he got trapped inside. Before they could drag him out, it burned his whole body, not just his face. That was a few years back, and he's on disability now. When Sam Dash started this church, Lloyd suddenly got religion. Now he's Sam's right-hand man. Which is ironic, because when Lloyd was on the force they were always on opposite sides of the law."

"So the Reverend Dash isn't just talking when he says he was a bad boy."

Oates shook his head. "No, not at all. It's like he said,

he was about as bad as you could get in a small town like Paradise, or the way the town was then. Petty theft, drugs. Then one of his buddies showed up dead from an overdose. I always figured that scared him. He left town for a few years. When he came back, he'd found God and found Him in a big way. Or at least it appears he did."

"You think maybe he didn't?"

The big man shrugged. "Margaret Masters let people know she didn't like the Reverend Dash and they're after her job. Sam Cain didn't think much of him either and look what happened to him."

"Are you saying that Dash had something to do with cracking the old man's skull?"

Oates squinted into the growing darkness and said nothing.

Chapter 4

Margaret Masters's house was in a neighborhood that seemed part of a different town or even a different world. It was much more what Thomas thought of as small-town America: a one-story, white frame place with a gabled roof, at the end of a clean, quiet side street. By the sidewalk there was a wooden gate and the lot was guarded by a shoulder-high hedge and shadowed by big elm trees.

The door was opened by an elderly cleaning lady, who led them to a study off the foyer, told them Miss Masters would be right down, and then let herself out. The shades were pulled, and an electric light in the form of an old oil lamp illuminated the room. It was on a wooden desk covered with papers, probably schoolwork. On the floor was

a wicker sewing kit and splayed out next to it on the rug
was an old-fashioned, full-skirted, high-necked gray dress
with lace at the wrists that someone was in the process of
making. Pins still held it together and scraps of lace lay
about. Above it on the wall hung a print that Thomas
recognized: Doré's engraving of Quijote madly charging
the windmill. But mostly the room held bookcases; wooden
bookcases, floor to ceiling, stuffed with both hardcover and
paperback books. From what he could see, it all had to do
with literature: classics and contemporary fiction, poetry
and criticism. The collection spoke of single-mindedness,
a passion, the kind that might possess a schoolteacher in
a small town that didn't have much else to offer.

Thomas and Oates sat in straight-back chairs across from
the desk, the editor with his long legs and tooled cowboy
boots stretched out before him. The singing from the
church was still echoing in Thomas's ears and the heat had
gotten inside him. Plus he was working on his first story
in two months. Thomas, who normally stepped from one
world into another without a hitch, still felt lost. He realized
he hadn't even asked Oates about the crime.

"Are there any leads on the beating of the attorney?"

Oates shook his head. "If there are, the sheriff isn't saying. Apparently no one saw anyone enter or leave Cain's
office. They can't even settle on a motive. He had money
in his pocket, and the secretary said there was nothing
missing as far as she could tell. It might have been vengeance or maybe just malice. Mindless violence."

"There's the religious angle," Thomas said. "The
weapon, right out of the Old Testament and then the conflict involving Margaret Masters and Dash's people."

"Yes, although Sam Cain wasn't involved in that conflict,
not directly," Oates said. "Sam let people know he didn't
like this movement against Margaret Masters. He kept his
distance from our local religious crusaders, even had some
choice words to say about them. In private, that is. But
when Margaret asked him to represent her before the

school board, he turned her down. He figured it was too risky politically. He was covering his back."

He paused. "I guess he didn't cover it well enough. As for the weapon, it was right on his desk. Nice and handy."

Thomas was frowning at him. "You said over the phone that the sheriff came to question Miss Masters. Did he really think she had something to do with it?"

"I don't know what Jim West thinks," Oates said. "Margaret called Sam the day before the attack about representing her and he turned her down. The secretary told the sheriff about it. Maybe that's why he wanted to see her, maybe only that. I don't think people in this town are ready to accuse Margaret Masters of being a murderess, or attempted murderess. They'll believe a lot of other things though."

"That she's an immoral woman and a corrupter of youth, a Harlot of Babylon."

"It's a witch-hunt, like you said."

Oates was about to say more, but then he looked up and across the room. A woman stood in the doorway and Thomas sensed she had been standing there for several moments, listening. The two men stood as she came into the room and Oates made the introductions.

"Welcome to Paradise, Mr. Thomas," Margaret Masters said in a voice that was gravelly and low for a woman.

"Thank you for making time for me," he said, taking her proffered hand.

At first glance, she might have been the small-town English teacher from central casting. She was a tall, slender, square-shouldered, small-breasted woman, in her mid to late thirties. She wore her dark hair tied in a bun. The face was pale, longish and her features were sharp, especially her high cheekbones. They gave her some of the flinty, ascetic quality of a spinster schoolmarm. She also dressed the part, keeping herself well covered in a long black skirt and a dark, high-necked, modest blouse.

But the type casting ended there. First there was her mouth, which was large and full, a sensuous mouth. To

Thomas it spoke not of West Texas, but of the Mediter-
ranean, and it softened her other features. Then there was
her distinctly low, suggestive voice and the way she had
said welcome to Paradise. And finally, there was the look
in her eyes. They were dark eyes, almost black in her pale
face, watchful near the surface, but with a depth, a know-
ingness in them. They said, "I know the facts of life. I've
been around."

Her hand was still lying in Thomas's.

"You can call me Margaret," she said, "Margaret Masters, the Wicked Witch of the West." She gave it a surprisingly sultry delivery and exaggerated the accent. Then
she cast a wilting, sardonic glance at Oates, who had just
been talking of witch-hunts, and she turned away from
them.

"Can I get you gentlemen a sundowner?" she asked,
crossing the room and opening a liquor cabinet to reveal
several bottles, glasses, and an ice bucket. "I have the
works. I even had some white lightning in here not too
long ago that a cousin brought me from Arkansas, but it
got finished off."

She turned to them, feigning regret. "What can I get
you?" Oates asked for a gin and tonic. Thomas, following
the regimen he'd been on since his "incident," asked for
plain soda. She reacted by furrowing her brow and looking
at him dubiously. Then she shrugged at Oates.

"Each man his own poison."

She made their drinks and topped off her own, which
was already sitting on the desk. It was a healthy volume of
gin. Then she sat in an easy chair next to the desk and in
front of a full wall of books, crossed her long legs under
the long black skirt, and gestured at the dress on the
floor.

"I've been putting together costumes for the senior play.
It's a period piece. This is how I spend my Friday nights,
Mr. Thomas. Although my enemies in town, I'm sure, will
tell you a different story."

She gave him another wilting look and sipped her drink.

Thomas sipped his and watched her. Margaret Masters, on first impression, was not what he had expected. She was certainly not the poor spinster teacher he had described to Marshall Mundy. But Thomas suspected she was not what she pretended to be either. She was trying to throw him off. Her tone was sardonic. Her style, in general, was offhand. But it seemed out of character, a fiction. In part it was the collection of literature around him, its seriousness. And what he knew of her situation. But it was also an intuition. Maybe his journalist's intuition about people trying to deceive. And maybe it was the last chapter of his own life, which had taught him that there were dark currents running under cool surfaces in people. He sensed that right away in Margaret Masters. If you read between the lines, you saw that her solitude was no joke.

"Excuse me for keeping you waiting, Mr. Thomas, but I had a call from an out-of-town friend. It was a treat. So many of the calls I'm getting these days aren't from friends at all."

Thomas took out his notebook. "Who is it calling these days?" he asked.

She shrugged. "They call late at night, and they don't leave their names. If you know what I mean? That explains the dark circles under my eyes."

She touched her face. The eyes were dark around the edges, but still attractive.

"You're being harassed?"

She wrinkled her nose. "Just a bit." She gazed at the window shade, as if she could see through it and into the town. "I had one character, a man, who called two nights ago at one in the morning, to tell me I was full of the devil. I told him he was the one who apparently couldn't sleep, and maybe he was the one who was possessed."

She lifted her eyebrows, punctuating her cleverness. When she sipped her drink Thomas noticed that her hand shook. Maybe it was lost sleep because of the calls, and the resultant nerves. But again Thomas thought it was more.

His hand had shaken like that at first. In his case it had come from a life hitting the rocks.

"But I imagine you're here, Mr. Thomas, because of what happened to Sam Cain," she said, bringing him out of his own thoughts.

"That's right, although your problems with the school board also interest me. The whole issue of freedom of expression."

"It's all the same context, isn't it?" she said. "These people trying to drive me out of the high school, trying to brand me as a witch, and then one of them goes after Sam with the jaw of a mule because he told people what they were doing was unjust and oppressive."

For the first time a real emotion, anger, crept into her voice.

"Do you believe that's why Mr. Cain was attacked?"

"Given what society has become for us in Paradise these days, yes I do. It's as if the Inquisition has come to town. It's quite an atmosphere we live in." She looked at Oates. "I went to see the mother of a friend today at the hospital. Still, I received some interesting looks from the other citizens around, people I've known all my life. As if I were one of the original Salem witches." She shook her head in disbelief.

"You seem to be at the center of the storm," Thomas said.

"Yes, and against my will, I want you to know."

She got up to put more ice in her drink. The emotion of her last words stayed on her face. There was anger in the English teacher, and also, it seemed, a disposition to tangle with those she called her enemies. No shrinking violet, Margaret Masters.

"Just what is it you did to provoke the wrath of the populace?" Thomas asked as she sat down again.

"Nothing," Oates said before she could answer. "She didn't do anything. It's just small-mindedness, prejudice."

"Why prejudice? What kind of prejudice?"

Oates looked at the woman and she turned to Thomas.

"What Dan is referring to is my family background. More specifically my mother, which is all the family I had. You'll hear accounts of her from other citizens, I'm sure, so you might as well hear it from me."

The voice had grown even more gravelly and the West Texas accent more pronounced.

"My mother was a character in this town, Mr. Thomas. She came here in the beginning with the boom."

"Nineteen thirty-eight," Thomas said, writing it down.

"That's right. She was twenty years old, an only child, and her parents had died and left her orphaned. They owned a small farm in east Texas and by herself she couldn't work it. But she told me once that even if she could, she wouldn't have. She was restless and she wanted off that farm. When she heard they'd hit oil out here, it was the sign she'd been waiting for. She sold the place and headed right for Paradise."

"An adventuress," Thomas said.

She nodded. "She liked the energy of the place right off, the excitement. She liked the dreamers who came here looking to get rich. She had a little bit of money of her own from the sale of the farm. It wasn't much, but she was smart with it. She bought a plot of land near where the two state roads intersect now and she began a business." She looked at Thomas. "It was the smartest business to start at the time although one that people hardly considered polite for a lady: she opened a bar." For a moment, she had a stern, censorious look on her face, like one that must have greeted her mother back then.

"I take it some citizens of Paradise let her know they didn't approve," Thomas said.

"Yes. But she ran that bar for the next forty years anyway and she never got tired of oil people. There were good times and bad times, but she got through. It allowed her to buy this house and to send her only child to college and even to graduate school."

"So certain people don't like you because their fathers

used to go drink their paychecks at your mother's saloon?"

"There's that, although she did her share of lending to regular customers. But there's also the question of how my mother kept the place afloat all those years, even during the bad times, the busts. She had to give her clientele what it wanted, Mr. Thomas."

"What was that?"

She shrugged. "Lots of the bars featured backroom poker games where the boys could lose the money they made on the rigs, and, of course, there was the need for occasional female company. If you didn't offer those services you went out of business, and Mother wasn't about to let that happen." She arched one sweeping eyebrow. "Some of the gossips insisted that even Mama herself was available to a man with enough money. It wasn't true at all, but that was the rumor."

She held his gaze brazenly as if she herself were a hustler. But she was just someone who refused to color the truth: that the high school English teacher was the daughter of a woman who was not only a bar owner, but a gambling den operator and a madam, and was suspected of being a hooker.

She turned the glass in her hand. When she spoke, her voice was softer.

"My mother did what she had to do to survive here, Mr. Thomas. To me, she was my mama, and she was good at it. She loved me, as much as any mother in this town loved her child or even more. And she had lots of friends in Paradise. Dan's father, who founded the *Chronicle*, was one of them."

"That's right," the big man said eagerly. "One of her best."

"But there were always stories, whispering in certain sectors of the population," Margaret said. "As well as whispering about me when I first started to teach. I probably never would have gotten the job if a friend of my mother's hadn't been superintendent at the time. But the gossiping started then."

"And all of it was unjust," Oates said. "Margaret's a fine teacher."

"But that's not the main reason why people are trying to drive me out of the high school," she said abruptly. "They want me fired because I attempted to teach literature," she said. "It's an uncomplicated as that."

"I take it they don't want you to teach certain kinds of literature."

"No. What they object to is just what makes writing real literature. That's what I believe." The passion that went with that collection of books surrounding her was obvious. "Literature isn't the simple story, the official story, or accepted story. It's the story that maps human complexity. It's about the evil side of people who are supposedly good and vice versa. It isn't black and white. That's what some people don't like. Another reason is that it's often composed by misfits, in the literal sense of the word, individuals who don't fit easily into society. That's why some people won't hear it and don't want their children to hear it. And finally, it's a world in which there is sex. Not pornography, but sexuality. And there are parents who seem to think this is a deep, dark secret that should be kept from their kids."

She stopped and went to her drink. Thomas could see how Margaret Masters might ruffle some feathers in a place like Paradise. He could also see how her concept of literature neatly fit her own experience: the desire to see the good side of supposedly bad people, as in the case of her mother; the misfit, which was maybe the image she had of herself; and the sexuality, because that's what it was that infused those dark eyes.

He understood the brass in her too, now. That disposition to fight. She probably had needed it all her life, growing up in the shadow of her mother's reputation.

She reached over to the desk, shook a cigarette from a pack, lighted it, exhaled, looked at it, then at Thomas.

"Yes, the complete Jezebel. I stopped smoking these things four years ago and I've started again with all this madness."

"What is the literature you assigned that caused all this trouble?"

"The complaints started about three years ago," she told him. "First about one book, then another, until I had to change almost every work of literature in the curriculum. They wouldn't let me teach Salinger because one of the characters was a prostitute; Hemingway because two unmarried people, stuck in the middle of a terrible war, dare to make love; Steinbeck because a woman suckles a man, a black man, who's starving to death. Anything that had to do with sex, with intimacy, had to be stricken from the curriculum and even taken off the shelves of the school library. I ended up teaching a course, supposedly about literature, which means about human beings, in which no person ever touched another person with love."

She paused, took a last drag from her cigarette and stubbed it out.

"It turned out that wasn't good enough. One day a woman, a mother of one of the students, stood up at a parent-teacher meeting and complained that the books her daughter was reading were too secular, that they didn't speak of God. That it was wrong to give children a version of life in which God wasn't in evidence. That wasn't reality. Sex couldn't exist, but God had to. That was the perspective, and other parents at the meeting got on the bandwagon. It was suggested that I find literature in which God was in evidence."

She stopped, her drink poised next to her face, and begged a question of Thomas.

"So what did you do?"

She cocked her head and assumed a canny expression. "I went right to the source."

She got up, took from a shelf a copy of the Bible, sat again and opened it.

"I brought it to class and read to them parts of Genesis, the Psalms, and a bit of Job, which I thought they would empathize with given the trials Paradise has been through."

She was flipping through pages. "That was all well and

good, but then one of them asked what was my favorite scripture."

"And what did you answer?"

She turned more pages and then stopped. "Have you ever read 'The Song of Solomon,' Mr. Thomas? It's a paean by a woman to what she considers God's most beautiful creation: her lover."

She ran her finger down the page.

> "Let him kiss me with the kisses of his mouth: for thy love is better than wine."

She looked up, and Thomas nodded. He recognized the line. Her eyes dropped, she turned the page. Her voice was even lower and more gravelly after the gin.

> "By night on my bed I sought him whom my soul loveth: I sought him, but I found him not.
> I will rise now and go about the city in the streets and in the broad ways I will seek him . . .
> The watchmen that go about the city found me: to whom I said, 'Saw ye he whom my soul loveth?'
> It was but a little that I passsed from them, but I found him . . .
> I held him and would not let him go, until I had brought him into my mother's house and into the chamber of her that conceived me."

Her finger went up the page.

> "My beloved is mine and I am his:
> he feedeth among the lilies.
> Until the day break, and the shadows
> flee away, turn, my beloved,
> and be thou like a roe or a young gazelle
> upon the mountains of Bether."

Her hand had strayed to her breast. She stayed staring at the words. Then she closed the book and sipped her drink.

"You read it to your students?" She nodded. "Why that particular scripture? You must have known with the sexual references it could cause trouble."

Her chin came up combatively. "Religious conservatives believe that the Bible isn't just a story, but that it's history. That it really happened. If that's the truth, then people involved must have had some warm blood in their veins. At least, this woman did. She was a real human being."

Thomas nodded slowly, studying her. Of course she was not just defending a warm-blooded woman five thousand years dead, but herself as well.

"That was why those parents moved for your dismissal?"

"Yes. That and a discussion we had in class about those readings. I was asked in which genre I placed the Bible: fact or fiction. One of the little devils put me right on the spot."

"And?"

"And I said I believed it was allegory," she said readily, "but that others believed it was historical fact. That both were opinions that should be respected." She shook her head. "You can ask Dan what happened after that. The reaction was apocalyptic."

Thomas looked at the editor.

"There was a ruckus," he said.

"Dan is a master of understatement," she said. "These people won't accept any challenge to the Bible's historical legitimacy. They said by using my position in the classroom to cast doubt on that legitimacy, I had challenged their religious beliefs and those of their children. They demanded my dismissal. Right away they started piling wood around the stake. They had themselves a witch to burn.

"Overnight a group of parents organized. Some of them didn't even have students in my classes, but they wouldn't have missed it for the world. They insisted on a meeting with my principal, a man who is retiring soon and doesn't want to risk his pension. A man who doesn't want the boat rocked. Officially, they charged me with using materials in class that had not been approved by my superiors, which is technically a violation of my contract. In this case, it was the Bible, a nice irony. But they really came to that meeting to cast stones. They would have cast real ones if they could. One mother I'd never laid eyes on called me an immoral woman. Do you know why?"

Thomas shook his head although she wasn't looking at him. Her tone was flat, emotionless.

"She said not only had I profaned the Bible by using it for my salaciouis purposes, but I'd also been married for some time and hadn't had children of my own." She shook her head in disbelief and her voice fell. "As if that's a crime and not just a sad fact of life.

"She also brought up my broken marriage. A divorce which wasn't my idea, I should tell you. It was my husband's. He said it was because I gave him too little attention and my work too much. Now isn't that ironic as well."

A bitter smile pulled at her full lips and she drank from her gin. Just then a clock on the wall rang nine o'clock. She glanced at it.

"The bell tolls for me, Mr. Thomas," she said dryly.

"So they want your job."

Her hand shook just a bit as she lit another cigarette. He wondered how much she'd had to drink. He also noticed lines around her eyes, cracks in the tough exterior.

"Yes, they're trying to get me removed from the high school, and that means they're trying to take away my life. Because teaching is my life, Mr. Thomas. Make no mistake."

She said it matter-of-factly, not as a play on Thomas's sympathies. It was a declaration of her state of affairs: divorced, childless, approaching forty, married to her work, her students. Her dilemma was naked before him. The half-finished dress on the floor and the glass of gin on the desk were evidence. It must have been clear to the citizens of Paradise as well. Thomas, who had seen his own life shaken during the past three months, thought he could actually feel the tremor coming from her.

"The school board makes that decision?" he asked.

"That's right. They make their decision after a public hearing next week and based in part on the recommendations of the legal counsel to the board."

"Jack Eames, the county attorney."

She raised her eyebrows. "You know him?"

"Not yet, but I've read his name in the articles," he said. "Can you count on support from him? After all, he's a lawyer and there are constitutional issues here."

She tasted her drink and her mouth puckered with the bitterness, of the drink or maybe of her thoughts.

"I don't know if anybody can trust Jack Eames about anything these days," she said. "He used to be a liberal. Now he's supposedly a moderate. But this town is very conservative lately and Jack wants to run for state senate. Every vote counts."

She said it snidely, cynically, smiled to herself, then stared out the window for several moments.

"You're also going to hear from others about another chapter in the life of Margaret Masters, so you might as well hear it from me," she said. Her words made Oates shift in his chair. The look on his face was one of extreme discomfort.

"I was divorced five years ago," she said. "Two years after that Jack Eames and I became lovers. When he started talking about running for office, he broke it off. That was late last year. And in a town like this, everybody knows it happened. I wasn't the first woman in this town to have an affair and I wasn't the first to be linked to Jack Eames. But then, other women here aren't also corrupters of children who also have shady family pasts." She focused on Thomas with her dark, almost black eyes. "Now do you understand, Mr. Thomas, why I'm being hauled before the school board, why the witch-hunt?"

Neither Thomas nor Oates said anything. There was nothing to add. Thomas watched her and wondered if the affair, like the reading of "The Song of Solomon," had also been an act of rebellion against a town that had whispered about her all her life.

"And Sam Cain's connection to your case?"

"Old Sam let people know he didn't like the movement against me."

"That's why you went to him for help?"

"Yes, but he said he couldn't spare the time."

"He couldn't or he wouldn't?"

She gave him a sharp, cold glance, then shrugged.

"Is that why the sheriff came to see you?" Thomas asked.

"The day before Sam was attacked, I called him. That was the only reason the sheriff wanted to talk to me."

"Do you have any idea who would do that to him?"

"Go ask the Reverend Sam Dash," she said, giving a sarcastic twist to the title. "He's the one leading the Inquisition. He should know all the deep secrets there are to know in this town."

She went to her gin as if to wash a bad taste from her mouth. Thomas wrote down the quote.

"Is this the first time you've had dealings with him?"

"I wish," she said shifting restlessly in her chair. "I had him as a student in a speech class about ten or twelve years ago. I believe it was the only course he passed. They tell me he's very good at it these days, especially when he's asking for my head."

"Is there any reason he would go after you now?"

She nodded. "A few months back his name came up in conversation with a parent. I said I didn't like him or his ideas and that I thought he was a fake, a hustler. I didn't know it, but the woman was a member of his church and it must have gotten back to him. It was only a short time until the show of vengeance began. That's why all this started. I challenged his veracity, his authority. Me, a lowly woman. I think that's the true reason he came after me." She looked at Thomas with mock sheepishness. "I'm afraid I'm sometimes careless with my opinions."

She shook her head again.

"This is a crazy town with all its booms and busts, Mr. Thomas. Mercurial. Unstable. But it used to be a fair place to live and work. Before this bust hit, that is. Before it started breaking apart and this madness took over."

Thomas watched her. She was staring into nothing, a troubled expression on her face. An intelligent woman who was besieged by forces, by demons she didn't believe in, but which were certainly undoing her life. She had been less than diplomatic with her antagonists, but she was still the victim of fanaticism and small-town prejudice. He pictured her as the heroine at the center of his article.

Thomas wrote down the last quote. Then he began to go back over his notes, asking her details: her education, graduate study, teaching experience, past evaluations. Dates, places, the names of parents involved.

When he was finished, he and Oates stood up. Margaret Masters took them toward the door, stopping next to the Doré engraving of Quijote.

"Dan is trying to help me and maybe you too can write something that makes a difference, Mr. Thomas. Maybe you can be my knight in shining armor."

Her look was acute, delving. Over the years Thomas had found the women in his life almost always in the stories he was covering. It came with the rootless lifestyle. The relationships were necessarily short, as he'd told the psychiatrist; exchanges of warmth and information, but not much more. They had ranged from policewomen to congressional aides, from starlets to a lady lieutenant colonel. The affairs had almost always started with an interview and, somewhere along the line, that sort of gaze.

One of those affairs had ended in marriage. It had lasted barely a year, during which he'd had to cover an earthquake in Iran, fighting in Nicaragua, famine in Ethiopia. Meanwhile the relationship had turned into a disaster as well. It had fallen apart altogether during a five-week period when he'd been away covering a hostage taking. He had received a telegram from New York: "I'd rather be a hostage, anybody's hostage. Goodbye."

He said goodnight then and Margaret Masters saw them out, a dark silhouette disappearing behind a closing door.

"So what do you think of Margaret?" Oates asked as they went to the car.

Thomas glanced back at the house. "I think she's a woman afraid her whole life may be falling apart and she may be right."

But Thomas's thoughts went beyond that. Margaret Masters was a woman who had brought herself to the point of crisis. Deliberately. By assigning the sexually charged reading, she had tossed a gauntlet before the conservative majority of Paradise, a majority she felt had ostracized her all her life. She had finally said: "Here, this is who I am. Burn me for it." Maybe it had been the broken love affair that had brought her to it. Whatever the reason, she had placed her life neatly in the hands of her former lover.

Oates was just getting back into his car. "Let's go see Jack Eames," he said, as if he had read Thomas's mind.

Chapter 5

*T*he sun was all the way down now, but it felt just as hot and still. The constituents of Paradise were out on their porches, sitting, talking, escaping the heat of indoors. You could see them bathed in the porchlight, or sometimes they sat in the dark and you spotted only the embers of cigarettes glowing. Outside many of those homes were For Sale signs, making it seem to Thomas as if the whole scene was for sale: house, people, heat, despair. Name your price.

They passed the motel and Thomas saw no cars there, apparently no new arrivals. They turned right at the corner of the state road, right again into a cul-de-sac, and pulled up to a house at the end of it. Beyond the house there was only open prairie stretching west.

"This is Jack Eames's place," Oates said.

It was a long brick ranch house with a stand of white wooden columns outside; a little touch of Washington, as if the political hopeful were already getting in the mood. A car was in the port, and a light was on in the living room. They walked up to big white doors and rang the bell; it echoed inside, but nobody answered.

"I called Jack this morning and he told me he'd probably be here," Oates said, pressing the bell again. Thomas peeked in a small window that looked through the foyer and into the living room. He saw a card table there with cards and chips on the table. No players, though. On one wall hung a print of a Norman Rockwell painting: a campaign platform draped with red, white, and blue bunting, and an old pol, mouth agape, finger waving, working the voters. But he was apparently the only pol around. Jack Eames wasn't home.

"Maybe he went to Austin after all," Oates said. "He told me he might have to talk to the powers that be about his political future."

"Just who is Jack Eames?" Thomas asked.

They stopped next to an old-fashioned mailbox with a red flag on it.

"Jack's a local boy, born and raised here," Oates said. "He's been county attorney about five years. There's been a lot of crime in Paradise because of the economic conditions and he's been tough but fairhanded. A lot of drug activity, particularly these last couple of years, and Jack's been trying to get at the roots of it.

"Margaret has her reasons for disliking him, but they're personal. Like she said, he's gotten more conservative these last years, but then, lots of people have. And he *does* have political ambitions, but whether that had anything to do with the end of their relationship, I don't know."

Oates was talking like a man caught in the middle of a fight between two friends.

"He has an affair with her," Thomas said, "breaks it off, and now has to make recommendations that will affect her career, her life."

"Exactly."

"So why doesn't he exclude himself? Why doesn't he cite a conflict of interest, his personal complication?"

"I'm not sure there is a conflict in Jack's mind," Oates said. "To him it's a legal matter."

"Although he'd also be publicly admitting the affair," Thomas said, "and given that he's been mentioned for elective office, maybe he doesn't want to do that. The wrath of God and the God-fearing might come down on him. And she's afraid he's going to sell her down the river at this hearing in order to win a certain block of voters."

Oates looked at the house as if he could see through the walls and fix on the man who lived there.

"I wouldn't think that of Jack, but you can't always know what ambition will do to a man." Oates was a journalist in a small town who had to write about his friends and neighbors. He didn't have the luxury of distance and cynicism that Thomas had.

Oates was about to say more, but then a car turned into the cul-de-sac, came toward them, and stopped in front of the house. Thomas followed Oates as he walked through the beams of the headlights and leaned in the driver's window.

"Hello, Landon."

Oates was talking to a middle-aged, narrow-shouldered man in a light-colored cowboy shirt sitting in an extremely old and beat-up white Rolls-Royce. He had dark stubble on his face, and even standing next to the car Thomas smelled alcohol. The man looked at Oates and then at Thomas suspiciously, as if he wasn't expecting to see them there.

"This is Landon Turner, one of our local ranchers," Oates said, and he introduced Thomas.

The other man nodded. "My pleasure," he said, although he didn't seem too pleased. He tried to smile, but it came out crooked.

"If you're looking for Jack Eames, he's not home," Oates said.

The other man stared at the house.

"I was just making a run to the store and thought I'd pass by. I'll have to come back later."

"How are things with you, Landon?"

"Oh, I can't complain, Dan. It wouldn't do any good anyway." He smiled his crooked smile again.

Then he said good evening, nodded to Thomas, glanced one last time at the house, and pulled around the cul-de-sac, seeming in a hurry to be away. Oates watched him reach the corner and turn right, out of sight.

"Landon Turner," the big man said, shaking his head. "He had to declare bankruptcy about two years ago. He's one of the citizens around here who let the boom go to his head. He branched out into businesses he didn't know anything about. He got his ways and means all fouled up. They say he went out to California and spent a lot of time with racehorses and television actresses. Then he sent to Africa, had animals shipped over and started a zoo, a safari land, on his property. He drove around it in his Rolls-Royce."

"A high roller."

Oates nodded. "He ran crazy, and then it all came down around him like a house of cards. He even lost most of the family ranch his father left him. On top of that, his wife divorced him and took what she could. He's got a small patch and a house out there that Sam Cain, his family lawyer, saved him with his legal work, and he looks after the rest of the place for the company that bought it. Some Japanese outfit. He's had the trials of Job lately, Landon has."

Oates looked back at the house. "I guess Jack isn't gonna make it. Let's go to the hospital and check on Sam Cain."

They got into Oates's Bronco and drove back through the darkened center of town until they reached the small, one-story hospital on the northern outskirts. It was a relatively new brick building that Oates said had forty beds in it. He bragged about its highly trained staff and modern technology.

"It was built when times were good and there was plenty of money around," he said.

It was after visiting hours and the lobby was dark and quiet when they walked in. Oates simply waved at a white-capped woman at the nursing station and led Thomas to a private room on the main hallway.

Attorney Sam Houston Cain lay on a hospital bed in an oxygen tent. The room was filled with floral arrangements and the night table was crowded with get-well cards. Coming out of the clear plastic tent were various connections, including one that led to a cardiograph. The electronic green line rose weakly as his heart beat, fell into a loose scribble for several seconds, and then rose weakly again.

They moved closer and looked down on the old man whose head was almost totally concealed in bandages. Oates gazed down at him somberly, as the slow heartbeat punctuated the silence.

"I saw this coming for a long time," he said finally.

"What do you men?" Thomas asked.

"Not that something would happen to Sam Cain specifically, but that politics around here would be turning bitter, even violent. That bad times were coming. Yes, I did."

The editor took a last look at Cain and then led Thomas out of the room. Just across from it was a visitors' waiting room with a stainless-steel coffeepot in it and Styrofoam cups. Oates poured them each a cup and they sat in adjacent red Naugahyde chairs, from which they could see into the room and watch the wavering green line that represented Sam Cain's tentative hold on life. The hospital was quiet around them.

"Something like this has been coming ever since the town was founded back in the thirties and it broke down into two tribes," Oates said, "the religious conservatives and the others."

"It was always that way?"

Oates nodded. "When they first hit oil here, this place filled up with people overnight. Some of 'em were farm boys from around the Southwest, hardworkin' and almost always religious. They worked the wells and were the ones who got baptized by oil when the gushers came in. They were, in that sense, the anointed of the oil fields even back then." He paused. "Then you had the other arrivals."

"The sinners," Thomas said.

"Exactly. People trying to escape the Depression that had hit all over the country. Salesmen and lawyers, like Sam Cain, merchants and teachers, gamblers and ladies of the night. When that first big boom passed, when the gushers slowed up, many people left, but others stayed on, from both tribes, and they became the permanent population of Paradise."

"And there was always friction, the way Margaret Masters said?"

"Some maybe, in cases like Margaret's, but not politically. Those religious people didn't get mixed up in politics. Strict fundamentalist Christians paid their taxes, they rendered that much to Caesar, but politics was profane."

"For some reason things changed."

Oates nodded. Somewhere up the hall a voice called out in sleep, a nightmare. Then it quieted.

"Fundamentalists everywhere got militant politically, but here there was extra reason: the last boom," he said. "The Arabs turned off the spigots over in the Middle East and the price of oil here went through the roof. People were making big money, more than they had ever dreamed of, and it turned this town into Babylon."

"How so?"

Oates's face wrinkled with distaste. "We had women flying to Dallas to get their hair done once a week. We had people buying Mercedeses and Rolls-Royces, sometimes more than one at a time. Gem dealers were setting up in the motels, selling their trinkets, drillers and roughnecks were walking around with diamonds on their fingers and gold around their necks. We had more prostitutes and gamblers. And we also got something we never had before during the other booms, the other epochs of sin in Paradise. We got heavy drugs."

"Cocaine?"

"Cocaine, some heroin, and, of course, high-grade speed, so that people could work those long shifts and make that big money. There had been some drugs around here ever since the late sixties. But very little and always in the transient community. Drugs had never touched the townspeople. Not until this last boom. Kids from the old families, the backbone of the town, got into cocaine and even into heroin in a couple of cases. We had one boy, from a Mexican family, who died of an overdose." He pointed out the window. "Then drug planes started coming over right outside town, dropping the stuff. Big-time smugglers working shipments worth lots of money. Jack Eames started looking into it. About six months ago, the sheriff's department managed to shoot one of the smugglers on the ground. Another of them got away after a chase. It was the biggest story we had all last year."

"All of it the work of the Devil," Thomas said. "At least in some people's minds."

"The Reverend Sam Dash showed up in town just about the same time that really heavy drug traffic started. He'd been gone about three years. In the meantime, he'd found God and found Him with a vengeance. He was younger than the other preachers, more fiery, a real crowd pleaser. He told folks the end of the world was comin'. He knew it for fact. That it was the duty of the God-fearin' to take over the town and get ready for the Lord's comin'. That's what they're doing."

"Let's go back a moment," Thomas said. "You said the smuggling started about the time Dash came back?"

Oates shook his head.

"Don't try and make anything outa that. I brought it up once with Jim West, the sheriff, who was staking out those drug drops. I mean, with Sam Dash's past history and all, it was something of a coincidence. But he told me to forget about it. That it had to be outside people, from Abilene or Odessa. Maybe even Dallas. Sam Dash, as far as he was concerned, was exactly what he appeared to be."

Still, there was doubt in Oates's voice.

"But like a good journalist you didn't quite buy that, did you?"

Oates cocked his head. "Let's just say it was an election year and Sam Dash and his people already had control of a big block of votes in this town. They still do."

"And that's the buzz saw Margaret Masters had gotten caught in by challenging Dash," Thomas said.

"Margaret and many of the rest of us in town. During the last elections Dash got his people out to vote. They won all the seats on the school board that were up for election. That gave them almost half the board. The ones who aren't theirs figure they have to keep Sam Dash happy or lose their seats in the next election. In fact, every politician in town has to keep these people in mind."

"Fanatics," Thomas said.

Oates winced at the word and fixed on Thomas with his sad eyes.

"Not all of them," he said. "You have to try and understand what's happened to these people. They really do feel like they're in captivity in a country and in a culture that is immoral and ruinous. You can't blame them for that, when you live in a small town, in the middle of nowhere, and suddenly you find some of your children are doing heroin. Some of their own kids are becoming criminals because of it. You can't understand your child anymore, as if he's become a different species of human being. I think most of these folks truly believe we are in the last days of the world.

"These are mainly people who've worked all their lives in oil and now they have to face the fact that they no longer control those lives. The Arabs do. That's just the truth of it. But they can't accept that. So they say that God controls their lives, a God that's gonna take them outa their misery and end the world any day, because for them, the world as they knew it *has* ended."

"Do you believe in God?" Thomas asked him.

Oates mulled over the question, the way he might have

if asked to state a political position. In Paradise maybe it was a political decision.

"I try to believe," he said finally. "But you write a story like this and see what happened to Sam Cain and you start thinking it's the Devil who has sway in Paradise and not the Lord." He focused on Thomas. "Do you believe?"

"In the Devil?" Thomas asked. "I guess I do. I've seen him at work often enough over the years and I've come here looking for him." He quickly drew a horned Beelzebub on the cover of his notebook. "God? That's a different question."

Oates got up, threw away his coffee cup, and gave a last glance at Sam Cain's waning heartbeat. Thomas followed him back past the empty nursing station and outside. It was hot and close. Instinctively, Thomas looked for the skyscrapers he was accustomed to, but there were only those stunted buildings and the sky, vast, dark, empty and still.

Oates drove Thomas back to his car. They said goodnight and Thomas headed back to the motel.

Right next door to it was a hamburger stand that was open, and Thomas realized he hadn't eaten dinner. It wasn't the Broadway Deli, but it would do. He went in and ordered a cheeseburger, fries, and a Coke, and sat at a table by himself. Right in front of him, one table away, sat the only other customer, a heavy-set man about sixty, in a cheap green plaid sport jacket that was too small for him. On his pudgy fingers the man wore rings, four of them, all flashy gold and stones, none of which looked real. A small-brimmed Panama hat lay on the table next to a Styrofoam coffee cup and an overflowing ashtray. The man took a drag off a cigarette and nodded at Thomas.

"I'll bet you're from outa town," he said. When he spoke he exposed bad teeth, generously inlaid with gold and silver. He also revealed an accent that wasn't at all Texas. Maybe the West Side of Chicago, but no more western than that.

"That's right," Thomas said.

The fat man nodded. "On the road, huh?"

"Just here on business."

The other man flicked his eyebrows avidly.

"Me too. Lots of opportunity in a town like this."

Thomas frowned. "I hear differently. I hear the place is bust."

The fat man nodded sagely. "That's exactly when you want to be here. Not when everybody is reachin' for the same pot of gold. This is when you pick up the change." He tapped the Formica table with a long, yellowed fingernail. "Right now. I know this town."

"You've been here before?"

"Lots of times. And I've made a bunch of money here."

"Is that right?"

"You can bet your bottom dollar. My name's Claude Denison," he said, as if his name and riches were synonymous and Thomas would recognize it. "All you need is a little bit to invest. This is when people are looking to get out and this is when you get your bargains."

"What do you buy?"

"What is there to buy around here? Land, that's what. That's all there is, land and what's under it."

"But it's not worth anything these days."

The other man squinted through his own smoke. "Is that right? Well, show me people who have some land and think it's not worth anything and we'll talk business."

He got up, grabbed his coffee cup, and sat down across the table from Thomas. He leaned forward and spoke under his smoke-laden breath. "I know this place. I worked as a land man here once."

"What does that mean?"

"That means I worked for the oil companies, buying land and drilling rights for them. Years ago I did that. But that was a sucker's game, workin' for the companies. After that I worked for myself as a promoter. I put together my own land deals, worked with independent drillers. Made bundles for me and for my investors."

Thomas studied him. His eyes went from the pale, un-healthy-looking face, to the worn jacket, to frayed cuffs that stuck out of the sleeves. Denison noticed and gri-maced, pulling down a sleeve.

"Lately I had some trouble in the market, like lots of people," he said.

From the looks of him, the only market Claude Denison had ever been in was one where he'd gone to shoplift. If you held him upside down and shook him, you wouldn't get a dime—maybe some old tote tickets, losing tickets, but not much else.

He reached into his shirt pocket and took out another cigarette without exposing the pack and lit it.

"There's big business to be done in this town. There's a lot of natural gas under us right where we sit and all over these ranches. I've got some inside information that the government is gonna make it profitable to get that gas outa the ground any day now and things will be cookin' around here."

"Maybe somebody beat you to it. I understand the Jap-anese have bought some land around here recently. Maybe that's why."

Denison scowled. "The Japanese." He didn't like that. They had invaded his territory, had snuck in on him. He shrugged it off. "Well, that's all right. There'll be enough to go around. But right now I don't have the ante. I had some problems in the market, like I said. If you have a little bit to invest, I can tell you how to triple your money in a matter of days. I've got some inside information."

Thomas nodded. He was looking beyond Denison, through the window, where a sheriff's-department car had pulled up outside. A large, brown-shirted policeman in a Stetson stepped in and was headed for the counter when he noticed the man in the green plaid jacket.

Denison had leaned toward Thomas across his table.

"I know somebody who's sitting on a fortune and doesn't know it."

The sheriff's man sidled over and touched Denison's shoulder. Denison turned and looked up the length of him, then he frowned.

"What's this?"

"You're supposed to be out of town," the deputy said sternly. "You were told to go somewhere else."

Denison's pale face stormed over. "The sheriff said twenty-four hours." He jabbed at his hairy wrist, although there was no watch on it. "I have until noon tomorrow."

The sheriff's man looked at him stonily.

"You be on that bus tomorrow, or you'll be back in jail and this time you'll spend your whole summer vacation there. We don't need more swindlers here."

Denison scowled at him, but said nothing. He watched the deputy pick up a coffee at the counter and leave. He didn't speak again until the police car was pulling out.

"I don't know who that guy is trying ta push around."

"You had a bit of trouble?"

Denison turned on him.

"I didn't do a thing. Like I said, I have a bit of a cash-flow problem, that's all. But I can solve that. I know how to make money around here and make it fast. In fact, that's why they kept me in jail three days. The county attorney would probably like to make some of that money himself. So they run me out. They know I have this place wired for sound. All I need is someone with a little bit of working capital."

"Well, I wish I could help you," Thomas said, "but I'm not positioned for it at the moment."

"You said you're in business."

"I'm a journalist. A writer."

Denison grimaced, showing his yellow teeth. "That's not business."

Thomas sipped at his Coke. Then the door opened and the heavy-set Latin man from motel room number three came in and went to the pay phone in the corner. There were phones in the rooms, but maybe his was broken, Thomas thought. Or maybe he didn't want the skittish desk clerk eavesdropping. Whatever the reason, he pressed himself into the corner, dialed, got someone at the other end, and talked. His voice rose once, but Thomas didn't make out what he said. After less than a minute, he hung up. Thomas watched him walk out looking upset and turn away from the motel and up the road.

Thomas finished his food and said good night to Claude Denison. The "land man" nodded, but didn't look at him. He was grimacing into his coffee, maybe worrying about the Japanese.

Thomas went back to the motel. The night seemed warmer and even more still. Inside, he tried the air conditioner, but found it didn't work. He cranked open the windows, undressed, and was getting into bed, when he noticed the Bible on the night table. It was the same Bible that was in hotel and motel rooms all over the world, part of the decor. Thomas could never remember opening one because it had never been source material for the story he was working on. This time maybe it was. He picked it up, flipped through it, and came, at the back, to Revelation, the scripture cited by Lloyd Haynes about the end of the world.

He thumbed through it, skipping from chapter to chapter, stopping at words, phrases, images; a slain lamb, a great red dragon in the sky, a man with flames for eyes holding stars in his hand, the heavens splitting, "hail and fire mingled with the blood and were cast upon the earth"; the pale horse of death riding through eternity. They were the plagues and horrors Haynes had talked about.

Thomas closed the book before reaching the end. He had seen the murals at the Revelation Temple. He didn't need to provoke more nightmares than he already had. He turned off the light and lay in the heat and stillness until he went to sleep.

Chapter 6

*T*homas lay on the bed listening to the hail pelt the roof of the motel. It had started maybe five minutes before and drummed him out of sleep. He looked at his watch. The numbers flicked and now it was 6:44 A.M. In New York you learned to sleep through the clanking pipes and the angry taxi horns, but they weren't as loud as this.

He closed his eyes, but he couldn't doze off again. He lay blinking at the racket and then swung out of bed, put on a towel, opened the door, and saw the hailstones ricocheting off the tarred parking lot. Some of them were the size of Ping-Pong balls and made a crackling noise on the asphalt, as if the outer skin of the earth were splitting. He had parked the car under the adjoining carport, and it was riding out the storm without damage. He watched the mad bouncing of the hailstones a moment longer, then closed the door and headed for the shower.

As he walked toward the bathroom, the noise on the roof suddenly stopped. It happened from one second to the next and created an abrupt silence that was as loud as the noise had been. He turned, looked back at the door, and strained to hear something, anything. He waited several moments, but there wasn't the slightest noise. He put his palms up to his ears, actually afraid that he'd suddenly gone deaf. He still heard nothing, only the tension of his own body. He frowned; it was as if the walls around him had sucked up every sound. He went to the television and pushed the On button. even static would satisfy him. Light started to dawn on the screen, then it went black. The overhead light also went off. The electricity was gone. When he looked toward the curtained window, he saw that it was dark, darker than it had been just a minute ago. Thomas felt something now he hadn't felt in almost three months: a vertiginous fear that he was losing his mind.

He quickly slipped into pants and opened the door. He stared at the parking lot. It was covered with hail and reflected a strange light. It was seven o'clock in the morning, but he was looking at twilight. The day had shifted in reverse and daylight was being sucked back into the sky. It was dead quiet and still. He wondered if mornings were always like this in Texas. Thomas stood there, facing down the stillness, as if he could make it end, but it didn't. Then he stepped away from the door, turned and glanced back over the roof of the one-story motel. And that was when he saw it.

In that first moment before the word could form, it looked to him like a monster in the sky, a colossal manta ray. Its enormous body blocked out all light and its long, tapering, pointed tail dangled near the earth. But its body was whirling and churning and it was sucking into itself all the light and sound, and all the soil of the earth, which made it bigger, murkier, darker every moment.

A door flew open down the motel row, slammed against

the wall, and Thomas saw the hesitant, slow-moving clerk of the night before come hurtling out of it in flapping yellow pajamas and go sprinting across the open field, toward a culvert, but also in the direction of the monster.

"Tornado-o-o!" he screamed.

His one word was snatched out of the air as if the man had shouted it from a speeding train. Thomas heard it and then looked up again at the towering column of blackness. He stood stock-still moments more, planted like a tree, ready to be ripped from the ground. And then finally he uprooted himself and began to run headlong after the clerk, in a way that could only be generated by terror.

Thomas ran right at the tornado; right at death. It was growing darker and bigger as it swallowed the earth of the prairie, sucked in more and more of the light out of the air. And now he could hear it. The sound, like a tremendous rock slide, vibrated all around, all through him, as if the earth underneath him were about to give way.

Thomas ran, gasping for breath, as the black cloud suddenly dipped and its sharp tail touched the ground for the first time. It was maybe a half mile away from him and it began to move with an erratic, frenzied motion, like a dancer driven by unbearable tension, by madness. It undulated one way, then another. His eyes pinned open by fear, Thomas watched as the funnel hit the first houses on the outskirts and he saw pieces—a roof, a fence, a wall— being sucked up into the air like so many toothpicks. He saw an entire house twist and fold and disappear into the cloud and thought he could hear the nails wrenching from the wood. A tree took flight like a twig. He saw an animal— maybe a dog, maybe a coyote—swirl along the outside of the funnel clawing madly at the air and get sucked into it. And there was the roar, louder, enveloping him, reaching his bones.

Then he tripped and fell. Staring up into the blackness, he hadn't watched the ground. His toe smashed into a large rock and he went sprawling flat on his chest. He rolled over, grasping for his bare foot, and he felt the rumbling in the earth right through his back.

He rolled over, tore at the soil with his fingers until he was able to get to his feet, and ran again, limping now in pain, moaning with it.

The tornado was closer, larger, darker. The air pressure hurt his ears. Above him the electricity wires began to tug and flap, twirling like a jump rope spun by invisible hands. Death was playing with him. He saw the telephone poles start to fall one by one. Wires snapped, spitting electricity, and went into convulsions.

Thomas saw the motel clerk run right off the edge of the darkening field and disappear, falling into the culvert, a madman who had run off the edge of the earth. Thomas was gasping from the pain in his lungs and in his foot and from his fear. The funnel was no more than a hundred yards away now, a black cone with strange yellow light around its edges, as if yellow were the color of life, of its essence, and it was seeping out of the cone as people died. The funnel sucked more of the light into itself, so now it was almost night again. The air was starting to gust around him, dirt was thrown against him and stung his chest and face.

Then he felt the first tug of it on himself, a plucking at his clothes. He started to scream. Screaming to keep the roar of it out of his ears. Screaming in terror.

Suddenly he felt weightlessness, as if he were being lifted toward that black roaring. As if he had lifted from the earth like an angel, someone no longer human. The way they said God harvested the souls of the dead. It plucked him easily from the earth toward its black heart, toward Death. His feet were still running, clawing the air, looking for earth. His hands flew over his head, trying to hold it off. And then the earth tilted. His legs flew over his head and it was as if he were falling, not rising, falling and falling.

He landed on his side in the culvert; like the clerk, he

had run off the edge of the earth. The fall knocked the
wind out of him. He was as breathless as a dead man. When
he opened his mouth to gasp for air, all he got was soil.
There was no air, only dust and the howling. Then he felt
it pull at him again. His eyes opened wide in terror and
he saw a pipe running along the edge of the culvert a yard
off the ground and he dived for it. He wrapped his arms
and legs around it belly up and held on as it tried to pull
him off. He was looking up toward the sky and saw the
air full of soil. He was breathing soil, lying on the air. The
world was upside down, inside out.

Pieces of Paradise began to fly over the culvert. Pieces
of wood, a small tree, parts of houses. Shingles and planks.
Furniture tumbling in the air. Clothes. Sheets that whirled
like ghosts. More trees. Everything was being ripped out
of the ground. Thirty feet above him Thomas saw a mobile
home fly by, as if it were driving, but upside down, tires
in the air. He thought for a moment he could see a face
in a window. A face like his, screaming.

Branches and leaves and soil fell into the culvert. Then
a large mirror came and shattered on the edge of the
concrete; a piece of it grazed his head. The pull was strong
now. It had him pinned to the pipe and the pipe was
shaking, bowing, threatening to be plucked into space.
Thomas held on, screaming against the twister's scream.

Suddenly, just as had happened back in the motel, everything went still. The pull stopped and the roaring died.
All Thomas could hear were the sounds of the clerk somewhere farther down the culvert, crying, jibbering, praying.
That and a barely audible sound of wind. Thomas loosed
his grip on the pipe. He should have fallen to the sand,
but he didn't. He was held against the pipe, maybe by sweat
that had escaped him in fear. But it wasn't that. He again
felt the terrible weightlessness. The feeling of a disem-
bodied, weightless, dead soul. The sudden silence was the
silence of the dead and it terrified him. He grabbed hold
of the pipe again. He was afraid he was losing his mind.

Without warning, a black gust blew into the ditch and

pulled the air out of his lungs with a screech and threat-
ened to suck the lungs right out of his chest, to turn him
inside out. Thomas's hair stood up in flames and he uttered
a long, pulsing scream as the air came out of him, as the
life was sucked from him. "Oh God!" he cried. "Oh God!
Oh God!"

But then the black gust ended as abruptly as it had come.
It had been the tail of the twister cracking its whip one
last time. The pull weakened and the roar died. There was
dust in the air, but he could breathe. And he felt his heart
pounding. He felt the muscles straining in his arms and
legs now, which he hadn't felt before. He could no longer
hold on to the pipe. He let go and fell the three feet to
the sand, landing on his back. He began to cough the dust
out.

Thomas tried to call to the clerk, but what came out
wasn't language. It was an earth-clogged shout. He got to
his knees and coughed more dirt out of his lungs and dug
it out of his eyes. He tried to get it out of his hair and
when he brought his hand down, he saw blood on it. Not
much, but some. It was where the piece of mirror had hit
him. He was staring down into its broken pieces, his reflection splintered, as if he himself had been shattered.

He looked down the culvert. It was littered with debris:
broken furniture, tree limbs, clothes. Then he saw the
clerk. He was sitting, his pale eyes staring out of a mud-
covered face. He was rocking and jibbering with fear.

Thomas climbed over the junk toward him. He didn't
see any blood on the man. The clerk looked up and saw
Thomas. An inhuman wailing sound escaped him. He
jumped up, lunged suddenly, and swung a fist that hit
Thomas on the side of his neck. Thomas grabbed his arm,
twisted him around, and pushed him back to the ground
on top of some broken branches, kneeling on his chest.
The man was thrashing and screaming. He was out of his
mind, and with his blue eyes staring out of the mud face,
he looked even crazier. Thomas held him until he stopped
thrashing. The man looked up at him and began to sob.

Thomas scrambled up the concrete side of the culvert. He looked in the direction the tornado had gone, but saw nothing. It had cut a trench through the field maybe four feet deep, with soil, stones, and old cattle bones scattered on either side of it. He followed the trench back to where it started and looked into the adjoining neighborhood, which had also been hit.

What he saw made no sense. One house was untouched by the twister, as was another. Then right next to them, where there had been a third house, there was nothing but a fractured foundation, like the root of a broken tooth. Another untouched house and one more that had disappeared.

He realized he was looking from the rear to the street on which Jack Eames lived. The brick house with white columns had stood at the end of the street, but now the columns and roof were gone and there were just two walls still standing. He moved toward it.

People began to come out of the standing houses. They walked slowly, stopping, staring, maybe in shock. Thomas heard his first sound, a moan for help that came from the rubble of one of the houses. The cry seemed to snap the people out of their trances. They stumbled over the broken tree limbs and the crumbled walls toward the cry.

He cut through a yard and was on the street when he saw Margaret Masters. She had come from behind Eames's house, or maybe, miraculously, from inside it. She stepped over the rubble and was walking down the street right toward him, but staring straight ahead as if she didn't see him. She lived at least ten blocks away, and he wondered what she was doing there.

There was no emotion on her face, no fear. Thomas thought she was in shock. He saw blood on her arm and hand, although she didn't look seriously injured. He called to her, but she didn't turn or even blink. She continued down the street, insulated, carefully picking her way through the debris as if she had radar. He called to her again, started to go after her, but then stopped. She, at least, was walking. Someone would take care of her. He turned and ran to Eames's house and into the front yard.

Thomas had covered natural disasters before, earthquakes and hurricanes, but never a tornado. He had heard the amazing, surreal stories spun around twisters, and now he was seeing one with his own eyes. The roof to Jack Eames's house had been torn off, as had two walls and most of a third. You could stand in the street and look into the living room. There was the card table standing exactly where it had been the night before, the chairs around it and the glasses still on the table. Even the pack of cards was on the table, unmoved. The Norman Rockwell print remained on the side wall.

Thomas climbed over broken Sheetrock. In the air there was a bright pink fluff like cotton candy. It was insulation and when it touched his sweaty skin, he itched. He maneuvered over splintered beams and yelled for Eames. He felt the dirt under his eyelids, and tears were flowing to flush them out.

The house, behind the living room, had all caved in. It appeared that the roof had been lifted off the walls and then fallen back down, crushing them. He picked his way across, kicking the shattered red tile of the roof out of his way. The television antenna had fallen straight down and was now planted in the rubble like a metal tree. There was broken glass everywhere. The large limb of a tree had blown into the house. The furniture was outside and the trees were in. It was mad.

Then he stopped. Jutting out from under a beam and shattered Sheetrock was the end of a collapsed bed and sticking out from that was a pair of bare feet. They were pointing in opposite, unnatural directions. Thomas began to pick and scratch at the shingles and the wood, shouting Eames's name.

Behind him, sirens were coming closer. He could hear other noises, other voices. Then someone was helping him move the rubble, a young, red-faced man in a blue fireman's uniform. Together they hefted a section of roof.

They grunted and struggled with it until they pushed it up off the bed and it fell with a crash into the backyard. It exposed the body of a man and on top of him two crisscrossing beams.

"Jack Eames," the fireman gasped, trying to catch his breath.

Thomas looked down at the man lying on the bed, knew right away he was dead and knew right away he had seen him before. It was the tall man in the checked shirt he had seen the night before at the motel talking with the Mexican. He was still wearing the checked shirt, although the front of it was now covered with blood. Some of the blood had come from his head, a beam apparently glancing off his skull and then crushing his chest. His eyes were wide open, staring up at eternity. Jack Eames hadn't gone to Austin to talk over his political future. Now he didn't have a future at all.

The fireman was kneeling over him, his ear to Eames's chest.

"He's dead," the fireman confirmed. He turned Eames's head to look at the wound, bent over it closely.

"What is it?" Thomas asked.

The fireman didn't answer. He got up, clambered across the rubble and yelled for help. Thomas stayed, matching stares with the dead man. Sirens sounded around him mixed with cries and moaning.

Suddenly someone was grabbing him by the arm. He turned and saw a small, purposeful Latin woman with red hair, wearing a white smock with a large red cross on it. She was looking at him in disbelief.

"Were you in this house?"

Thomas shook his head.

She watched him with enormous, soulful eyes. Then her gaze moved to the body of Jack Eames and fear suddenly filled those eyes. "*Dios mío,*" she said. She swallowed, reached out and grabbed his arm again, and for a moment Thomas thought the woman would faint. He held on to her. When she spoke her eyes were still on the corpse and her voice quavered.

"Is he dead?"

"Yes, he is."

She gaped at the dead man.

"We better move away from here," she said, but she didn't let go of Thomas. It was he who turned her and led the way out of the rubble. On the street they saw an old man wrapped only in a sheet. He was being led away by a fireman.

Thomas and the woman went to a station wagon with a red cross painted on it, parked across the street in the field. They sat down on the tailgate.

"Are you all right?" he asked her.

She nodded, but she was still shaking. "I'm sorry, but I'm not used to seeing that much blood."

Then she noticed the cut on his head.

"That cut is bad. I should take you to the hospital."

Thomas put his hand to his scalp, looked at the blood on his fingers. It wasn't much. There were sirens sounding everywhere now, on all sides.

"I can't go to the hospital," he said, getting up. "I'm a journalist and I have to work."

The Latin woman, recovered from her own fright, looked at him as if he were crazy. "You can work later. Now we need to look at your head."

Thomas touched the cut again. It was almost dry.

"I need to see what happened to the town." He turned around as if he weren't sure what direction it was in. Then he started for the motel.

The woman called after him, but he continued across the field. When he reached the culvert, he found the clerk still sitting there, praying. Without a word, Thomas lifted the man by an arm, helped him climb out of the ditch, and led him back toward the motel.

Chapter 7

*T*he motel had been spared. Thomas found it exactly as it had been except for what appeared to be an apple tree, roots and all, lying in the parking lot. He led the clerk to his quarters behind the office and got him to lie down. He told him to sleep, that he was all right. The man was still excited, wild-eyed, but he didn't argue.

Thomas went to his room. The door was still open and everything was as he had left it, which in itself seemed unreal. He stepped in, passed by the mirror, stopped and looked at himself. He realized now why the civil-defense woman had looked at him so strangely. Even more than the clerk's, his body was covered with red dust. He was caked with it, from head to toe, except for white rings around his eyes that had been flushed by tears. He looked like a man made of clay; or maybe a member of a primitive tribe whose members wore only mud. Or even a man risen from the grave. One of those beings described in the Bible, the walking dead resurrected on Judgment Day, when the earth has been destroyed. For a moment, Thomas was frozen by his own image, as if it were another man standing there. After all, at the height of the storm, Thomas—the journalist, the agnostic, the man wedded to the photographable, the recordable—had heard himself scream "Oh, God." It was the closest he had come to praying since he was a child. Now the image of himself had spooked him.

Thomas closed his eyes and let the moment pass. He had to get to work. With the fatigue that follows terror, he took off his pants and took a shower. The tank on the roof had not been hit, so there was water, at least for now. When the stream hit the cut on his scalp, he winced and the dust on his face cracked and fell like a mask.

Thomas dressed, grabbed his equipment—tape recorder, camera, notebooks—got in the car, and drove toward the edge of town where the tornado had entered the city limits and where he had seen houses flying into the air. The sky there was still darkened with black, roiling, fast-moving clouds, like wolves waiting to feed on the victims.

He took the state road, which hadn't been hit, but he still had to wind his way through the litter left by the twister: tree limbs, pieces of houses, furnishings, clothes. At one point, on the median line, he found an upholstered sofa, its cushions in place. Just beyond it, on the side of the road, outside a weathered wooden shack, he saw a family: a man in coveralls, a woman in a housedress, and children. Some were standing, some kneeling, but all looked in the direction the storm had gone with their hands raised in the air. At first, it appeared they were waving at the sky. But then he realized they were praying. As he drove by slowly he heard the children mumbling and the man calling, "Thank ya, Jesus."

Near the edge of town he turned off the state road. He had to park two blocks away from the first serious damage because the streets were impassable. Sirens sounded on all sides. A black horse, loosed by the storm and frightened, galloped by him across yards.

Thomas turned onto the first block the tornado had hit. It was May in Texas, and the streets he had just left were green. But here the twister had pulled every leaf off the trees, those that were still standing, so that branches were as bare and brittle as if it were the dead of winter in New York.

He started down the block. Here again he saw evidence of the nature of the storm, erratic, inexplicable, capricious. One house was totally destroyed and the place next door untouched. He saw an old white frame house flattened, but two rocking chairs still sitting on the porch. He saw planks and limbs driven through cars, large trees emerging from houses.

He went down the street slowly, in a state of suspended belief. Many of the other people he saw along that route appeared to be in similiar states, or in shock. Outside one standing house, he spoke to a pale, ethereal-looking old woman, still dressed in a white nightgown, so that she looked like an elderly angel. She claimed her husband had disappeared.

"He was in the house, but now he's gone," she said, her eyes glazed as she looked in the direction the tornado had taken. Thomas tried to comfort her, saying he would be found. He taped her, a voice that sounded lost, dispersed by the wind.

The twister had seemingly made the corner onto a cross street. On that block, Thomas helped dig out a survivor. It was a heavy-set man who had been trapped when the roof caved in. He emerged pale as a ghost, another of the walking dead. On the next block, he saw his first real dead person; a terribly still shape under a sheet. Next to the body sat a young woman, both hands dug into her blond curls, as if she were tearing them out.

Thomas followed the drunken, destructive path almost a mile, until it veered out of town and across the grazing lands to the north. He toted the arithmetic of disaster, the number of houses destroyed and the people who were homeless. He knew of at least six persons who had died, including Jack Eames. There were also several people still missing. And then there were those who, apparently, had lost their minds. He had seen disturbed people wandering the streets of cities all over the world, but this was different. He wondered what the unit was to measure madness, because there was much of it in the streets of Paradise. The scenes of destruction. Pieces of buildings from one street mixed with sections of houses from another. Sirens eerily sounding. The trees, leafless in the heat. In the midst of that shattered landscape, people moved like zombies or talked at the sky. He could feel their confusion and despair, and it made him flash back to his own fear as the twister had pulled at him and his own despair when he had lost his mind down in Latin America.

At one point he found a group of residents gathered in a circle, looking down at where the street had buckled and the ground cracked open. They were staring as if the force which had hit the town had erupted from the darkness below, as if a god that had not been appeased had taken his vengeance against them. Much, Thomas remembered, as the Reverend Sam Dash and Deacon Haynes had prophesied. Thomas hurried away.

After he reached the edge of town, the end of the destruction, Thomas turned back and walked to the hospital. By the time he got there, ambulances and medical personnel had arrived from nearby towns and from as far away as Odessa. The semicircular driveway leading to the emergency room was crowded with them. A helicopter with a red cross painted on its underside was above and heading down to a nearby field. For a moment, the sight of it took Thomas to scenes he'd lived in other countries, on other continents. Scenes of war.

He saw Oates standing just outside the emergency-room door. Thomas remembered the editor of the *Chronicle* the night before, like a somber Old Testament prophet, saying he had seen bad times coming. Now he stood covered in dust and sweat, with a look of terrible regret on his face, watching the injured being carted in and out.

Thomas came up next to him. Oates looked right through him at first, then frowned.

"I'd forgotten all about you."

Thomas nodded. "Jack Eames died," he said.

Oates looked at him with strain in his eyes, trying to remember if that had been part of his premonition, that Jack Eames would die.

"The roof of the house collapsed on him. He was still in bed. I found him," Thomas said.

"He'll be in the morgue in the back," Oates said, but he didn't move. He stood at the door with his notebook. First he would deal with the living and then he would worry about his obituary page.

A stretcher came out of emergency, bearing a middle-aged woman with a bandage on her head and a dazed expression on her face. She was mumbling something unintelligible. The hospital was sending her to Odessa. As the ambulance doors were being opened, Oates leaned over, took the woman's hand and squeezed it, whispered something too her. Then she was shoved in, the doors slammed, and the ambulance took off, its siren wailing painfully.

"You know her?" Thomas asked.

"I know all these people," Oates said. "I've seen people from two and three generations of the same families carried through these doors this morning. I saw a woman who taught me in kindergarten and a grandaughter of hers who I taught when I was at the high school. The girl didn't recognize me and I've known her all my life. I've seen others come in here who don't even recognize their own kin."

A police car pulled up at the foot of the emergency entrance, another siren added to the madness. A man got out dressed in a brown uniform, a white Stetson, and mirror sunglasses. He carried a pearl-handled pistol in a tooled leather holster.

"That's Jim West, the sheriff," Oates said, and he called to him.

The sheriff's head swiveled. He saw Oates and came over.

"Yes, Dan?" But he was looking at Thomas.

"This is Edward Thomas, a journalist from out of town. What can you tell us?"

West was a tall, slim man of about forty-five, with a graying mustache and a grim, tight-lipped mouth. There was a gold star on his chest and another on the crown of his hat. As he scanned the scene, his mirrored glasses reflected the chaos and suffering around him.

"I can tell you it's bad," he said. "The whole west side of town was hit. We have dead, lots of injured, a couple of fires and tremendous loss of property. A company of Texas National Guard from Odessa is due here by mid-afternoon to help us patrol the streets, keep order, and stop looters coming in from outside. All roads into town will be blocked and no one will be allowed in or out of town, without police permission. There's an eight o'clock curfew for everybody. We hope to keep this from turning into a worse nightmare than it already is."

"How about the number of dead?" Oates asked.

"At least seven are dead and there are still people missing. We don't know the total number of casualties."

"My friend Thomas here says Jack Eames was killed, crushed by his roof. Thomas found him."

West looked at Thomas with more interest. "He's dead, that's all I know. The medical examiner should be looking at the dead right now. I'm sure he'll have something to say soon."

West ducked into the emergency room. There was moaning coming from it, sobbing. Thomas watched the Stetson disappear into the turmoil.

"Steady fellow."

Oates stared after the sheriff.

"Jim West fought in Vietnam," he said. "He's witnessed scenes like this before, I imagine. Maybe even some more terrible."

After a while the flow of injured, in and out, stopped. Thomas and Oates took the time to compare notes on the damage they had seen and the stories they'd heard. Along the way Oates had found a Mexican woman who swore she had seen a large statue of the Virgin Mary fly around her living room in circles and then set back down on the floor. Her house had not been destroyed because of the intercession of the Blessed Mother. And he heard about a man who had been picked up by the tornado, carried high into the air, and then put back down. He had been taken to the hospital, badly hurt, but still alive. People talked about him as if he had been to heaven and back.

Then Thomas saw the sheriff and another man, older and bearded, come out the door.

"That's Dr. Earl Muller, the county medical examiner," Oates said.

Muller was wearing a long white surgical gown stained with blood. He and the sheriff exchanged some words. West appeared irritated. He stalked by them without a word, jumped into his car, and sped away, with a squeal of tires and the siren wailing.

Thomas and Oates met the medical examiner as he came out the door. He had a lugubrious face and large bags beneath his eyes. He was staring at the police car as it drove away.

"Any more dead, Earl?" Oates asked.

"So far the death toll from the tornado is six. It may change," he said.

Oates frowned. "But Jim West told us there were seven dead."

The old man turned on him as if his professional competence were being challenged.

"There *are* seven dead, but only six of them died in the tornado," he said deliberately. "The seventh body is that of County Attorney Jack Eames, who died of a gunshot wound in the head. Apparently a homicide." His baggy, sad eyes narrowed. "He was dead before the tornado hit the house. He never knew it happened."

Then he turned and disappeared back into the madness.

Chapter 8

*L*ate that afternoon the National Guard marched into town. By nightfall they had taken up positions, one to each street corner in the affected areas. The sight of the soldiers, bayonets in place, in that setting, seemed unreal: nightmare within a nightmare.

Oates got police permission for him and Thomas to stay on the street after curfew, and they continued their rounds. Along the way Oates kept up a running monologue about Paradise and about his life here. When he had met certain persons, aspects of their lives, his feelings for them. He went from sadness to fondness to humor, and inevitably back to grief. He showed Thomas his own home, where he lived with his wife and children and which had not been hit by the storm. He took him to the houses where he had been born, where his brothers lived, where he had met his first girlfriend and even, somewhat sheepishly, where he'd first had sex. He pointed out the houses of friends who had died long ago. It was as if by recalling the places where all these things had happened they remained real. It was a way of keeping himself sane.

Electricity had returned to the center of town, but most parts of Paradise were still dark. In that darkness the wreckage of houses looked even more frightful. Occasionally they heard crying, sometimes a baby, sometimes not. Dark figures moved through the lightless streets; relief workers, they assumed.

About 9 P.M. another body was found. It turned out to be the last one. It was a young man Oates knew, a high school athletic star. The body was pulled from the wreckage of a house on the north side.

They made a last stop at the high school, which had not been hit and was being used as emergency shelter; power was supplied by a generator. People were resting on cots on the basketball court. Oates drifted around, talking to friends, commiserating, listening to accounts of the storm. Thomas stood by until he noticed on a cot in a corner the recumbent form of Claude Denison. He was in his shirt-sleeves, his stomach sticking up, sloping down on either side to a sunken chest and skinny legs. The shape of his body was that of a bad economic curve. He was smoking and staring at the ceiling when Thomas walked up.

"How are you, Mr. Denison? Not hurt, I hope."

Denison looked at him and frowned. He was a businessman who forgot faces. Thomas jogged his memory.

"We met last night at the hamburger stand."

Recognition dawned on the grizzled, unshaven countenance.

"You're the writer."

"That's right. Where were you when it hit?"

"Where do you think I was? In my car on the street where the sheriff put me," he said angrily. "Right out in the open."

"I thought you had friends here, business contacts, you could stay with."

Denison's face closed up. "They were out of town on business."

"Well, it doesn't look like business will be good around here, the way you'd hoped."

"Don't bet on it," the land man said. "It depends what business you're in. Construction outfits'll be wading in money. You got yourself a building-supply company nearby, you're in the gravy. You'll see. People will be in here selling everything from drinking water, to food, to good-luck charms against tornadoes. There's always a way to make out. And here I am without capital."

He drew on his cigarette. "I hear there were people killed."

"Seven have died so far." Thomas remembered the night before, Denison saying the authorities had it out for him. Now Jack Eames was dead from a bullet in his head.

"One of them was the county attorney," Thomas said. "But he didn't die in the storm, he was shot to death. You didn't know him, did you?"

Denison scowled at him. "No, I didn't. The sheriff put me in jail. I didn't have any dealings with the county attorney."

He took a last drag on his short cigarette, stubbed it out in the ashtray next to the cot, reached into his pocket for another one, but came up dry. He balled up the empty pack and dropped it on the floor.

"You don't have a cigarette, do you? You could make a living in this place just selling smokes."

Thomas told him he'd take care of it. He left Denison staring at the ceiling as if it were going to cave in on him. He found a nurse, gave her some money, and asked her to see that Denison got his cigarettes. Then he caught up with Oates.

They left and headed back to the *Chronicle*. Electricity was back, but telephone and telegraph were still out, so

Paradise continued to be cut off from the outside world, at least for the average citizen.

They pulled up in front of Oates's office. From outside, the place had the look of an old frontier newspaper. It occupied a narrow storefront, with "Paradise Chronicle" arched on the window in old-fashioned gold lettering.

Inside was a different story. The front room contained two gray metal desks, each with a word-processing screen and keyboard. There was a high-speed printer and a fax machine against one wall. On Oates's desk was a radio telephone which he explained was used to make contact with outlying ranches that still were not part of the municipal telephone network. In the back room, the editor showed Thomas a bank of computers and other machines, all about seven feet high, that turned what was written on the screens into a newspaper. The *Chronicle* had moved from being a pioneer newspaper to one on the frontiers of modern technology.

In the front room, Thomas sat in a chair by Oates's desk. Framed front pages, marking important moments in the history of Paradise and the nation, hung on the walls: headlines of a giant oil-well fire in the thirties; the end of World War II; the Kennedy assassination; Lyndon Johnson, hand raised, taking the oath; men coming home from Vietnam; and a last headline that blared, "Arabs Pull Plug on Oil Price." That one marked the beginning of the last bust.

Oates sat behind his desk, unloaded his pockets of more than one notebook, and looked at Thomas.

"I have to get an Extra out," he said. "I have to let people know what has happened and what hasn't. It'll cut down the rumors and wild fears."

He glanced at the one other desk in the room. It belonged to a woman named Elsa Chisolm, who handled all the society and club news for the *Chronicle*. They had stopped by her house that day and found that she and her family were all right.

"I can't call Elsa in this late," he said, glancing back at Thomas. "I can't take her away from her family."

Thomas took off his camera, rolled up his sleeves, threw his notebook on the desk, and sat down.

"You do the main story," he said to Oates, "all the facts and figures. I'll do a sidebar on people's individual re-collections and maybe a small one on my own experience."

"Exactly," Oates said.

Thomas flipped open his notebook, studied it for several minutes, let the facts jostle for position in his brain, and then began to write. He worked on instinct. He was halfway through with the first sidebar before he realized that, until now, he had not written a word in two months; that there had been a time two months before when he did not know when or if he would write again. It was as if his own disaster had put him off track and now this one had knocked him back onto the rails. Or maybe other people's nightmares had taken the place of his own. For that reason, he wrote like a man running just ahead of a storm.

Thomas finished his two sidebars in a little over an hour and a half. Meanwhile, Oates sat quietly, working on what had to be one of the most painful stories he had ever written. He finished a half hour later, proofread Thomas's work, giving him a nod of approval, and put the stories into the offset system.

Then he opened a small refrigerator near his desk and took out a can of Lone Star beer. Thomas declined. They sat in silence awhile.

Not once since they had left the hospital had they talked about Jack Eames. Thomas had tried to bring it up, but Oates had told him flatly that it would have to wait. He had been intent, in a manic way, on visiting the living, giving solace to the families of the dead. In a sense, it was a numbers game he was playing: many of his fellow towns-people had been affected by the twister, while only one had been murdered. But Thomas had sensed that the big man was thinking about Eames. He would fall into a silence that was more troubled than sad. Thomas had thought about it many times during the day: about seeing the body, recognizing it, having seen Eames the day before talking to the Mexican.

Thomas's face folded in a frown. He had totally forgotten about the Mexican. He had not seen him after the tornado had passed. Maybe he had checked out before, maybe he hadn't. He would have to find out.

Thomas thought again about seeing Margaret Masters hurrying away from Eames's house. The blood on her. The shock on her face. Thomas had not told Oates about that either. He glanced up at the other man, who was sipping his beer, new grief etched into his face that had not been there twenty-four hours before. He watched him and knew that he would not tell Oates about his friend Margaret Masters. Not now.

"What did you write about Jack Eames?" he asked.

Oates swiveled in his chair.

"I quoted exactly what Earl Muller said about Jack being shot, that it was an apparent homicide and that was all. There wasn't room or time left to do more."

Thomas sat and listened to a faraway siren. Oates listened as well, a journalist's natural reaction. Thomas looked back at him.

"Who had reason to do it?"

Oates shook his head. "He was county attorney. He put people in jail. They all had motives, if you want, but I can't think of one who would kill him."

"He's like this man Sam Cain in some ways," Thomas said, "a politician and a lawyer. The attacks came just days apart. Was there anything that connected them lately, apart from their involvement in the Masters case?"

Oates looked at Thomas. "Sam Cain wasn't involved in the case, not officially."

"He let people know he didn't like it. You said so yourself. And that probably angered certain individuals around here. Then he turned down Margaret Masters when she went to him for help. He irritated both sides."

"But Jack Eames hadn't angered the religious political

community, at least not yet he hadn't. It's true he had to decide Margaret's fate, whether she was protected by freedom of expression guarantees or not, but he hadn't decided it yet. Not like Sam, who had made up his mind."

"She was sure it would be thumbs down. That he would sell her out to Dash and his people for political reasons," Thomas said. "That gave her a motive."

"You can't just listen to Margaret. She didn't like Jack's change in politics, and then there was the affair. She had had an ax to grind, but it was just talk."

Thomas considered Oates carefully. "She had an ax to grind and maybe reason to kill him."

Oates was exhausted, depressed. It had been one of the worst days of his life. Now he had to consider the possibility that one friend of his had murdered another. He just glared at Thomas, drained his beer, and got up.

"I can't deal with this now. I have seven other people to bury."

He headed for the back room where he would make up the paper. Thomas caught up with him near the bank of gray metal file cabinets against the back wall.

"Do you mind if I look at your files for Jack Eames and Sam Cain?"

"Be my guest."

"Margaret Masters mentioned there was at least one other woman Eames had an affair with."

He could tell by the expression on Oates's face that the big man didn't like the question. "I assume she was talking about Laurel Davis," he said reticently. "At least those were the rumors. When you're finished, pull the door closed behind you."

They exchanged tired but pointed glances. Then Oates left and Thomas opened the file drawer.

Most of Paradise was still dark when Thomas left the *Chronicle* an hour later. The streets were abandoned, except for the shadowy figures of the National Guardsmen walking their posts. He was stopped at one checkpoint on the way to the motel, by men in helmets, carrying M-16 rifles and field radios. For Thomas, it was as if he had somehow made a wrong turn and driven into an episode from his past. He showed them a press pass from that past life and was let by.

He had read the clips until they had begun to swim in front of his eyes, until he had started to hallucinate the public events of Paradise. By the time he pulled up at the motel, he was possessed by that light-headed, atomized sensation that exhaustion produced in him.

He got out of his car and crossed to the room where the night before he had seen the Mexican. The curtains were drawn and there was no light on. Thomas listened outside the door, but heard nothing. He knocked and waited. Still nothing. He tried the knob quietly, carefully; it was locked. He thought for a moment about waking the clerk to ask him if he had seen the one other guest. He decided it would be better to let the clerk sleep.

Thomas crossed toward his room, but then stopped. Beyond the motel he could see the field he and the clerk had crossed that morning, where they had been brushed by death. The trench the twister had cut was visible in the sparse moonlight, and the edge of the culvert as well. And then there was open country beyond.

He walked past his room and into the field feeling like a sleepwalker, walking through a landscape that was not real, but of his memory, of the fears of that morning. He walked to the edge of the culvert and looked down into it.

Then he gazed out across that open country, until he realized he wasn't alone. He hadn't noticed him before because he had been very still, but it was a man sitting on a horse. The animal appeared white or gray in the moonlight, and it was when the horse moved that Thomas noticed the rider. All he could make out, at a distance, was the silhouette of a Stetson hat.

The horse and rider were maybe fifty yards on the other side of the culvert. But now that Thomas stood staring at him, the rider flicked the reins and started to trot away, back across the range from where he had to have come. Thomas squinted after him until he was swallowed by the darkness, a horseman of the apocalypse. He pressed his eyes closed against his fatigue, then turned away and headed back to the motel.

In the room, he undressed and got in bed. He closed his eyes to sleep, but suddenly everything began to spin as it had that morning. His hands crawled out and reached for the sides of the mattress and he opened his eyes and the dizziness slowed, but didn't stop. This time he was caught not in the twister, but in the vortex of his own fear. He had not felt this sensation since that day two months before in Colombia, the day his "international crisis" had been provoked.

That was the last time he had seen a dead body. Walking down a street in the city of Cali, he had witnessed the explosion of a car bomb. Just a block away when it happened, Thomas had been knocked back by the concussion and showered with flying glass. While others had fled from the ball of fire, Thomas, the journalist, had run right at it, notebook in hand. The street had echoed with screams and crying.

One young girl, maybe sixteen years old, her flowered dress charred, her long raven hair matted with blood, had been thrown into a doorway where Thomas had found her. She was still alive, clutching a small black patent-leather purse as if it were life itself. Thomas had crouched over her, shouting at scrambling policemen for help. But it had taken too long. The light gradually had faded from her deep brown eyes and then suddenly had gone out altogether. Thomas had stayed motionless, pen and notebook poised. Her dead stare had remained fixed on him until he had taken off his jacket and covered her face with it.

It was by no means the first time Thomas had seen someone die or written about it. He had gone back to his hotel intending to do what was expected of him: to sit down at the computer and compose a firsthand account of the bombing scene. Halfway through his article he had stepped out to get a beer, and the rest, as they said, was history. He'd had beer after beer, rum after rum, day after day until he had fallen apart.

The psychiatrist had wanted to know what drew him to other people's tragedies. Thomas's wife had had an explanation for it: she said he had no interior life. "All you do is run from yourself." Well, yes, that was true. Thomas was the only child of a bad, battle-ridden marriage. He joked that he had been covering war since the cradle. The desolation in the house had caused him to look for life in the streets and in books. When it came time to pick a profession, he'd put them together: he'd become a journalist. Life was outside one and one's problems. Life was what was new, not what was old. Tragedies happened to other people and were to be visited and written about; then one moved on to the next tragedy. And moved on again and again, without wear and tear on the soul. Or so he'd thought.

Now Thomas lay holding on to the sides of the bed, as if it might leave the ground and take him away again. He held on tight, fighting his fear, and for now he made the world stop spinning. He lay there a long time making sure and then he closed his eyes and fell into sleep.

Chapter 9

*T*homas was dreaming about his parents, who were both dead. In the dream they were sitting in chairs outside the house where Thomas was raised, and they were staring at each other in silence. Thomas's mother was dressed as a gypsy or a sorceress, a red silk scarf around her head. His father was white-haired as he had been only in the last years of his life. Thomas was watching them from a second-story window, and when he looked out to the horizon he saw a tornado.

He opened a window and screamed to them, but they didn't move. Thomas ran down the stairs, outside, and opened a trapdoor leading to a storm cellar. He shouted to his parents again to hide from the storm, but they sat motionless, staring at each other, except for the red scarf flapping in the wind. The storm was right on top of them now, and Thomas could feel it tug at him. He dived into the cellar, the door slamming above him and shutting him in darkness. He heard the storm outside, and he held on to the door as the tornado tried to pull him to his death. He realized his parents hadn't moved because they were already dead. He felt the wind pull at him again, trying to take him to them.

He woke up with a start and sat straight up in bed.

The phone rang. Thomas watched it in the mirror, then he reached for it.

"Hello."

"Mr. Thomas?"

"Yes."

"This is Sheriff Jim West."

Thomas frowned at himself in the mirror. He recognized the voice now.

"Yes?"

"I understand you found the body of Jack Eames yesterday."

"That's right."

"Could you please meet me at the scene in thirty minutes? I have some questions for you."

Thomas hesitated as the question got caught in the cobwebs in his brain left by the nightmare.

"Can you?"

"Yes, of course." The other end went dead.

Much of the rubble had been cleared from the streets, and Thomas managed to drive into the neighborhood until he was a block from Eames's house. He parked next to West's police car.

Eames's block, however, still looked like a war zone, a street that had been bombed. Removed from the tornado itself and his own fear, he saw the destruction more clearly: the splintered beams, the cracked streets, the crater where a tree had been uprooted, the exposed housing foundations like broken teeth. Workers picked through the rubble.

A rope had been strung around the Eames property, hung with yellow pennants that said: "Police—Keep Out." Beyond the rope, Thomas saw West crouching down, sifting through the wreckage. The sheriff glanced up, saw Thomas, but went back to his rummaging.

Thomas made his way toward him. "Good morning."

West didn't reply, but he stood up. He was carrying his pearl-handled pistol on one hip and a squawking walkie-talkie on the other. He turned the volume down.

"Can you show me just where he was?"

Thomas pointed to the bed. They picked their way across to it. "He was lying with his legs sticking off the end of the bed. Those beams were on top of him and lots of tile and Sheetrock. He was faceup, wearing a sport shirt and pants."

West nodded, looking down at the bloodstained sheets with an eerie detachment.

"Nothing lying on the bed with him or nearby? Nothing that caught your attention?"

"If you mean a weapon, no," Thomas said.

"Oh, we found the weapon," West said. Thomas raised his eyebrows. "Or at least a .38-caliber pistol that seemed to have been fired recently. I found it under some Sheetrock right near the bed here. Unregistered. It's on its way to Odessa for ballistics and fingerprint analysis."

Thomas nodded and looked around him at the wreckage. "Can't be easy to find clues in a mess like this. Then again, if it weren't for the tornado taking the roof off the place, you might not have known he was lying here dead."

West didn't answer. He bent over and picked up some legal papers and studied them as if he were expecting to find a signed confession by the killer. He didn't look at Thomas when he talked.

"How was it you came to find him?" He asked it casually, but with an edge.

Thomas told him of running from the motel after the clerk, diving for cover in the ditch, and then seeing the destruction on Eames's street. How he had been there the night before with Oates, but hadn't found Eames.

The last bit of information caught West's interest. He squinted at Thomas through his already narrow eyes.

"You came here the night before?"

"That's right, about nine-thirty. We came looking for him, but he wasn't here." Thomas stopped and looked down at the bed. "Or maybe he was here, but he was already dead. The car was here."

His frown deepened and he looked at West. "Although he wasn't dead at seven o'clock because I saw him at that hour and he was alive."

West had become very still. "Where did you see him?"

Thomas told him of seeing a man he now knew was Eames talking with a Mexican, and of seeing the Mexican again later. He knew nothing else about it.

West crouched back down and sifted through some broken roof tiles.

"Why were you coming to see him?"

"To talk to him about the Margaret Masters case."

West nodded. "You know Margaret Masters, do ya?"

"Yes, I talked with her Friday night."

"What time was that?"

"About eight P.M. Oates and I talked to her for an hour or more."

West picked up a piece of broken tile and scaled it across the yard.

"Did Margaret Masters mention Jack Eames at all?"

"Yes, she talked about her case before the school board and Eames's role in it."

West stood up and began kicking rubble out of the way again. "What did she think his role would be in it?"

"You mean, did she think he would sell her down the river?"

West met his gaze but said nothing. Thomas didn't like

the game the sheriff was playing, extracting what could end up as testimony from him. He spoke carefully.

"She was worried, but she didn't say anything definitively one way or the other. That's all I can tell you."

West crossed to where he had his evidence box and came back carrying a black duffel bag.

"Did you see this here yesterday when you found the body?"

"No, but I didn't see much except Eames himself," Thomas said. "When a man is staring at you, dead . . ."

West put the bag down in the rubble next to the bed and pointed at it.

"I found it right here this morning," he said. "Right next to where you said you found him. You're sure you didn't see it?"

The sheriff was pressing for some reason. Thomas shook his head.

"Why is it important?"

West's tongue licked his thin lips. Then he crouched down again and unzipped the duffel bag. He dug his hands into the bag and brought out a small clear plastic bag containing maybe two pounds of a white substance.

"This is why."

"Cocaine," Thomas said.

"Right." West dropped the packet back in the bag and brought out a larger package wrapped in black plastic. He unwrapped it and showed Thomas what appeared to be about three kilos of the stuff.

"They kick these duffel bags out of small planes over the ranches," West said. "They're carrying heroin, cocaine, marijuana. Lots of open land around here. Hundreds of thousands of acres of grazing land. Impossible to patrol it all. They have a contact person on the ground who sits at an arranged place, in a car or truck on a dirt ranch road, with his lights off. When he hears the plane he blinks his lights. They drop it to him, he picks it up, and within hours it's being sold on the street, some of it here, the rest all over West Texas and beyond."

West looked down and sneered at the white powder as if it were a dangerous explosive, plastique. He glanced back at Thomas.

"We got lucky one night last year. A patrol car out west of town spotted a plane flying low over the grazing lands. Heard the plane, got a look at it, shot at it, but it got away. We managed to trap one of the guys on the ground. He died in a shoot-out and we didn't get to talk to him. We also recovered a few of these black bags. But another guy on the ground got away. He took off over the grazing land in a truck and we couldn't get him. It seemed like he knew the lay of the land here. I thought that night that maybe it wasn't some dealer from Amarillo, Lubbock, or Odessa, but a local. Maybe I was right."

"What are you thinking?" Thomas asked.

West shrugged. "I'm wonderin' where this came from. That's all."

"It was probably evidence from a case he was working on."

"Then it should have been locked in the evidence locker at the courthouse, shouldn't it? Not laying around his home."

Thomas scowled. "You're not saying the county attorney was involved in drug smuggling, are you?"

West just looked at him under the brim of his Stetson. "When you live all your life in a town built on greed, when you see what it does to some people, you can believe just about anything, mister."

He punctuated his words by zipping up the bag. Going through the files at the *Chronicle* the night before, Thomas had read about recent tensions between the sheriff's office and the county attorney. Apparently Eames had complained about the lack of arrests in drug cases. West had complained about the impossibility of covering thousands of square miles of prairie with a handful of men and had accused Eames of politicking with the drug issue. Bitterness was evident in Sheriff Jim West now. Oates had mentioned West's stint in Vietnam. Thomas wondered how much of that bitterness he had brought back from the war and how much was due to the recent in-fighting.

"Let's assume it belonged to Eames," Thomas said. "Maybe he had gotten somewhere with his drug investigation or, as you suggest, maybe he was the one who needed to be investigated. That means there was somebody else with good reason to kill him. Not Margaret Masters, but somebody involved with drugs. Maybe that's what he was talking to the Mexican about."

West, who just a minute before had been gathering evidence against Margaret Masters, eyed him suspiciously. He wasn't a stupid man, just bitter. He picked up the bag. "I want to see that Mexican."

They climbed back over the rubble, reached their cars, and drove separately the short distance to the motel. Thomas led West to number three, the Mexican's room. He told the sheriff of knocking and trying the door the night before.

West knocked, but got no answer. He tried the door. It was unlocked now and he pushed it open. The bed was tousled and looked as though it had been slept in, but who knew what night that had been? There was a suitcase open on the dresser with clothes in it. A half-empty bottle of whiskey on the night table. Cigarette butts in the ashtray. A radio next to the bottle. West crossed the room and shoved open the bathroom door. Thomas could see shaving equipment on the shelf, but there was no one there.

West stopped and looked around. "When was it you saw this man talking with Jack Eames?"

"Friday, about seven P.M."

"What were they talking about?"

Thomas shook his head. "I didn't get close enough to hear."

West frowned at Thomas as if he'd screwed up. Then they went out and headed for the office. There was no one in it and no TV noise from behind the beaded curtain. West rang the bell and, after a few moments, the clerk stuck his head out, looking even more reticent than the day before. This time he didn't just have a journalist but a cop.

"Hello, Robert," West said.

The clerk shuffled out. "Hello, Jim." He nodded skittishly at Thomas as though he was afraid Thomas would be angry because of the swing he had taken at him in the culvert.

"I need to know about the man in number three," West said.

Robert nodded. "Mexican fella."

"That's right."

He dug into a drawer, brought out the registration card, and laid it in front of West and Thomas. It said the man's name was William Vega, and gave an address in McAllen, Texas, which was way down south on the Mexican border near Brownsville. There was no phone number listed. West looked at the card a moment longer; something on it had caught his attention.

"What is it?" Thomas asked. West shook his head and then started questioning the clerk.

The Mexican had arrived five days before, on Tuesday. His English was unaccented. No, he hadn't been there before, not that Robert remembered, and Robert had worked there eight years ever since moving up from Odessa. No, he hadn't seen the Mexican talk to anyone. He had made no phone calls, at least not through the motel switchboard. But Robert had seen the man head over to the hamburger stand a couple of times, maybe to eat, maybe to make phone calls, he didn't know. He hadn't seen him since Friday. But no, he hadn't checked out.

"He owes a day," he said. "It'll be two at noon."

"It looked like he was here last night. If he shows up back here, Robert, you get on the phone and let me know right away," West said. "I need to talk to him."

The clerk looked bleakly at West. He had a journalist in the motel, a policeman, and now, possibly, some kind of criminal. Things weren't good.

West and Thomas went outside again.

"Same thing goes for you," West said. "If you see him, I need to know about it right away."

"Have you ever heard of him?"

West shook his head. "No, but in Texas everybody and his brother is named Vega."

West got into his car. He rolled down the window. "You're not thinking of goin' anywhere, are ya?"

Thomas shook his head. He couldn't tell if West thought that was good or bad.

"If you change your mind, you let me know first." It wasn't a request. It was an order. He pulled out of the parking lot with a squeal of tires.

Thomas watched West disappear up the road. He decided to find out what had happened to Margaret Masters. And to ask her what she had been doing at Eames's house with a dead man. He hoped she had a good answer. He hadn't told Oates about seeing her there, and now he hadn't told the sheriff either.

Chapter 10

*I*t was near nine when he reached Margaret Masters's place. The street was still littered with tree branches, but damage there had been minimal. As he approached, he saw a window broken on the western side of her house, in the study where they had talked the other night. Apart from that, everything appeared intact.

He parked in front, went up the walk, and rang the bell. He waited, pushed it again. It was Monday morning, but it had been announced the day before that schools would be closed all week, so Margaret Masters was probably not at work. A car was parked in the port. Thomas stepped off the flagstone path, went to the window that was broken. Through it he could see into the study.

Margaret Masters sat in one of the rocking chairs. Her

hands lay limply on her lap, and she was staring at the floor in front of her. She wore the same dress she had been wearing the morning before when he had seen her outside Eames's house. That had been more than twenty-four hours earlier. Her face was streaked with dirt, and there was still blood on her hand. She appeared to be in shock.

Thomas went back to the front door and tried the knob. It turned. He went into the study. A branch had shattered a window, knocking over a tall bookcase, and volumes were scattered all over the floor.

Margaret Masters continued to stare at the rug. She didn't seem to notice that Thomas had entered. Her chest rose and fell slightly with each breath. The lamp next to her was on, and next to it was an empty packet of cigarettes, an ashtray full of butts, a bottle of gin, and a glass.

Thomas crouched before her. "Margaret?"

She stared at the rug.

"Are you all right?"

She cocked her head to one side and spoke in a flat, emotionless voice. "Oh, it depends."

"On what?"

Thomas saw that her cheek wasn't just soiled, it was bruised. "Do you know where you are?"

A sly smile pulled at the corners of her full mouth. "Well, this ain't Kansas, Toto." Her smile grew larger, but it pulled the skin around the bruise. She touched it and it made her grimace with pain.

He took her hand and brought it away from her face. "We have to get you a doctor."

She shook her head.

Thomas looked at the gin bottle. It was still half full, if it was the same bottle from the other night. If it was, then she hadn't been drinking much. The haze she was in didn't seem to be caused by alcohol. It was a mixture of shock and exhaustion. It was much like the look she'd had when he saw her outside Eames's house.

Thomas thought of calling for an ambulance. But with the ambulance might come police, and he wouldn't have a chance to talk to her.

"Margaret, do you remember what's happened in the last day or two?"

She didn't answer.

"Do you remember being in the tornado? Do you remember seeing me on the street after it was over? Walking down the street and my calling to you?"

Her eyes narrowed slyly. "You must have me mixed up with someone else. I'm the Wicked Witch of the West."

Thomas scowled. He wondered just how wicked she had been. He hadn't wanted to mention Eames, not knowing how she would react, but her glibness exasperated him.

"You were outside Jack Eames's house. You were coming from it. Do you remember?"

Her lip twisted at the sound of Eames's name.

"The tin man," she said. "No heart. No courage either."

Thomas grabbed her by the shoulders, and she flinched. "This isn't funny, Margaret. Jack Eames is dead." Thomas suspected for a moment that she was putting on an act to throw him off, but the shock and fatigue on her face seemed too real.

Her eyes focused now, although she didn't take them from the floor in front of her.

"Did you go there after the storm?" Thomas asked. "No, you must have been there already. What happened?"

She stared at whatever it was she was seeing in her mind's eye, seemed about to speak, but then said nothing. Thomas squeezed her shoulders. "Did you kill him?"

She lifted her gaze and finally looked at him. Behind her eyes there was not shock but thought. "I wish I *had* killed him."

"But you didn't kill him," Thomas said, squeezing her shoulders hard.

She reacted to the pain and shook her head no, so that her hair flew around her head. She looked exhausted. He would call the ambulance, but first he had to know how she had gotten that bruise on her cheek and the blood on her.

"Tell me what happened, Margaret."

Her eyes narrowed. "I went to talk to him."

"To ask him about your case?"

She nodded.

"What happened?"

She met his gaze. "He was dead."

"He was dead when you got there?"

"Yes."

"Then what?"

Her face stormed over. "The tornado hit," she said and she fingered her bruised cheek and turned away.

He pressed her shoulders again. "Now listen to me. The sheriff found a black bag with drugs in it near the body. You were with Jack Eames two years. Did he ever keep drugs around? Did he use them?"

She frowned, then shook her head.

"Did you ever know him to have contact with a Mexican man named William Vega?"

Again she shook her head.

"Did you see a gun on or near the bed where Jack Eames was lying? Try and remember."

Now she was pressing her temples and shaking her head. She wouldn't answer anything else. She wanted it to be over.

Thomas gave up. He went over to the phone, but found that service had not been restored on Margaret Masters's street. He went out the door, planning to drive to the hospital and get a doctor or flag down a police car. But right up the block, he noticed a civil-defense van parked and saw its driver come out of a doorway across the street. It was the small Latin woman with the soulful eyes whom he'd helped out of the wreckage of Jack Eames's house the day before.

"It's you," she said. "Did you get that cut looked after?"

Thomas put his hand to his head. He had forgotten it.

"No, but right now you have to take care of someone else. Margaret Masters."

He led her back into the house. Margaret was still sitting in the chair. The nurse's face furrowed in concern. She looked at the broken window and then at the blood on the English teacher. She knelt down in front of her.

"Margaret, it's Esperanza Clark. Are you all right?"

Margaret frowned at the woman and then nodded. The nurse looked up at Thomas.

"I guess she was in this room when the bookcase went over," he said. "She must have gotten hit in the face by one of the flying books and the window glass cut her." He looked at the teacher, who didn't offer any argument. "But I think the worst of it is shock and exhaustion."

The nurse nodded, full of concern. "Help me get her into a bedroom where she can lie down," she said. "When I'm finished with her, I'll look at that cut of yours." She became stern. "And don't argue."

Thomas did as he was told, helping Margaret Masters walk into a bedroom that was also lined with books. He left the two women and went back to the study. He sat down in the rocking chair, looking at the mess around him. He had told Esperanza Clark that Margaret had been cut with flying glass from the broken window, but, of course, she hadn't been there when it was broken.

He wondered just what had happened at Jack Eames's house. When had Eames died? How long had Margaret Masters been there? All night? Just that morning? Her car had not been moved from the front of her house. Had Eames picked her up and brought her to his house? But she said she had gone to talk to him. When Thomas had seen her Friday night, she had seemed at the end of her rope. Her job, her life, had probably been in Jack Eames's hands. Had she arranged to see him and demanded to know what he would recommend to the school board? What had he said? Had he told her he had to rule against her? Had she killed him that night and stayed there? Or gone in the morning? Because, despite West's talk of drug connections, it was still possible she had killed him. Thomas remembered now the bitterness with which she had spoken about him. And that look on her face as she stumbled away from the house; a woman in shock, but maybe at the sight of her own crime.

He was still sitting there thinking when the nurse came back in.

"I've gotten her undressed and given her a sedative. She'll sleep."

"Shouldn't you take her to the hospital?" Thomas asked.

"She isn't so bad, and the hospital is wall-to-wall people. There aren't enough personnel there to look after everyone they have. Anyway, Margaret's a tough girl. I've known her all my life."

She came over to Thomas and turned his head. "Now let's look at this."

She took hydrogen peroxide and cotton out of her bag. When she pulled the hair away from the wound, Thomas winced. He had combed around it that morning.

"How is it you know Margaret?" the nurse asked.

Thomas told her he was a journalist and that he had interviewed the English teacher.

"It's terrible what some people are trying to do to her," she said. "Margaret is a good teacher."

She finished washing the cut, then opened a bottle of Mercurochrome. Thomas flinched when it hit the open cut.

"Calma, calma," she said.

Thomas turned to her and read her name plate. Esperanza Clark.

"You're Latin," he said. "Esperanza."

"That's right." She was applying gauze. "It means hope. My family is Mexican. In fact, it was my great-granddaddy who came here from Mexico." She snipped tape. "He was a cowboy and worked on lots of the cattle ranches around here. They don't show you that in the movies, that lots of the cowboys were Mexicans. They were some of the best."

"And Clark?"

She grunted. "I made the mistake of marrying an oil-man. When the bust came he took a powder, as they say." She shrugged. "I've had the same kind of luck with men that Margaret's had. Not too good."

"Did most people know about Margaret and Jack Eames?"

She studied the question a moment and then nodded. "Maybe not at the beginning, but by the time it was over they did. You don't hide much in a town this size."

"How about a Mexican named William Vega? You ever hear of him?"

She stopped and made a face. She was thinking. "No, I can't say I have. Why, who is he?"

"He's somebody the sheriff is looking for. He was here Friday night at the motel and after the tornado there's no sign of him. He knew Jack Eames."

That made her eyes open, as if she were seeing Eames again, dead.

"I'd like to talk to him too," Thomas said.

"If he was staying at the motel he probably wasn't from here," she said. "But then, lots of Mexican guys have worked the oil fields, and they come back again and again. So maybe people know him."

Thomas described what the man looked like and told her he might be from McAllen.

"I'll ask around and let you know," she said.

She went then to call Mrs. Castle, the housekeeper whom Thomas had met briefly on his first visit, and have her come sit with Margaret. Thomas agreed to wait there until the woman showed up, and the nurse headed for the door.

"I'll come by and check on her every once in a while to make sure she's all right," she said. "And you find me tomorrow so I can change that dressing." She gave him a stern look, and he said he would.

Thomas waited fifteen minutes until the housekeeper arrived and then left. As he came out the door, a woman approached walking along the sidewalk. She was about thirty-five, of medium height, with thick, chestnut-brown hair. Her skin was honey-colored and her eyes, even at a distance, were startling hazel green, like a cat's. She wore a modest, high-necked dress, but it was still clear that she was possessed of a statuesque body. She carried a black-bound Bible in her hands.

She stopped at the foot of the walk as Thomas approached and he recognized her. She was Laurel Davis, the other woman with whom Jack Eames had had an affair, according to Oates. Thomas had seen her photos the night before in the *Chronicle* files. Her folder had been thick with clips. Fifteen years earlier she had won every beauty contest sponsored in the town: Miss Paradise for the Fourth of July parade; Miss VFW; the Lions Club queen; and more. Before that she had reigned as queen of the high school prom and captain of the cheerleading squad.

Two years out of high school, she had married a former University of Texas football star who had gone into the oil business in Paradise, "a prize catch" as the social column had put it. She had then proceeded to win prizes for her pies at the county fair and had garnered other homemaking awards. But the marriage had ended in divorce after eight years; she had accused her husband of alcoholism and extreme cruelty. She had been represented by Jack Eames and her husband by Sam Cain.

The last clip had been dated just two years before, and made it known that Laurel Davis had not only recently joined the Paradise Revelation Temple, but had been named head of its Women's Auxiliary. This had to be after her affair with Eames.

Now she stared at Thomas, the Bible clutched to her ample bosom, beautiful cat's eyes fixed on him.

"I'm here to see Margaret Masters," she said with a pronounced local accent. "Is she home?"

Thomas stopped in front of her. "She is, but she's sleeping, Ms. Davis. A nurse just gave her a sedative."

She frowned at him. "Do we know each other? You're not from around here."

"No, but I was looking at your photos as Miss Paradise

last night. You haven't changed much." The fact was she *had* changed. In the photos she had been smiling and youthful, and now she was somber.

She looked at him suspiciously. "Why were you looking at my photos?"

"I'm a visiting journalist. I was researching different personalities in town."

She pulled the Bible even tighter to her breast. "I wouldn't do that again."

"Do what?"

"Enter those contests, walking around in bathing suits. All it does is incite men to lust, to sin. It leads them away from the Lord." She sounded as if she were reciting from memory.

Thomas thought she could probably still win if she did enter, but he didn't say so. He didn't have to. He was looking into her eyes, beyond their pious glaze, to the woman behind them, and he knew that she could tell what he was thinking. She watched him as well, not totally displeased. There was a part of Laurel Davis, Thomas thought, that had not totally embraced the Lord.

"Is Margaret sick?"

"Just tired," Thomas said. "Are you a neighbor of hers?"

"Yes. I live on the next block, although we hardly ever see each other."

Thomas remembered another fact from her files. "You're part of the parents committee that demanded her dismissal from the high school."

Her chin came up and her tone hardened again. "Yes, I am. I have two children, one already at the high school and another who will be soon. I need to see that they get good, wholesome education."

"And Margaret Masters won't provide that? She doesn't come up to local moral standards?"

"You're not from Paradise, Mr.—?"

"Thomas."

"Mr. Thomas. You don't know the story of Margaret Masters." She spoke the line with the perfect intonation of a small-town gossip; just the right mixture of censure and shrewdness.

Thomas, suddenly feeling protective of the teacher, decided to give her a little taste of it himself.

"I know her family background and I know a bit more," he said. "I also know she's not the only one in this town who has violated the public standards of morality. She's not the only girlfriend Jack Eames ever had."

Her beautiful jaw tensed and her fingers tightened around the Bible. She held it like a life preserver that was keeping her afloat in a sea of seamy scandal.

"We've all sinned, Mr. Thomas," she said stonily. "I've committed my own transgressions, but I've made my peace with the Lord and He saved me. Now I have to do His work."

"Like asking for Margaret Masters's dismissal."

"Yes. The end is coming and we have the Lord's work to do. That's what the storm told us."

"Had you seen Jack Eames lately?"

"Only regarding the school issue," she said.

"When was that?"

She thought a moment. "Thursday."

"He died either Friday night or Saturday morning," Thomas said. "Where did you see him?"

Her beautiful eyes narrowed. "At his home. I tried to make an appointment to see him at his office, but he was busy. He said he could make time for me that evening. I went to try to convince him to support our position. That was all we discussed."

"Was anyone else there?"

She shook her head in tight jerks. "No. At least I don't think so. We never left the foyer. I didn't go farther into the house or accept as much as a glass of water," she said chastely.

"What did Eames tell you his position was?"

"He didn't say. He listened to me and that was all. Then I went home to my children."

Thomas wondered what had happened between Eames

and Laurel Davis. She was a completely different woman from Margaret Masters. Had Jack Eames jilted her for Margaret? Had Eames tired of her small-town ways and turned to a less beautiful but more sophisticated and brighter woman?

"Who do you think killed Jack Eames?" he asked her.

Her eyes shifted momentarily to the house and then back to him.

"I don't know."

He hesitated, but then spoke what was on his mind. "You think it was Margaret Masters."

She tensed. "I didn't say that."

"But you think it, Ms. Davis. Why did you come here?"

She held the Bible out. "To pray with Margaret."

"Or to ask her if she had killed him?"

"I said to pray with her, Mr. Thomas." She glanced again at the house. "I'll have to come back later, when she's feeling better."

She turned and walked back in the direction she'd come, looking once over her shoulder at him. She was a woman who had learned to live without Jack Eames and was willing to teach someone else how to do it, too. At least that was what she let on.

Thomas found Dan Oates at his desk, unshaven. He wondered if the editor had been home at all. A pile of Paradise *Chronicle* "Extras" was next to him on the desk. A seventy-two-point headline read: "Twister Rips Paradise." It was the kind that would get framed and end up on the wall with the other big stories in Paradise history. In the middle of the page was Thomas's article of interviews with townspeople and under it his own brief first-person account. Oates had put Thomas's byline on both of them. At the bottom of the page, in a box outlined in black, was a smaller headline: "Police Investigate Death of Jack Eames."

The brief story said that Eames's body had been found in the wreckage of his house, that he had died of a bullet wound, and that it was an apparent homicide, according to the medical examiner. The article did not speculate on why the county attorney had been killed, only that the police were investigating.

Thomas pulled up a chair and told Oates about meeting Laurel Davis outside Margaret Masters's house, without telling him why he had gone to see the teacher in the first place, and how the former beauty queen suspected the English teacher was a murderer.

"I've had a few calls this morning from some of her fellow church members," Oates said. "They called Margaret a witch and let me know witches were for burning. And there are lots of them out there who think that and that the tornado is proof that Sam Dash is right. God only knows what they'll do."

Thomas then told him about his early-morning meeting with Sheriff West and finding the pistol in the wreckage of Eames's house. The other man nodded.

"They expect ballistics and fingerprint results back from Odessa this afternoon. I have a friend over at the sheriff's office who'll call as soon as it comes in."

Thomas couldn't expect to scoop the big man that easily on his own turf.

"How about the duffel bag with drugs in it that was found next to Eames's body?" he asked.

This time Oates lifted his head and looked suspiciously down his nose. So Thomas filled him in on the finding of the black bag that morning and West's speculation about Jack Eames.

"Well, that's just crazy," Oates said. "Jack Eames had nothing to do with drug smugglers, except trying to put them in jail. Jim West knows that."

"How about a man named William Vega? Heard of him?"

Oates shook his head and Thomas told him what they had found at the motel and that he had seen Eames talking to the man Friday evening. Then Thomas asked to see the files on the sighting of the drug plane.

Oates went to the file cabinets and brought back a folder full of clips. He took out one and slid it over to Thomas. It was a big front-page *Chronicle* headline, dated November of the year before: "Police Spot Drug Plane"; "Smuggler Killed: Narcotics Captured."

The article, written by Oates, mostly quoted Jim West as to the sighting of the plane, the black duffel bags falling, the shoot-out with one smuggler, and West's chasing the pickup truck. The article ended with the name of the dead man—Ricardo Ramirez, thirty-eight years old, of McAllen, Texas. Thomas frowned at it.

"What's wrong?" Oates asked.

"This man, William Vega, he was from McAllen too."

Thomas recalled the look of interest on West's face as he had studied the registration card. He thought about the connection and the other connections of the past two days.

"I see Eames talking with this man Vega," Thomas said. "Then Eames is shot to death and next to him is found evidence that might have to do with this drug drop and this other man from McAllen, Ramirez. So maybe Jack Eames had made some progress on the drug-smuggling question. Maybe that's why he was killed. Maybe by this man Vega. Which is why Vega isn't anyplace to be found. But only if that's all true."

Oates' face clouded over with doubt.

They stayed staring at each other, looking for answers. Suddenly something occurred to Thomas, and his gaze brightened.

"Then there was your friend the rancher who drove up to Eames's house while we were there and said he'd come back."

"Landon Turner."

"I wonder if he did go back. We should go ask him."

Oates looked at his watch. "The county commissioners are meeting in a few minutes. They're discussing emergency recovery measures. I still have to get out a newspaper."

"Then I'll go see him. He should remember me from the other night. Where do I find him?"

"He owns the first spread out north of town. It's called the Buckknife Ranch."

He gave Thomas directions, and they agreed to meet back at the *Chronicle* later in the afternoon.

Chapter 11

*T*homas went north on the state road. He had been told to go about three miles west, to look for a cattle guard and a small sign on the north side of the highway. He was to take that dirt road and after another two miles or so he'd run into it.

"You can't miss it as long as you don't get lost," Oates had told him.

Thomas remembered that in the *Chronicle* file on Sam Cain there had been mention of the Buckknife Ranch and its owner, Landon Turner. According to the clips, and what Oates had told him, Turner had been forced to sell off a large portion of his family ranch lands in order to pay off debts from the stock-market downturn of 1987 and other bad investments. The clip also mentioned the zoo Turner had imported from Africa, which he had also closed down. In the end the lands had been purchased by a soft-drink corporation, which in turn was owned by a Japanese concern. Turner had retained a ranch house and a few acres, only a small fraction of what the ranch had been. The deal had been arranged and the legal aspects handled by Sam Cain, who had been attorney to the family since the thirties. Turner, given the looks of him, had taken his losses very hard. From what Thomas had seen Friday night, he looked like a man going down the tubes. Thomas wondered not only if he had returned to Eames's house that night but why he had been going to see the county attorney in the first place.

He clocked three miles and then spotted the turnoff. Buckknife Ranch, the sign said and showed the shape of the cattle brand used on those lands: a jagged, saw-toothed line with a straight line over it.

Thomas turned off, rolled slowly over the pipes of the cattle guard and went up a straight red dirt road. He kept going, past two miles of fencing, all in good repair. The land was extremely dry, and the midday sun made the prairie look that much flatter. Here and there he saw a windmill and drinking troughs. A few stray white-faced cattle looked up and watched him go past. And there were the pumpjacks, all frozen at different angles.

Finally, he saw a stand of trees ahead, the only ones in sight, and under them the ranch headquarters. Thomas rambled over another cattle guard to get into the compound, then pulled to a stop in the yard and looked at the complex of buildings. He had never been on a cattle ranch before and it wasn't at all what he had expected. There were four two-story brick houses, built roughly in a circle around a carefully manicured lawn. The grass had automated sprinklers crawling across it. In the middle of the large lawn was a swimming pool, the shimmering blue water inviting. This so-called cattle ranch looked more like suburban townhouses, or a resort.

Thomas heard a motor behind him and found a man approaching on a red lawn tractor. He was an older man, tanned and leather-faced, wearing a Stetson, a brown cowboy shirt, jeans, and a blue bandanna around his throat. He stopped right next to Thomas, turned off the mower, and dismounted.

"Can I help ya?" Up close Thomas could see just how cracked the skin of the man's face was from years of blazing sun. In the midst of those cracks were two extremely blue eyes, like pieces of the sky above.

"Yes, I'm looking for Landon Turner."

The other man pointed a knotty finger up the road. "For Landon, you have to keep goin' another mile. He don't live here."

"Who does live here?"

The old cowboy shook his head. "Nobody now. Landon and his family used to live here before they sold it off to the soda company. Landon and I run it for 'em now. They send some executives out here every once in a while, supposedly to check on the operation. It's more for a vacation, if you ask me. Ride a horse, look at the sunset. Because they really don't know nothin' 'bout cattle. They just own 'em."

He had a blade of grass in his mouth and he moved it now from one side to the other. "You ain't seen nothin' until you seen one o' these Japanese fellas up on a horse."

"A samurai," Thomas said.

The other man didn't respond to that. "They say lots of ranches in Texas are owned by corporations today. Know why they buy 'em?"

"Why's that?" Thomas asked.

The other man took the grass out now in his callused fingers.

" 'Cause they wanna lose money. Ain't that somethin'?"

"Tax write-offs."

The other man nodded. "That's right. That's what they're lookin' to do, lose money." He shook his head.

"Damn, it's too bad that tornada that hit town didn't come through here. They woulda loved that." A boyish smile spread across his weathered face.

Thomas held out a hand to introduce himself and the other man took it. It was like shaking hands with a piece of buckskin.

"My name's Vachel Niles," the man said. "I work for Landon Turner. In fact, I've worked on this ranch, on and off, for fifty years." The skin crinkled around his blue eyes. "I used to be a cowboy, when there was such a thing. Now I ride this thing instead of a horse." And he kicked the tire of the lawn tractor.

Thomas shaded his eyes from the sun. "So you were a working cowboy."

"That's right," the other man said. "Startin' when I was twelve years old. That's when you'd spend your life on a horse, roundin' up cows for brandin' and curin', checkin' fence and windmills. Ridin' a horse was just as natural as walkin'." He glanced at the beverage company compound. "Now there ain't no need for cowboys."

"Why's that? You have cattle."

Niles grimaced and pointed to a shiny new pickup truck parked in the gravel lot.

"You got trucks," he said. "You don't use horses no more, hardly ever. You gotta check a fence, you get in the truck and you do it in a fraction o' the time. You wanna put feed out, you kick it out the back of the truck. You know how we round up cattle for brandin' these days?"

"How?"

Vachel Niles pointed at the sky.

"Helicopters," he said. "Goddamn helicopters. They swoop down on those cattle, scare the devil out of 'em and make 'em go the way they want. This week one'll be here and this place'll look like Vietnam."

He leaned over, spit, and put the straw back in.

"Ain't no cowboys actually livin' on ranches no more. Sometimes you need a hand or two, you hire 'em by the day. They drive up in their own pickup, with a horse trailer on the back. Lots o' times these fellas have their own place or some other business. Why, last year we had a hand who came to work with us, a young fella, who's gettin' his master's degree in mathematics over at the university." He shook his head.

"I guess that makes sense," Thomas said. "When international corporations own ranches, the cowboys have master's degrees."

Niles shrugged. "I guess so."

"From what I hear, Landon Turner had to sell the place," Thomas said.

"That's right. He didn't have no choice. Investments went bad." He looked off across the flat, dry distance. "It's a shame. Coy Turner, Landon's father, ran one of the best operations anywhere. Landon did the same. He ran a real ranch as long as he could. Everybody'll tell ya that. We didn't brand with butane, we did it with wood fires and we didn't scare the hell outa the cattle with helicopters."

Thomas studied the old man.

"Is that why he went under, because he wouldn't modernize?"

Niles shook his head hard, the way a horse might. "Naw. Part of it was just that he went crazy with his money. Invested in all sortsa things he didn't know nothin' about. Television stations, companies that made computers, rocket ships. God knows what all. And then his third wife divorced him and went after him in court. She wanted a piece of the money he made from the oil companies."

"I didn't see many pumpjacks working as I came in."

"There ain't many workin'. This field is almost dry. And there ain't no new drillin' at all, which is why there ain't no work. But there was a few years back. When the price of oil was way up, it was like they were pumpin' money right outa the ground. It went ta Landon's head this time. He started investin' in junk bonds too, whatever those are." He shook his head again. "Some people investin' in order ta lose money and others buyin' somethin' they know is junk."

He looked out across the dry land as if there were an explanation for all of it out there. Then he tapped his chest.

"On top o' that, I went and got sick," he said. "Bad ticker. They put a clock in there now to keep it goin'. A pacemaker. I didn't have no insurance for somethin' like that. Landon had to pay for it. That didn' help either. Shows what's left o' me, my own heart don't know when to beat."

He grimaced then as if his pacemaker was experiencing heartburn.

"And then, of course, Landon got swindled."

"By who?"

Vachel Niles shuffled his boots and looked away.

"That's not for me to tell ya."

"Was it the Japanese?"

Niles's troubled blue eyes settled on Thomas, who was no longer just a stray visitor, but a stranger from back East asking pointed questions.

"You'll have to ask Landon about it."

He threw a leg over the lawn tractor and got on.

"Is he there now?"

"He's there," Niles said. "Just follow the road, you'll see it. Not like this here. It's the old original ranch house from the time of Landon's dad. You'll find him there."

Thomas thanked him and headed for his car. As he pulled away he saw Niles starting to cut the grass.

The car had sat in the sun and was like an oven. He headed up the dusty road, and the air-conditioning was just starting to dry his sweat when he saw the old ranch house. It was a white wooden place and a bunch of run-down old outbuildings, including a barn, under an isolated stand of elms. Just behind the house, feet away from it, was a pumpjack, poised with its head up. Thomas crossed another cattle guard and went under an old wooden archway into the dirt yard. He parked under a tree this time.

The complex of buildings around him was considerably different from the one down the road. It was more what he had expected of a place called the Buckknife Ranch.

The main ranch house wasn't large, but it looked comfortable enough. A big bell hung outside the front door, probably once used to call the hands in to eat. He saw a barn and a couple of corrals, one holding a white-faced steer, and the other, two beautiful red-brown horses. There was a long bunkhouse and a couple of smaller houses, maybe for married help. All those buildings were run-down and obviously uninhabited, windows clouded with dust, the paint almost worn off completely by the elements.

The horses' big, round eyes followed Thomas as he crossed the yard. He poked his head in the barn. It was stacked floor to ceiling with bales of hay and sacks of other feed. The whole place smelled of wet grass and manure. There was also a gas cylinder and, hanging on the wall, a couple of branding irons with the saw-toothed brand of the Buckknife Ranch. That was the butane can Vachel Niles had complained about.

He went to the ranch house and found the door open. He called out, but nobody answered, and he stepped into the front room which had been converted into an office. On a desk was a home computer system with various components and next to it what appeared to be a radiotelephone. There were charts on the wall, listing pastures, numbers of cattle, and what appeared to be schedules for feeding and medical care. On a table next to the desk were a slew of magazines and journals. Thomas read the covers. The top one said it was dedicated to "The Science of Ranch Management" and contained articles on endocrinology and embryo transplants. Next to that was an advertisement for a helicopter service, the new cowboys, according to Vachel Niles. All very modern and systematized, the way a Japanese cattle ranch should be.

Thomas looked around, and suddenly saw something else: a closet was open a crack and he could see an automatic rifle leaning there. It was an M-16, a weapon that could fire thirty rounds in about four seconds or fire one bullet at a time. Also very modern.

He heard a board creak behind him. He turned and found Landon Turner standing in the doorway. Thomas had only seen him in the dark and sitting in a car. He turned out to be a big man, probably six-three, with narrow shoulders, a large, soft gut and a heavy, pallid face. He was probably in his mid-forties, but he appeared younger or at least tried to. His hair was longish and styled, he wore rimless plastic glasses, a wide-collared shirt, a gold chain around his neck, and jeans that were too tight for him. His weak eyes also had the same look Thomas had seen the other night. He looked not just nervous but desolate.

"Hello, Mr. Turner."

Turner scowled. "Who are you?"

Thomas reminded him. Turner watched him, not quite convinced and then came into the office. He glanced in the direction of the closet.

"I was just admiring your assault rifle."

"We have that for shooting coyotes," the big man said. "We take it up in the helicopter with us."

His tone was defensive, as if he didn't know what Thomas was doing there and how he should treat him. Thomas glanced around.

"It looks like quite an operation," he said. "The latest developments applied to the cattle business."

Turner didn't comment. He moved his large body to the desk, sat in the small chair, and turned on the computer. As he passed, Thomas caught a whiff of alcohol, just as he had the night before. Thomas followed him.

"I hear you even have Japanese business partners riding around the grazing lands," he said. "Vachel Niles was telling me."

Turner swiveled hard. "They're not business partners. They own the Buckknife Ranch," he said flatly. "This is a corporate holding. Vachel doesn't understand these things."

Thomas nodded. "Yes, from what he told me, he's having trouble adjusting to modern ranching."

Turner stared at Thomas for several moments, his expression turning sour.

"Vachel Niles comes from a breed of man that's extinct," he said. "He's like the dinosaur—he didn't adapt to changing times and new ways. He doesn't understand the modern world and doesn't want to live in it."

He punctuated his pronouncement by turning and tapping a computer key.

"You, on the other hand, didn't let the world leave you behind," Thomas said. "I'm told you branched out into all kinds of businesses, that you diversified."

Turner eyed him suspiciously. "You probably also heard that that's why I went bust. That I got in over my head. And that I had it coming."

Thomas shrugged. "I guess I have heard that."

"I'm sure you have," Turner said testily, "and I'm sure people made it sound like I desecrated the graves of my ancestors too, since they were original homesteaders." He tapped the computer angrily and turned back to Thomas. "Our family survived the droughts here that drove most other homesteaders off their land sixty years ago. But that was only because my granddaddy showed some initiative," Turner said. "With the cattle dropping around him, he had to find other ways to create cash. At first, he shot coyotes for bounty. Then when they put the railroad through, he found a way to get a small piece of the shipping business. When there was no town here at all, just a road passin' miles away, he bought gasoline and sold it to people crossin' country. All so he could stay on his land. Other people went bust. And when the oil people came nosing around here, he was smart enough to buy up all that abandoned land. Some people didn't like it, but that was the law. If you didn't stay on the land, you lost it."

"Survival of the fittest," Thomas said.

"But when another member of the family shows some initiative, shows some ambition, people take potshots at him."

"You mean when you went into other businesses."

Turner nodded sullenly. "When the boom came, there was lots of money around and opportunities. The early eighties was a boom time just about everywhere you looked." He frowned, hearing his own words. "At least it seemed that way."

Thomas nodded, but Turner was looking past him.

"Who wants to spend his whole life on a cattle ranch anyhow? There's other life-styles out there. There's other people to know, and why not if you have the capital?" He gave Thomas a worldly look. "There's no sense spendin' your whole life in the slow lane, especially when it's nothin' but a dirt road."

Turner had stated a philosophy, a creed. He stayed staring at his own words, convinced at first, but then watching them fade the way he had probably seen those other life-styles crumble and fade. Thomas remembered what Oates had said about Turner in California—television actresses and racehorses. Thomas could just see certain folks in the fast lane feasting on a big, rich boy from Paradise, Texas, like Landon Turner.

"Then the bust came," Thomas said.

Turner bridled, the sound of the word apparently causing him physical pain. He nodded silently.

"Your investments went bad and you ended up having to sell to the Japanese."

"Japanese cattlemen."

"Vachel said you also got swindled."

Turner looked at Thomas warily. Behind his eyes thoughts could be seen dashing from one side to the other and then scrambling for cover. He shook his head. "Vachel doesn't know what he's talking about. Just because Sam Cain owns a small bit of land that used to be part of the Buckknife Ranch, Vachel feels like it was a piece of him that was taken. That's how he feels about his ranch. That's why he talks the way he does. I've had trouble with my cash flow, so I paid Sam for his legal work with a piece of land instead."

Thomas was surprised to hear Cain's name pop up in this context. "How much land was it?"

Turner waved his hand carelessly at the distance. "It's just one section, a piece of scrubby land with an old dry hole and a beat-up trailer on it. I think Sam was thinkin' of drilling for natural gas out there when the economic situation improved. He had Walt Gamble, an old geologist, out there nosing around. In fact, he's been wanderin' around the ranch lands too. Breaking the law. Trespassing."

"Is that why you were going to see Jack Eames on Friday night, to talk to him about this Gamble?"

Turner froze a moment. "That's right," he said, although it wasn't right at all by the looks of him.

"After Dan Oates and I saw you that night, did you go back to see Eames?"

Turner shook his head emphatically. "No, I didn't. I came back here and decided I'd see him the next day. Of course, then the twister hit."

"And Jack Eames was dead, murdered."

"That's right."

"Do you have any idea who might have done it?"

Turner shook his head again, but not as emphatically as before. "No I don't."

Thomas watched him carefully, not looking at this large man sitting very still before him but at those thoughts that were scrambling and dodging for cover behind his eyes. He didn't believe Turner when he said he hadn't gone back to see Eames that night. According to Vachel Niles, Turner had been swindled and it might have been by Sam Cain. Now Cain was lying almost dead and the man who would have prosecuted his would-be murderer was lying completely dead. Thomas didn't believe him when he said he had no idea who might have killed Eames. Landon Turner had lots of ideas. But they were all running for cover behind his desolate eyes and Thomas wouldn't get anywhere with him now. He could probably find out more in town. Thomas said he would be heading back there and Turner followed him out onto the porch.

"I'm sorry I couldn't help you more," he said.

"Maybe you can," Thomas said. "This plane they spotted, the one where they gunned down that smuggler—just where was that?"

Turner thrust a finger into the distance. "Way over west of town," he said eagerly. "Nowhere near the Buckknife Ranch."

But it didn't matter where the smuggler had fallen, Turner had the same look on his face. Fear and guilt. As if all the grazing lands around Paradise were his soul and any sins committed on them were his. Thomas left him and headed back down the road.

Chapter 12

*T*homas drove back out the dusty road and passed the compound of brick buildings. He didn't see Vachel Niles or anyone else. He kept going until he hit the highway, but instead of heading south back to town, he went north. Landon Turner had said there was a mobile home on the land Sam Cain owned and about a mile down the road he saw it. It was the only dwelling in sight, everything else was scrub. Next to it was parked a beat-up gold Cadillac, maybe twelve years old or more.

Thomas pulled up behind it. The mobile home was a long one, old, soiled by the dust and the scarcity of rain. It was hooked into the power line that passed on the highway and an air conditioner was running. Thomas got out, climbed the portable wooden stairs, and knocked on the screen door. He could see into the living room. It was crowded with furniture, imitation antique, he'd call it. On the floor was a fake Persian rug and hanging on the back wall, a gilt-framed mirror.

Suddenly his view was blocked and a tall, white-haired old man was standing in the doorway, looking at Thomas through a rip in the screen. He had an apple in his hand and was just biting into it. He chewed a couple of times, then said:

"What's up with you?"

"Are you Mr. Gamble?" Thomas asked.

"That's right," the man said, chewing. "On good days, that is."

Thomas introduced himself. "I'm a writer and I'm trying to find out a bit about the oil business in these parts these days. I understand you know quite a bit about the oil fields."

The old man's bushy eyebrows rose. "I should know it. I've put more holes in the land around Paradise than anybody else." He opened the screen door. "Come on in before you drop dead from the heat." He let Thomas into a miniature living room and pointed him at a stuffed chair. "You wanna drink?"

"Some water will be fine."

"Fine for you maybe," Gamble said and disappeared into the kitchenette. Thomas looked around. The trailer was cramped and dark. The ceiling was low, especially for a man of Gamble's size, and the walls were covered with oppressive imitation wood paneling. The furniture was worn, but it appeared to be of good quality. What most attracted Thomas's attention was the rug. It was a very good imitation antique Persian. Thomas had worked the Middle East, had gotten to know a thing or two about rugs, and had bought one himself. This one was scarlet and deep blue and was very good. The old geologist had some granite-colored rocks lying on it.

Gamble came back in, handed Thomas his water, sat

down across from him, lifted his highball glass, and said, "Cheers." He drank a quarter of it, then wiped his mouth with the back of his hand. Thomas pointed at the rug.

"Nice rug you have."

Gamble nodded. "It should be. Cost me five thousand dollars to buy the thing and that was years back. God knows what it's worth now."

Thomas frowned at it and then at Gamble.

"It's real," Gamble said. He pointed at the gilt mirror on the wood-paneled wall. "That's real gold too," he said. "Got it in Saudi Arabia. Forget what I paid for it." He thumped the armrest of his chair. "Everything in here is top o' the line."

Thomas looked around and believed Gamble.

"I bought all this stuff when times were good and I had a big house," Gamble said. "Always figured if you had the money you should buy the best." He pointed toward the back of the trailer. "I have a closet full of five-hundred-dollar suits, too. Not that I have any cause to wear the things. Always figured if you had money . . . and there been times when I had money over the past fifty years. I had my ups and downs. You're just seeing me durin' one of my downturns."

He took another long pull of his drink.

"You've been here a long time, I hear," Thomas said.

Gamble nodded and his eyes lit up with enthusiasm.

"Since the first boom back in the thirties. That was a time when there was nothin' but luck around here. That's what came outa the ground, good luck."

"Lots of oil," Thomas said.

Gamble nodded avidly. "You could do the backstroke just in the spillover." He pointed to the small window. "This land around here was dry as hell from the droughts. Cattle was dyin' from thirst, and the families they was leavin' before they died of it too. Then some old boys hit oil right near here and it was like the whole damned prairie was paved with gold. Nobody was thirsty anymore, I'll tell

ya that. There were so many wells workin' out here at one
point, you could read the newspaper in the dead of night
just from the light of the burnoff flares."

"It must have been quite a sight."

"You'd be standin' there next to a hole where they was
drillin'. They'd been goin down into the ground for days,
maybe a couple weeks. Then you'd feel that earth rumblin'
right through your boots. I mean it'd shake right underneath ya, and you knew it was comin'. You watched and
all of a sudden it just come up outa that hole, black as
black could be. All over you. Your face, your clothes. But
nobody cared. Everybody would laugh. They'd jump for
joy. Yes sirree, it was somethin'."

His eyes had filled with wonder and happiness.

"Ta tell ya the truth, there wasn't no trick to bein' a
geologist in those days. You went around makin' believe
you knew what you were doin', checkin' the ground and
charts. But just about anywheres you put a hole around
here, you hit a formation in those days. Nobody had ever
tapped it before. They was pumpin' so much outa here,
they had to slow themselves down. The stuff was sellin'
for peanuts there was so much of it. Had to get the price
back up. That was about the time I stopped workin' for
the oil companies and got in independent drillin'."

"You were a wildcatter?"

Gamble cackled gleefully. "That's exactly right. That was
the only way to live. By your own luck, the seat of your
pants."

He fixed on Thomas with bright gray eyes.

"I been rich a half dozen times and most of it went to
the same place, back into a hole in the ground."

"You've had your own booms and busts."

"I've been lucky and unlucky, rich and poor, a winner
and a loser." He pointed a finger at Thomas and took a
bead on him, one eye closed. "But I always been in the
game."

Gamble sat nodding to himself. He sat that way for what
must have been twenty seconds and Thomas saw the light

in his eyes start to dim slowly but steadily, and the expression on his face change, until he sat staring as if he were looking at something painful or had just watched someone die.

"Of course, sometimes things ain't too good." His voice had gone lifeless. "Then everything goes ta hell. Everything, underneath the ground and on top o' the ground. And it goes on a while. All your holes come in dry. Yer life dries up on ya. Yer marriage goes bad, you lose your house, yer friends move away. You look around and you're just in some desert, just as if there had never been oil around in the first place. When things ain't good, you feel like a dry hole yourself. Like right now things ain't too good. Sam Cain got his skull cracked, ya know."

He said it out of nowhere, assuming that Thomas knew who Cain was.

"Yes, I know," Thomas said. "I understand he was going to give you some work?"

Gamble was suddenly disturbed. "Sam Cain wasn't gonna give me nothin'. I was gonna give him somethin'."

"What was that?"

Gamble's eyes narrowed and he looked canny. "My knowledge and experience." He winked at Thomas. "I was gonna make both of us rich."

"You were going to drill for natural gas, I'm told."

The light momentarily flared again in his eyes.

"I was gonna be in the money again."

Thomas watched the old man, who was staring away into that munificent future that was to have been. Gamble appeared to have a state of mind ruled by his chances of fortune, his being hooked directly to the price of oil. Now he was gazing at a bright future he had planned to make with Sam Cain. Two old men near eighty. Thomas brought him back.

"Vachel Niles says that Sam Cain swindled this land from Landon Turner. Is that true?" It wasn't what Niles had said exactly, but Thomas felt it was what he had declined to say.

Gamble scowled at him now. "Vachel Niles should get off his high horse and stop accusing people of anything," he said. "Vachel never had no use for nobody who wasn't a cattleman. He said oil people were nothin' but grease monkeys. Meanwhile he hasn't changed in fifty years. He's an old fossil, no use to nobody and he doesn't know anything that goes on around here. Landon Turner had to pay Sam Cain this land because Landon lost all his money livin' a high-falutin life and bein' stupid. Plain and simple."

He took another long swill of his drink and remained scowling at nothing in particular.

"When was the last time you saw Sam Cain?"

Gamble's face stormed over and he glared at Thomas. "I saw him on Tuesday when he come out here to see how the work was goin'. I didn't see him none after that. I been studyin' the holes around here. I been busy."

"He didn't say anything to you about being afraid for his life? Anything he was worried about."

Gamble shook his head, his face closed and obstinate. "No, he didn't, and I ain't answerin' any more questions." The old man had turned ornery.

"Why's that? You don't have anything to hide, do you?"

Gamble screwed up his eyes. "I know a lot about a lotta people round here, but I got nothin' ta say."

"How about Jack Eames, who was shot to death? Do you know about him? Do you know if he had any contact with Sam Cain in the past days? Do you know why someone would have gone after the two of them in the same week?"

Gamble was again shaking his head, but it wasn't at Thomas's question. The mention of Eames and death, apparently, had sent him off on his own. His mood had swung again. He was gazing out the window with a faraway look in his eyes.

"Some people say you dig in the ground and what you're going to find is the devil," he said finally. "You're gonna find Old Satan. The preachers been sayin' that forever. I never believed it. Da you?"

"I don't know."

"They say all oil ever brought was greed and more greed, sin and more sin. That's what some people say. That oil is somethin' sent up outa hell by the Devil to turn men into sinners and lead them right back down ta hell. They say we should never put holes in the ground because we're diggin' ourselves right inta hell. And they say if there's a God, then there has to be a Devil."

His eyes brightened suddenly. "I seen God. I seen 'im here in Paradise when we hit oil in those first years. I seen men give thanks to the Lord for that oil. I felt the Lord in me when I hit oil. It was a miracle. I know I felt 'im."

He looked ecstatic, but then his gaze slowly darkened again. "And I known men around here who been the Devil himself. Who done terrible things."

"Like who?" Thomas asked.

The other man didn't answer. He stared into nothing. If he knew more, he wasn't going to say, not right then. Thomas got up, said goodbye, and left him sitting in his trailer in a trance, with his Persian rug and his gilt-framed mirror, like a millionaire living in exile.

He drove back toward town. The sun had started on its way down, softening its light and giving the grazing lands back some of their definition.

Thomas reached the entrance to the Buckknife Ranch and passed it. As he did, he noticed someone traveling parallel to him, but on the other side of the barbed-wire fence on the ranch lands. It was a man in a Stetson, galloping on a dappled white horse that was moving quickly, eating up land.

The man didn't notice the car. But Thomas was sure that it was the same man and the same horse he had seen Saturday night near the ruins of the Eames house. The rider, the horseman of the apocalypse, was Vachel Niles.

Thomas drove back downtown and went right to the *Chronicle*. He found Oates at his desk. He sat down and told him about his talk with Turner and what Vachel Niles had implied about his being swindled by Cain and how

Walt Gamble had claimed that he and Cain would be rich off that piece of scrubland. He also told him about seeing Vachel Niles near the Eames's house the night after the twister.

Oates sat and listened to him with a somber expression. "I have news for you too. Sam Cain died this morning."

Thomas grimaced. "So now there are two murders."

"That's right." They sat in silence a minute.

"The question is, who had reason to kill them both?" Thomas said.

Oates looked at him acidly. "You mean besides Margaret."

Thomas nodded. "Maybe Sam Cain did swindle Landon Turner somehow. But what could Turner have against Eames?"

"Nothing that I know. I still think it may be somebody from the outside."

"There's the Mexican. He was talking to Eames, but what could he have to do with Sam Cain?"

Oates said nothing.

"And then there's Sam Dash," Thomas went on. "He came back to Paradise about the time the drug drops started. He had a history of drug involvement and he had reason to dislike Jack Eames. Maybe because Eames had decided to back Margaret after she'd been bad-mouthing Dash, but maybe, more importantly, because he was investigating smuggling."

Oates drank it all in. Then he glanced at his watch. "Sam Dash's Sunday service out west of town starts at eleven. Maybe we should go hear what he has to say."

Chapter 13

*T*hey drove west in Oates's Bronco on another perfectly flat, straight road. The buildings gave way to mesquite, shin oak, cattle fences, and the occasional idle pumpjack. It looked like a desolate area for religious services and Thomas said so.

"Sam Dash picked a spot on a small creek out here about three years ago in order to do baptisms," Oates said. "They got a bulldozer and dug out the creek so it was deep enough to totally immerse people. Then later he built an altar and I'm told they've performed sacrifices on it. Heifers."

Thomas frowned. "That's not the standard ritual for churches around here, I take it."

"No, but then Sam Dash isn't your standard preacher. He's taking these people back into biblical times. As if he

were Moses and he's leading them out of the desert to the
Promised Land. They say he comes out here into the wil-
derness sometimes by himself, like Moses did, to commune
with that Old Testament God of his." He shook his head.
"I'm not sure whether it's part of the show or if maybe
he's really crazy."

Thomas gazed across the landscape, which was flattened
even more now by a late-morning sun.

"Where's the place where the smuggler was killed, where
the drug drop happened?"

Oates pointed off ahead of them. "Out this way, but
farther off the road. Not far away."

The big man turned off the state road and rumbled over
a cattle guard and onto a dirt track. They went about a
half mile and the road was lined on both sides with cars
and pickups baking in the sun. They parked in back of the
last one and walked toward the sound of singing. The
refrain of the hymn Thomas heard was "When the day of
reckoning comes."

The creek ran on their left and they came to the spot
that had been dug out and where a concrete bath had been
constructed for the baptisms. Further on was the tent
where the service was in progress. It was big like a circus
tent, but the sides were up to allow ventilation. There were
no chairs or pews and people were packed together. At
one end was a raised stage made of earth. On it was the
altar Oates had talked about. It was a slab of what appeared
to be sandstone resting on other stones. It was stained with
what must have been the blood of sacrificed animals.

Seated on one side of the altar was Sam Dash and next
to him, Lloyd Haynes. The hymn ended and Dash got up,
Bible in hand, and went to the lectern in front of the altar.
Today his robe was white and it made his complexion look
even more flushed than the last time. The lectern was
placed just right to let the sunlight slanting in through the
seams in the tent illuminate him.

He opened the Bible, read to himself for several moments, and then looked up as if he were seeing right

through the canvas to the sky. Once again, he seemed to be listening to something, or someone, whom no one else could hear. Then the message was over. He lowered his gaze and looked at the crowd. His countenance was stern, reproving.

"What does the Bible say? What does it say about people who double-cross the Lord? Who transgress against Him, rebel against Him, reject His judgments and His laws? Who commit abominations? Those who have become guilty in their blood?"

He stared out at the silent congregation knowingly, as if he could actually visualize the scenes that were appearing in their imaginations, scenes of divine retribution. Then he looked down at the Bible.

"Behold, I, even I, am against thee and will execute judgments in the midst of thee, in sight of the nations. I will send mine anger upon thee and will judge thee according to thy ways, and will recompense thee all thine abominations and mine eye shall not spare thee. Neither will I have pity.' "

He scanned the crowd and then looked back at the Bible, turning to another scripture.

" 'Oh, thou that dwellest in the land, the time is come, the day of trouble is near.' " He flipped quickly to another page. " 'Destruction cometh and they shall seek peace and there shall be none.' "

He looked up now, excitedly, and jabbed the Bible with a rigid finger. " 'They shall seek peace and there shall be none.' It was right there all the time, wasn't it?"

Someone yelled, "Praise the Lord."

"Right here in the Good Book," he said, "and not in general terms, not in veiled language, but in detail. Right in Ezekiel, Chapter One."

He read: " "And I looked and, behold, a whirlwind came, a great cloud, and a fire infolding itself, and a brightness was about it, and out of the midst thereof, as the color of amber, out of the midst of the fire."

He looked up in amazement.

"Did you see it yesterday, brothers and sisters? Did you see the color of it?" He jabbed the book. "Black with amber, that yellow light, just like Ezekiel said."

Thomas observed the solemn faces around him. These were people who, he knew, at the moment of the storm, had prayed to their God to intercede for them. And not, like Thomas, by mistake. They were like those other people he had seen all over the world who at moments of crisis, of terror, when reason was pulled inside out, turned to the heavens. He had always thought it innocent, naive, quaint. But now he stood there with them, having prayed himself, not out of faith, but from naked fear and delirium of the moment, maybe out of the chaos of his life "behind the scenes." He might not be a believer, but maybe he could understand why other people who lived with poverty and fear for years, if not entire lifetimes, did their praying.

Someone yelled, "Help me, Jesus," and Dash went on.

"The Lord sent that tornada to Paradise, just like He sent that one to Ezekiel thousands of years ago. It's in here clear as a bell." He looked down and read: " 'In all the dwelling places, the cities shall be laid to waste and ye shall know that I am the Lord.' "

His chest was heaving with excitement. His wired eyes moved skittishly across the crowd, as if he himself didn't believe that his prophecy had come true. It freaked him some, Thomas thought. But then he nodded with assurance.

"I told ya this was comin', didn't I, brothers and sisters? Me, the Reverend Sam Dash. I let ya know in advance, didn't I? Look around ya today, brethren. Not one member of our congregation was killed in the whirlwind. Look around you and figure out what happened. Don't tell me it was accident or chance, 'cause I won't believe it. No, it was the hand of the Lord, just as if an angel had come down and painted the door of the faithful." All eyes were on him and it was as quiet as the prairie itself.

"I had ya ready, didn't I? And that's because I've spent

some time gettin' in touch with God. Gettin' high on the Lord. Yes, I have. Time with the Good Book and some nights right out here with nobody else around, gettin' to know the Lord." He looked out at the prairie and back at the faithful. "He lets me know what He's up to, brethren, just like He let the sons o' Israel in generations past know what He had planned. Like when He sent the plagues to Egypt and when He destroyed Sodom. He let his people know in advance, yes, He did."

"Love Ya, Jesus."

"Why do you think the Lord sent that tornada ta Paradise?" he asked. "Why has He sent whirlwinds, wars, plagues, suffering all through the ages? Why did He punish the people of Israel when they became idolatrous? Why did He destroy the Tower of Babel? Why did He destroy Sodom?"

The slanting sunlight caught him again. It sparkled in his dark eyes.

"Because He saw the Devil's hand at work, didn't He?" He scanned the crowd. "And the Harlot of Babylon's. Yes, He did. He saw it right here in Paradise just this week. God sent that tornada and one of the things He had it do was rip off the roof of a house. And what was underneath that roof? A man slain by the hand of another. And this came after another citizen had been brutally attacked. People of Paradise had started to prey on each other. And God said it's time to put them out of their misery."

"Love Ya, Jesus."

"Who knows when that body would have been found if that tornada hadn't come along? We don't know, but God worked it so that it would be found. He was a man who had to make some important decisions about our town. Who had to decide between God and Satan.

"He was a man searchin' his soul about what to do. I know, because he talked to me the day before he died. From what he told me, I think he was about to make the right decision. I think he was, but he ended up dead."

He shook his head as if he were looking at the corpse of Jack Eames. Oates had turned to Thomas and was staring at him in disbelief.

"Who do ya think killed that man, brethren? Who had reason to cut that man down, just as he was about to choose on the side of the Lord? Who had reason, but the forces of Satan. The Harlot of Babylon. That's who."

He looked down at his Bible and stabbed at it with a finger.

"And in her was found the blood of the prophets, and of the saints and of all those who were slain upon the earth."

He frenziedly flipped a page and stabbed again.

"And upon her forehead was written: 'Mystery, Babylon the Great, the Mother of Harlots and Abominations of the Earth. And the kings of the earth, who have committed fornication and lived deliciously with her, shall bewail her and lament for her when they shall see the smoke of her burning.' "

"Praise the Lord."

"What does the Bible say about the meting out of justice? It says an eye for an eye and a tooth for a tooth, don't it, brothers and sisters?"

Thomas felt Oates squirm next to him. Sam Dash was taking his revenge to the limit. He was accusing Margaret Masters of murder and asking for retribution. The big man was looking around him, and Thomas did too. The faces that surrounded them were chiseled in stone like the altar, possessed of the security of Old Testament justice. There were no dissident voices. Sam Dash had prepared them, as he said.

Then Dash raised his hands above his head, reaching into the bars of slanting sunlight.

"Lord, we have seen Thy power and Thy fury. We know that this is a sign from You, a terrible and glorious sign, full of Your wrath, but also full of Your love, Your mercy. We hope Your message will pierce the minds and hearts of our townspeople. We'll do our best to bring Your warn-

ing to every street, every home, every dark soul in Paradise.
For our time has come."

"Hallelujah."

Dash dropped his hands, and the congregation burst
into song. They sang a half-dozen hymns, finishing with
"Bathed in the Blood of the Lord." Lloyd Haynes offered
a final prayer, about how the world was in its last days,
and then the service concluded. Worshipers started to head
for their cars.

Dash came down from the altar and began to shake
hands and exchange words with some of his flock. He
worked the crowd in the tent as well as he did from the
pulpit, clapping a shoulder, pressing a hand. Lloyd
Haynes, round-shouldered and draped in black, looking
like a vulture, stood next to him. When the crowd had
thinned, Oates took Thomas over to Dash. A look of per-
plexity spread over the preacher's burnished face.

"Why, I do believe it's Dan Oates," he said. "I'm not sure
I believe my eyes when I see the editor of the Paradise
Chronicle in my congregation. But I'm not going to ask any
questions. I'm just going to thank the Lord."

He took Oates's extended hand and grabbed it with both
of his. Oates introduced Thomas.

"A pleasure to meet you, brother." Dash took Thomas's
hand and smiled benignly. When you looked closely
around the eyes and mouth you could see the wear and
tear of a misspent youth. He looked older than his thirty
or so years. You also saw that mischief. Sam Dash had the
eyes of a scammer. Maybe a scammer for the Lord. Maybe
not.

Dash noticed the bandage on Thomas's head.

"You didn't get hit by the whirlwind, did you, brother?"

"Just grazed," Thomas said.

"That's good. The Lord took care of ya." The preacher's
eyes narrowed cunningly. "Maybe He was just givin' ya a
little scare. To help ya find the way. He does that sometimes."

Thomas nodded, unsmiling.

"You must have been in Paradise before the storm," Dash said. "I wonder what brought you here. I don't think you had a tip that the twister was going to hit."

"No, my sources aren't that good. Not as good as yours."

Dash's eyes twinkled. "The Good Book is always way ahead of the game."

"It wasn't an act of God that brought me," Thomas said. "It was an act of man. The attack on Sam Cain."

"That was a terrible and cowardly act."

"He's dead, you know. He died this morning. That's what's keeping me here. His murder and that of Jack Eames."

Dash was grimacing and shaking his head. "The plagues don't end, do they?"

"It wasn't a plague that murdered Sam Cain and it wasn't a plague that killed Jack Eames. They were human hands."

Dash nodded solemnly. "Hands moved by the Devil, brother."

"Possibly, but it would still be good to know whose hands they were. You wonder what was in the mind of a person who beat an old man to death with the jawbone of an ass."

"The Devil gets inside a person and that person's capable of anything. Look at King Herod, or the Pharaohs of Egypt, or St. Paul himself."

"Or maybe it was someone who got a little too full of the Word," Thomas said. "When you say anyone not doing the Lord's work is doing the Devil's work, you make them free game for a certain kind of believer. A believer who is maybe a little crazy, who doesn't have a firm grip on reality."

Dash's eyes fixed on Thomas and his white smile suddenly blossomed to match his robes.

"I bet you and I have a different idea of what constitutes reality, Mr. Thomas."

Thomas nodded. "I would think."

"God is real, His love and His wrath."

"And Jack Eames is really dead with a bullet in his head."

Dash continued to stare at Thomas and his tone became steely.

"You're not saying that I'm preachin' murder, now, are you, Mr. Thomas?"

"When you say an eye for an eye and a tooth for a tooth, you are."

"I'm saying the law should follow what the Good Book tells us and mete out justice."

"But you might have some people who take it literally."

Dash smiled and nodded excitedly. "Oh, and I mean it literally, Mr. Thomas. Yes, indeed I do. When the Good Book says something, that's exactly what it means." He held up the Bible. "We believe everything in this book, and we don't think they're just stories either. To us, everything in this book is historical fact. Every bit of it happened in the real world. Yes, it did. Jacob wrestled the angel, the Red Sea parted, Lot's wife was turned to salt, David slew Goliath, Jesus rose from the dead. To you, the journalist, these are all pipe dreams. But the members of my congregation and I *know* they happened. Just as we *know* that God sent that tornado, which I'm sure you don't believe. Just as we know the end is comin' soon."

He continued to stare at Thomas, an incongruous smile on his face as he talked about death and destruction. Haynes stood just behind him.

"You said in your sermon that you spoke with Jack Eames on Friday," Thomas said.

Dash nodded. "He called me and asked me to go see him."

"What time was that?"

"It was a while after I got home from our prayer service here. Must have been about nine o'clock." After he and Oates had been at Eames's house and not found him, and after they had talked with Margaret Masters, Thomas realized.

"You went over there?"

"That's right."

"What did you talk about, if you don't mind my asking?"

"I don't mind. I've already spoken to the sheriff about it. We talked about the Margaret Masters case."

"What did he say about it?"

Dash paused. "He told me he had made a decision in the case, and that he wanted to talk to me about it."

"What was his decision?"

Dash's voice rose so that those standing around him could hear. "He said he'd decided that we were right. Margaret Masters had dealt with religious subject matter that wasn't part of her curriculum, and she had violated her contract and acted irresponsibly, and had deliberately provoked a segment of the population."

Thomas felt Oates stir next to him.

"Why would he call *you* and tell *you* that?" the big man asked, antagonism in his voice.

"He said he was calling because either that night or the next morning, before he left for Austin, he was going to contact members of the school board and tell them what he thought. He was worried about something, though."

"What was that?"

Dash looked at Thomas with an expression of pain on his face.

"Jack told me he was afraid that if Margaret Masters were told she was losing her job, she might do harm to herself. He told me she was bad off. He said me and my people should settle for a reprimand or maybe a suspension, not dismissal."

Oates was glaring at Dash.

"And what did you say?"

Dash shook his head the way he must have shaken it at Eames. "I told him I knew how folks felt about it and that wouldn't be enough. My people feel they have a duty to the Lord. They have to rid the school system of Satan's influences."

"What did Jack say to that?"

"He couldn't say much. He knew what he had to do. But as I was leaving I decided I'd go speak with her that same night, just in case the news leaked out. I would try to keep her from hurting herself."

Oates was gaping at him and his voice was full of disbelief. "Did you go see her?"

"Yes, I went. Miss Masters and I are opposite sides, and she's spread lies about me and my beliefs, but we've known each other a long time. You know that, Dan."

Thomas could sense the anger, the desire for retribution behind Dash's angelic countenance.

"What time did you go there?" he asked.

"I left Jack's place at about ten o'clock and went right over there."

"Did you tell her Jack Eames was going to recommend that she be fired?"

Dash was nodding again with that wired, keen gaze of his. "But I told her life wasn't over for her. That the Lord had His eye on her and wanted her. That there was not only a future before her, but life eternal. That, really, her life was just beginning. And that she shouldn't hate those who had opposed her in this matter, but should appreciate that they had saved her from eternal perdition."

Oates was staring at Dash, but you could see he was picturing Margaret Masters, suffering when she had been told.

"You told her that and then you left?"

"I prayed for her. I offered to stay longer or to send one of the women from the church, but she said no. She was calm. She promised me she wouldn't do anything drastic. Then I left."

"Do you have any idea what she did after you left?" Thomas asked.

Dash shook his head. "It was late, about eleven. I assume she went to bed."

Thomas looked at Oates. He knew the editor was thinking the same thing he was: if Dash were telling the truth, Margaret Masters would be the prime suspect in the killing of Jack Eames; the visit by Sam Dash would have given her an undeniable motive. Thomas recalled the image of the English teacher leaving the ruins of Eames's house the next morning, on her face that look of pain and distraction. It might have been the face of a woman who had just committed murder.

Oates was wearing an expression that was equally pained. He looked as if at any second he would reach out with his enormous hands and strangle Sam Dash. Thomas had wanted to ask the Reverend Dash about his past use of drugs, about the drug drops that had gone on nearby and his stays at night in the desert. About his finding the Lord, which was maybe nothing but a scam. But instead he took Oates by the elbow and pulled him away. He turned to Dash.

"I'd like to come back and talk to you again."

Dash flashed him his benign smile.

"Anytime, brother." He embraced Thomas, holding him for several seconds. He embraced Oates, who stared away blankly.

Oates and Thomas went to the car. Oates sat stonily behind the wheel as he drove. They were almost back at the *Chronicle* before he said a word.

"I don't believe 'im."

"You think he made that all up?"

"I think he could have cooked up the whole story about the conversation with Jack Eames, that Jack had decided to back Dash and his people." He shrugged. "Who's gonna say different now? Jack Eames is dead."

"But how about if he did talk to one of those school-board members? He told Dash he might speak to them that same night."

Oates shook his head. "I haven't heard a word about it, and I woulda heard somethin'."

They pulled up in front of the *Chronicle*. Thomas didn't move.

"You think he's making this up so that people will think Jack Eames had decided against Margaret. But why say he went to see her? Dash can't be lying about that. She's alive to talk."

Oates again shook his head, unable to untangle his own hypothesis. Thomas went on.

"If you're saying he went to Margaret at ten o'clock Friday night and told her of Eames's decision, even though it wasn't true, then he had to know Eames was dead, didn't he? All she'd have to do is check with Eames and he'd tell her it wasn't true. Dash had made it up. So if you're saying he made it up, you're saying Sam Dash is a murderer or at least knew that Eames was dead before the rest of the world knew.

"But would he kill Jack Eames just because he was going to rule against him on the Masters issue? Or was it that he had some other reason to kill him?" Oates looked at Thomas for the first time. "Was it that maybe Sam Dash isn't what he appears to be at all, just like you've suspected. That maybe he's still a bad boy."

They sat and stared at each other in silence. Then the phone sounded. They heard it ring inside the office and also on the mobile unit on the dashboard. Oates picked it up, listened, interrupted once, said thank you and hung up. He cranked up the Bronco again. Color had drained from his face.

"You can forget about Landon Turner and Sam Dash, too. That was the sheriff's office. They found fingerprints on the gun and checked them with prints they keep on file of all public employees in town. Also, a neighbor, three houses up from Jack Eames, saw a person walking away from his house right after the tornado."

"And?"

"They matched the two identifications. A judge issued a warrant an hour ago for the arrest of Margaret Masters for murder."

He put the Bronco in gear and they headed for the courthouse.

Chapter 14

*T*he courtroom was on the third floor of the county courthouse. It was a big place with room for a couple of hundred spectators. On either side of the judge's bench were two wooden columns in relief, a touch of classical Greece. In front of one column was a U.S. flag on a standard; in front of the other was the Lone Star flag of Texas. On the walls hung oil paintings of past judges with plaques marking their years of service. They were a uniformly stern-looking lot.

The judge's bench appeared to be of mahogany. It was high and impressive. The judge himself was an older man who was named, Oates told Thomas, William Octavius Forbes. He was also impressive and looked just as stern as his predecessors. But then, he had been hauled back from what was to have been a three-day fishing trip and he obviously didn't like it. You could see the collar of a plaid sports shirt beneath the judicial robes. He had arrived two hours before; then, for some reason, the arraignment had been delayed. There had been a commotion down in the sheriff's office. Oates had gone downstairs to see what it was about, but nobody would speak two words to him.

"They know I'm good friends with Margaret," he had said by way of explanation.

So they waited. Now there were a few other officials in the courtroom: a bailiff, a sheriff's deputy, a court reporter, and the assistant county attorney, a youngish blond man named Arthur Layton. Oates and Thomas were in the gallery. No one else.

It was just 10 P.M. when they brought in Margaret Masters. She was wearing a long, wine-colored skirt and a black blouse. She had on little or no makeup and her long hair was pinned up. She held her hands in front of her; they weren't handcuffed, but they had been when she'd been brought into the courthouse. The deputy had told them that. She held them the same way they had been then, as if it didn't matter that the cuffs were off. She was still a prisoner.

Standing next to her was a lawyer even younger than the prosecutor. He was a tall, pale boy and he wore tortoiseshell glasses.

"That's Charlie Young, public defender's office," Oates whispered.

Seconds later Sheriff Jim West entered and remained standing near the door. Then the bailiff rose and read out a case number.

"The County of Paradise versus Margaret Masters."

Layton, the prosecutor, was standing now.

"Your honor, we're very sorry for the delay in this proceeding, but earlier today we received some distressing news that has affected the state's case." He glanced down at a paper in front of him, then back at the judge. "At eleven o'clock this morning, our distinguished and longtime colleague, attorney Sam Houston Cain, was found dead in his private room at Paradise County Hospital."

The judge, who must have been a contemporary of Cain's, scowled at him with a look of pain.

"Your honor, the circumstances surrounding the death of Sam Cain are still being investigated by the sheriff's department. But it appears that he did not die of natural causes. Sometime between nine A.M., when he was last checked by a nurse, and eleven A.M. when he was found, someone entered his room and unplugged the respirator that had been keeping him alive. In other words, your honor, it appears that Sam Cain was murdered."

Oates, who had been taking notes, stopped. Everyone in the room was stock-still. They were all looking at Layton in disbelief.

"With the recent catastrophe that struck the town there has been considerable commotion at the hospital, as you can imagine, your honor, including disruption of the usual care schedule. Hospital staff say Sam Cain may have been dead as long as two hours before he was found. It's taken us all day to talk to everyone concerned. Those staff people say it was impossible that the machine was unplugged by mistake. Now, during those two hours he had no visitors who checked in at the reception desk, your honor; the three available passes were all still at the desk. But according to a nurse stationed on the wing in question, there was one person who did go to the room."

He turned now and looked at Margaret Masters.

"That person was the defendant who stands before you charged with the murder of attorney Jack Eames."

Margaret Masters stared at the judge as if it were he who had spoken the words.

"Your honor, the county presented in its application for a warrant for the arrest of Margaret Masters on evidence linking her to the death of County Attorney Jack Eames. For now we would like to proceed as originally planned with that one charge, but we would like to leave the door open, after the investigation has been completed, to bring against the defendant a second charge of murder."

The judge was staring at Margaret Masters. He had probably known her all her life, as had many other people in Paradise, and he seemed to be reviewing that life step by step, trying to understand how it was she stood before him charged with murder. The effort visibly troubled, confused, and, finally, tired him. He took a deep breath and looked away from her.

"The hour is late, ladies and gentlemen," he said in a thick Texas accent. "We won't take a lot of time here. I assume, Mr. Young, you've spoken with the defendant," he said, addressing the young public defender.

"Yes, I have, your honor." His voice was even younger than his face.

"Would you like to enter a plea at this time?"

"Yes, your honor. Ms. Masters will enter a plea of not guilty."

"Let it be so recorded that the defendant enters a plea of not guilty." The court reporter typed away silently on his machine. Margaret Masters stared straight ahead. The judge looked at her again.

"Miss Masters, do you have anything you wish to say to this court at this time?" She hesitated a moment and then shook her head.

The judge turned to the prosecutor. "Is there any recommendation on the matter of bail, Mr. Layton?"

"Your honor, the county would request that bail be denied in this case. We believe, given recent political events here that affect the defendant, not to mention these charges, that there is good reason to believe she might abandon the county and these proceedings."

Thomas thought, If you don't have a job anymore and your ex-lover is dead and you're accused of another murder, you might as well leave.

The boy public defender stood. "Your honor, we would recommend that Ms. Masters be released on bail. The defendant was born here and has lived in Paradise County most her life, owns property here, and she also maintains her innocence. She has no intention of leaving the jurisdiction of this court."

The judge mulled it over about ten seconds.

"The court orders that bail be set at one hundred thousand dollars. This case will be continued until further notice."

He stood up. The bailiff pounded his gavel twice and the judge was gone.

Margaret Masters stood talking with her lawyer, or rather, listening to him talk to her until the sheriff's deputy took her by the elbow and led her toward an exit that went to the jail. Just before she disappeared through the door, she glanced back to where Oates and Thomas were standing. It was Thomas she looked at, a look that said: "I thought you would be my Quijote, but you're my Judas." She had been told that she'd been seen leaving Eames's house and she thought it was Thomas who had told them. The look lasted only a second and it wasn't angry, it was resigned, as if she had expected betrayal.

Then she was gone. It had all taken about five minutes. Oates and Thomas approached Jim West.

"Can you tell us about the arrest, Jim?" Oates asked.

The sheriff looked worn out, after two days during which he probably hadn't slept. "We got ballistics and fingerprints results back around four P.M. Meanwhile a neighbor three houses down from Jack's house said she saw Margaret Masters at the scene just a minute after the tornado had passed. She walked right by this woman's house.

"When we got the prints back from Odessa, we compared them with prints in the files we have of public employees. They matched. We got the warrant and she didn't resist arrest. It was as if she was waitin' for us."

"What about finding that black bag at Eames's house?" Thomas asked. "The whole question of drugs."

"We're still looking into that," West said icily. "You'll excuse me now."

With that, he left. Except for Oates and Thomas, the

courtroom was empty. Oates stared at the jury box, maybe trying to envision the jury; who the twelve people would be; how they would decide the fate of Margaret Masters, if it ever got to that. He looked, like West, exhausted, and more than that, despondent.

"It's late. We better get going," Thomas said.

Oates didn't move. "Do you think she killed him?" he asked.

"Her prints are on the gun," Thomas said. "I don't know." It was too late to tell Oates that he too had seen her leaving the scene. Thomas finally took him by the arm and led him out.

Oates dropped Thomas at the *Chronicle* to pick up his car. Thomas told him to be sure not to fall asleep before he got home. Then he climbed into his own car and drove back to the motel.

It was ten-thirty when he got there. There were a half-dozen cars parked outside, probably emergency workers and consultants who had come to help with the cleanup. There were lights on in some of the rooms.

Thomas was on the way to his room when he noticed someone standing at the door of number three, the room the Mexican had occupied. It was a man who looked as if he were trying to get in. Thomas stopped and the man turned and stood staring at him. Thomas couldn't see the face, but he recognized that fireplug of a body, the thick arms.

The man started to walk away now, but Thomas headed across the parking lot at him.

"Hey!"

The Mexican started to run. He headed not toward the open field, but toward the state road. Thomas yelled at him again and took off after him.

The chase was short. Vega crossed the road into a residential neighborhood. Thomas followed not more than one hundred fifty feet behind and keeping pace. The neighborhood hadn't been hit by the tornado and there were no National Guards posted. The streets were empty.

Thomas stayed with him on a long street of ranch houses, shouting at him to stop. The Mexican turned a corner, and when Thomas did the same, the other man was gone. There was no sign of him, no sound of running. He had ducked between houses, through backyards. Thomas tried exploring in one, but all he did was get a dog barking. The Mexican had disappeared again.

Chapter 15

*T*he phone was ringing and Thomas opened his eyes to near-complete darkness. A thin beam of light from a lightpole outside squeezed through the curtain and landed on the bed. He looked at the illuminated dial of his watch. It said 4:10 A.M. Then he picked up the phone and made a noise in no known language.

"Hello, Thomas. It's Dan Oates." The voice echoed as if Oates were in a tunnel.

"Where are you?"

"I'm on the car phone. I'm at the park in the center of town, at the corner of Houston and State streets. There's something here you should see."

"It's the middle of the night."

"Yes, I know, but you should come. It's important."

"Is someone dead?"

"Not someone, but something," Oates said. "Just come."

Thomas, who hadn't had a full night's sleep in five days, dragged his naked body out of bed, dressed, grabbed a notebook, and left. The starlight barely illuminated the field next to the motel as he got in his car. He drove toward downtown, the National Guard watching but not stopping him.

He turned down State Street, saw the revolving red and white roof light of a police car, and pulled up next to it. His own headlights shone on Oates and a uniformed sheriff's man standing in the middle of the small, one-block-square park. They were looking down at something. There was no one else around.

Oates turned as Thomas approached.

"This is Officer Harvey Abrams," Oates said, and Thomas shook hands with the older man.

"He found something here and gave me a call."

Oates led Thomas to the center of the park where there was an old cement sun dial maybe three feet high. Abrams shot a beam from his flashlight at it. Lying on top of the dial was a lamb, a small creature, not more than twenty pounds, with thick white wool. Its throat had been slashed and its head hung awkwardly off the edge of the dial. Stuck right in the middle of its body was a knife pinning a piece of paper to the carcass.

Abrams moved closer with the flashlight. It was ordinary typing paper, written on in block letters with red crayon. It said: "Margaret Masters is a sacrificial lamb just like Johnny Campos." That was all.

Thomas frowned at it and looked at Oates.

"Harvey made several rounds tonight," the big man said. "He's still mainly keeping an eye on damaged houses. He doesn't know what time it was put here."

"Or who put it?" Thomas said.

Oates shook his head. He lifted a camera, focused, and shot.

"Who is Johnny Campos?" Thomas asked.

Oates led Thomas back toward the cars. The first light was just visible in the eastern sky seen through the alleyways of Paradise. They stopped and leaned up against the Bronco.

"Do you remember that first night, when we talked in the office I told you there was one local boy who died of a heroin overdose a few years ago?"

"Yes."

"That was Johnny Campos."

"How long ago was that?"

"About five years."

"What would he have to do with all this and why call him a sacrificial lamb?"

Oates stared off into the night. "Let's say there were doubts in the minds of some townspeople about how Johnny Campos died. His body was found in an abandoned house over beyond the railroad tracks. It was a house that some of the wilder kids used to smoke dope in. Johnny was found with the needle still in his arm."

"And?"

"And there were people who said that Johnny Campos was a bit of a troublemaker, not the best kid in town, had a few scrapes with the police, but that he'd never been known to do hard drugs. In fact, they didn't find any other needle marks in him but the one he died from."

"It could have been his first time and he shot up too much. It happens."

"That's what some folks said, but there were others who didn't believe he'd do something like that. It didn't smell right. His body was found by a policeman who it was known didn't like Johnny Campos at all and didn't like Mexicans in general: Lloyd Haynes."

"Our friend the deacon."

"There's something else interesting about it. Johnny's best friend, who might have been able to tell folks what Johnny was up to that night, left town after the police talked to him, but before anybody else could ask him what had happened. And he didn't come back for years. That was Sam Dash."

Thomas just looked at Oates, absorbing it all.

"Somebody is saying that Margaret Masters is innocent and that maybe there's a connection between the death of this boy Campos and the death of Jack Eames five years later."

"Maybe."

"Could it be? Drugs? Or Sam Dash and Lloyd Haynes?"

"Or both," said Oates.

"Or maybe neither."

The permutations visibly exhausted Thomas.

"It's gonna have to wait until morning," he said tiredly. "I'll see you then." He went back to his car, drove to the motel, undressed, got into bed, closed his eyes, and tried to get the nightmare out of his head.

Chapter 16

*I*n the end, he couldn't.

He went in and out of sleep, bothered by the image of the sacrificial lamb, and finally dragged himself out of bed at seven o'clock.

He made himself presentable and drove down the state road for coffee and breakfast at a place called Lurleen's Country Kitchen. It was a converted diner that, like the mobile homes across town, had been expanded by tacking on a red brick annex. The white gravel parking lot held the usual large, air-conditioned cars and pickup trucks. Inside, he found the drivers of those cars, red-faced men, some in baseball-style caps with company names on them, others in Stetsons. They sat around small tables holding large, steaming coffee mugs.

A few of the ol' boys glanced up as Thomas, a stranger in town, walked in. He recognized several of the men. William Octavius Forbes, the judge who had sat on the bench the night before, was still dressed in his plaid shirt. Layton, the assistant county attorney, sat at the same table. Thomas figured they were talking about the arraignment of Margaret Masters, because they had an avid audience around them. At another table Thomas recognized the young fireman who had heped him dig out Jack Eames. Or the corpse of Eames. He also saw Harvey Abrams, the sheriff's deputy who had found the slaughtered lamb. Thomas spotted other faces he had seen during his tour of Paradise after the tornado. He recognized them because, to a degree, they still wore those expressions of shock and disbelief.

He crossed the room and took a table by himself. Coffee at Lurleen's was probably one of the rituals that held Paradise together. It reminded him of Southeast Asia, where the Chinese merchants took tea together every day at mid-morning to talk over their trading. The small talk at Lurleen's, he imagined, would usually be about sports or oil prices. It would go with the decorations on the walls, which consisted of high school football banners and photos of old gushers. Today, however, they would still be talking about killer tornadoes, the murdered and the murderers. Plagues, as the Reverend Sam Dash would call them. There were many empty seats. He wondered how many of the regulars had been injured or even killed in the twister. Maybe Jack Eames and Sam Cain had been regulars as well. He could see their ghosts sitting in the vacant chairs.

A Latin girl in a violet uniform took his order: two over easy, links, hash browns, and coffee. He found a day-old Dallas paper on the table and read about the world for the first time in days: Bucharest, Bogotá, Beijing. People outside Paradise were killing each other, too. His food came and he was still reading when the door opened and in came a short, thin, silver-haired man in a white shirt buttoned all the way up to his throat. His pants were wrinkled and his shoes were covered with red dust, as if he'd walked a ways to get here. He held a worn black Bible in his hand. He stopped just inside the door and stared at the coffee drinkers. His washed-out blue eyes were pinned open in a strange way. It took a moment, but Thomas recognized him: the little man in the overalls who had stood next to him at the Paradise Revelation Temple. He peered around nervously, then lifted the Bible and shook it over his head.

" 'Alas, Babylon! Repent and I will come unto thee quickly.' " He spoke in a high, thickly accented voice as dry and cracked as the earth outside. "That's what the Lord says, brothers."

The collected citizens turned and peered at him under the brims of their caps and Stetsons. He stared back at them, wide-eyed, and shook his Bible again.

"Those who survived the first plagues, they didn't repent. They went on bein' sinners, still worshipin' the devil, still doin' dirt." His eyes opened even wider with fear. "So God opened the bottomless pit and out came worse plagues right up outa the earth. And that's what'll happen here, brothers. The Lord'll send more storms, more plagues. Sickness and ruin. Then He'll send the end of the world. If you ain't repented, He'll burn ya with the brand of Satan and send ya right ta everlasting damnation."

He stopped and the place was dead quiet. The kitchen personnel had come out, including a beefy, red-faced cook with a spatula in his hand, who had sweat beaded on his face as if he'd just come back from hell himself. The little man swallowed and summoned up courage.

"Our streets are runnin' blood," he said. "Our schools are fulla blasphemy against the Lord, our children are usin' drugs, the air's whipped up with the wrath o' God. And that's because the end is comin', brothers. The stars are gonna fall from the sky and the sea's gonna give up the dead."

He stood staring at them in terror several moments, then suddenly turned and bolted, slamming the door behind him.

The men kept their eyes on the door a moment, then went back to their coffee. Thomas finished his breakfast, paid the waitress, and headed for the door. On the way out, he stopped at the table of the young fireman whom he hadn't seen since the day of the tornado. He said hello, but the other man didn't recognize him.

"I'm the one who helped you dig out Jack Eames," Thomas said.

The other man squinted at him, working his way through the layer of dirt Thomas had worn that day, and then he nodded.

"That's right."

"I have a question for you." Thomas crouched down next to the table. "Do you remember when we found the body if there was a black duffel bag lying next to it? Maybe three feet long?"

Thomas held his hands apart measuring it. The other man's eyes narrowed as he looked at the empty space and back three mornings.

"It would have been right at the foot of the bed under his feet," Thomas said.

The other man thought and then slowly shook his head.

"I don't remember it. Why?"

"You're sure?"

"Yeah, I'm sure."

Thomas got up, thanked him, and went out.

He got in his car and headed downtown. At the corner across from the motel, he saw the little man who had just been in the restaurant. He was waving his Bible and preaching at the empty intersection.

As he made his way downtown, Thomas saw doomsday graffiti everywhere and more of the Reverend Dash's troops. This was the offensive that Dash had promised in yesterday's sermon. There was a man or woman on each street corner in the desolate downtown area, each with a Bible, hurling terrible images at the few pedestrians and motorists. Thomas slowed as he passed an older woman in a red checked dress with a ferocious cast in her eye. She warned him about the day it would rain blood, the day of reckoning. The town was beginning to look and sound like the inside of the Revelation Temple, apocalyptic.

He pulled in at the *Chronicle* and found Oates at his desk, as always. He sat down across from him.

"The news on the street is that the world is ending," Thomas said.

Oates nodded. "I've heard. They're all over town. One of them came in here a while ago to tell me, as if she were giving me a scoop. As if she expected me to lead the paper with it this week. She's a woman I've known all my life, used to work over at city hall." Oates shook his head. "It isn't just those people. It seems everybody's goin' over the edge."

Oates swiveled in his chair. "I went to the hospital this morning and talked to the nurse in charge of the emergency room. She says they've been full the past two days, not with people injured, but with head cases." He tapped his close-cropped skull. "People are having nightmares about the tornado, living it over again and again. Others can't sleep at all because of nerves. They're coming in for tranquilizers. We have these others preaching doom on every corner. Paradise is unraveling and all I can do is try and talk reason."

Oates tapped his screen. "Right now I'm writing an editorial in support of Margaret in her fight with the school board and calling for due process for her in the courts. Gotta let people know where the *Chronicle* stands. Especially if the world is ending. It's my last chance."

The editor looked at him sardonically. He was badly worn, but Thomas had to pick his brain. "I came by to take up where we left off last night," he said, "with the business about the Campos boy."

Oates rocked forward, picked up a file on his desk, and handed it to Thomas. It said: "Campos, John J. (Johnny) 1965–1983." Thomas opened it and found four old, yellowed newspaper clippings. The first three were short and had to do with relatively minor run-ins with the law.

Johnny Campos had been with a group of boys who had
gone joyriding in a neighbor's car. He had been arrested
once for loitering after refusing to leave the front of a
candy store, and another time, along with two other boys,
for possession of two marijuana cigarettes. These infrac-
tions all occurred when he was sixteen and seventeen years
old. He was no angel, Johnny Campos, but given the standards of teenage America, he was no child of the Devil
either.

What jumped out at Thomas were two other names he
recognized, just as Oates had told him. On two occasions
when Johnny Campos had been arrested, he had been
accompanied by and detained with another young man:
Samuel B. Dash. The policeman who had made those arrests was the same: Officer Lloyd Haynes.

The last clip, the one about Campos's death, was longer
and it was accompanied by a yearbook photo. It showed a
good-looking Latin boy with longish hair and a good-
humored, somewhat mischievous expression. It certainly
didn't look like the face of a hardened drug user. But then,
you never knew.

The clip said the body had been found by Officer
Haynes. He had answered a call at 10:35 P.M. about tres-
passers in an abandoned house. He had found the body,
the needle, and other paraphernalia lying next to it, as
Oates had said. A police-department paramedic had pronounced the boy dead on the scene at eleven-twenty. Pub-
lished two days after the death, the article also contained
the report by Earl Muller, the medical examiner, confirm-
ing that Johnny Campos had died of a heroin overdose.
Oates said Muller's reputation was beyond reproach and
there was no doubt that that had been the cause of death.

But Oates had also said there had been doubts in the
Mexican community. There was no article about those
doubts, and Thomas asked him about it.

"I couldn't write anything because no one would go on
record about it. And you can't challenge a policeman's

honesty on the basis of unattributed accusations," Oates said firmly. "But there were people with questions. Why did it take so long after the first call to declare Johnny Campos dead and who else had been with him? The original complaint had been about kids, more than one in that house, and Johnny never traveled alone. On top of that, Johnny was from a family that hadn't been in town too long, only a few years. Some people felt those late arrivals were taking work away from families who had always been here and sometimes they'd work cheaper. You still have some racism in Paradise, especially when things get tough. And Lloyd Haynes was an officer known not to like Latins."

"Yes, I'd say there were some questions."

Oates pointed at the file. "By the way, did you notice the name in that third clip, the boy Johnny was arrested with for dope?"

"Sam Dash."

"I mean the other one."

Thomas took out the clipping about the joyriding incident. He read it through again. According to the *Chronicle,* along with Campos and Dash in the car had been a boy named Guillermo Vega, eighteen.

"What was the name of that Latin man at the motel?" Oates asked.

"William Vega."

"Guillermo. Spanish for William."

Thomas told Oates about having seen the man the night before and the chase.

"I still don't remember him," Oates said, "and there's nothin' else in the files. Maybe it's not the same Vega. Maybe it's just a coincidence."

Thomas looked dubiously at Oates. "Maybe. But then why is he running? Maybe we should talk to Sam Dash and Lloyd Haynes and ask if they remember him and if they've seen him."

Oates glanced at his watch. "The lieutenant governor is coming this morning to view the damage and talk about state emergency funds," he said. "That's the main story today and I have to shadow him. I can't go looking for tracks left years ago."

Thomas got up. "Well, then, I'll go see them. It's probably better that way. You can avoid friction with some of your subscribers."

He was headed for the door when the phone rang. Oates picked it up, said hello, listened several moments, and held up a hand so that Thomas wouldn't leave. Finally he said thanks and hung up.

"That was the sheriff's office," he said. "Margaret Masters put up her house for security and made bail. She'll be out by noon."

Oates looked out to where the sidewalk preachers were working, then back at Thomas. "The Harlot is back on the streets," he said gruffly.

Thomas left him sitting there and went looking for Sam Dash and Lloyd Haynes. As it happened, he didn't have to go far. Turning off State Street onto Main, he spotted Haynes on the sidewalk preaching outside city hall. Someone had painted the word "Babylon" in bright red letters on a wall of the building. Thomas pulled over on the other side of the street to watch. The deacon wore his black robe and waved his Bible at people walking out of the municipal building. He talked to them through a scratchy portable loudspeaker telling them to repent, warning them of the approaching cataclysm. He stopped and pointed at the American flag on the flagpole and shouted so that his voice crackled down the block.

" 'And the nations were angry and wrath has come and the time of the dead.' Revelation, Chapter Eleven."

He turned and stalked back down the sidewalk, the round-shouldered, vulturelike harbinger of death. A sheriff's deputy in a brown uniform came out of city hall, going toward a police car. Haynes pointed at him and lifted the loudspeaker.

"In the past I worked for Caesar and I wore that uniform, brothers and sisters. Now I wear the uniform of the

Lord." He grabbed the black material over his heart. "I'm workin' for the real chief. I'm workin' for the Lord. Yes, I am."

He lifted his Bible above his head.

" 'And the fearful and the unbelieving, the abominable, the murderers, the whoremongers, the idolators and the liars will burn forever.' Yes, they will."

Thomas got out of his car and approached. Haynes watched him cross the street and lifted his speaker.

"The press," he crackled. "The unbelievers, the doubting Thomases."

He smiled at his own joke, his dark eyes lighting up. Thomas came up next to him. He was at least five inches taller than Haynes.

"Good morning, Deacon."

The police car was just pulling away, and Thomas gestured at it. "I understand you used to be on the force."

Haynes lowered the speaker and nodded, his eyes still smiling, or as close to a smile as they could get.

"That's right. And now I have the force in me." He tapped his chest with a finger and it sounded strangely hollow.

"I'd like to ask you about a boy you arrested once some years back. A fella named Guillermo Vega or William Vega."

Haynes focused on Thomas with a puzzled expression. "I detained a lot of people. They's always been lotsa sinners in this town."

"You arrested him about six years ago along with Sam Dash and Johnny Campos. You remember Johnny Campos, don't you? He was the high school boy who died of a drug overdose."

"He was a delinquent, a boy who lost his soul early on."

"He lost his life early on. That much is true," Thomas said.

Haynes nodded distantly. "The Lord decides those things. He took that boy out of his misery. It was an act of mercy."

"Or it was somebody's idea of an act of mercy. Just like maybe it was someone's idea to kill Jack Eames and Sam Cain and take them out of their misery."

Haynes's expression had become less distant, more wary. When he spoke, his voice was cold, emotionless.

"That Campos kid was a lawbreaker. He was guilty of various crimes over the years. He was headin' for a bad end. No way you could stop it. He fit the pattern of the lifelong criminal."

"Johnny Campos was awfully young to be called a lifelong criminal. He was eighteen when he died."

Haynes shook his head, dismissing what Thomas said. "He was on the track."

Thomas pointed at the Bible in Haynes's hand.

"They say a person can always save himself, even at the last moment, if he repents. Isn't that what you believe? Were you there during his last moments?"

Haynes scowled. "He was dead. Dead in the soul."

He turned away and approached a woman deputy entering the building. He lifted his bullhorn and told her to repent. She glanced at him, then disappeared into the station. Thomas followed him.

"But was he physically dead?"

Haynes turned and glared up at him. "I've told you," he said, strain showing. He began to head back toward the sidewalk and Thomas strode with him.

"In the records it said you were dispatched on the call almost an hour before you reported him dead. It couldn't take that long. Were you sitting there questioning a dead boy? Can you speak with the dead, Deacon?"

Haynes stopped in his tracks. "The facts are all on file. The case is closed."

"I'm not talking about the so-called facts," Thomas said. "I'm talking about the truth, which is sometimes a different thing." He pointed at the Bible. "I'm talking about that boy's soul and maybe your soul too. Let's talk about that. Let's talk about what the good Lord saw that night. What did he see Johnny Campos do and you and Sam Dash too?"

Haynes said nothing. He walked away again, but Thomas pursued him and cut him off.

"Sam Dash disappeared from Paradise after that night, didn't he?"

"Sam Dash was free to go where he pleased," Haynes spat back. "He wasn't in jail. He wasn't charged with no crime. He wasn't under investigation. He could go where he pleased."

"But he had some reason to run, didn't he? Some sin he'd committed."

Haynes walked along the sidewalk and Thomas kept up, like an evil spirit making suggestions in the deacon's ear.

"It was something that made him leave town. Made him roam the world until the Lord hunted him down. He himself testifies to it. He didn't even stay for the funeral, I'm told, and Johnny Campos was one of his best friends."

Haynes shook his head. "It was none o' my business."

A telephone-repair truck, fixing lines down from the tornado, stopped at the corner. Haynes crackled at them that the world was ending.

"Maybe it's your world that's ending, Deacon," Thomas said. "I've wondered what it was that made a man like you turn to God."

Haynes stopped and turned, showing Thomas his terribly scarred face by way of an answer. Haynes tapped his cheek with a finger.

"This is what made me see the light. This was the Lord's message to me."

Thomas winced. Haynes saw himself as living proof of God's wrath. He was exhibit number one in defense of his beliefs.

"Your accident," Thomas said, collecting himself. "A terrible thing. Why would the Lord send you such a terrible punishment? Was there some sin you hadn't atoned for? Is that why after the accident you turned to the Lord?"

Haynes blinked at Thomas.

"A man almost dies, he sees what's what."

"Yes, it must be something that goes on deep in a man's

soul," Thomas said, keeping a close eye on the strange man. "In fact, I was thinking just last night what must have been going on in the soul of whoever it was who killed Jack Eames and Sam Cain. Maybe it was the same person. And I was wondering what Sam Cain's sin was. Johnny Campos, he was a lost soul, a future lifelong criminal. A child of the devil. But Sam Cain was a pillar of the community, except that he didn't like the way some people forced their beliefs on others. Was that his sin? And how about Jack Eames, what did he do? Was he going to support Margaret Masters? Was he going to side with the devil? Is that why the Lord sent one of his agents to kill him? Who was the executor who acted as the right hand of the Lord?"

Haynes hadn't moved but his expression had grown more and more bitter.

"I don't know what you're talking about," he spat. "And anyway, who are you to talk about the Lord? About men's souls?"

Thomas nodded. "I know lies when I hear them. And I've heard a lot of them lately."

Haynes sneered and started to walk away. Thomas spoke at his back.

"Maybe you better repent yourself, Deacon." The other man whirled around as if he'd been hit. Thomas looked him in the eyes." Maybe you better repent before you lose your immortal soul."

Haynes looked even smaller now than he was. He looked drawn, shaken. He turned and stalked away. A gray-haired woman who had come out of city hall had witnessed the scene. She stared at Thomas, confused, until she saw him cross the street to his car, an avenging angel. He was going to Margaret Masters's house.

Chapter 17

*I*t was only 10 A.M., but the sun was already beginning to soften the tar on the street. On the way he passed more Revelation Temple members working the corners, preaching nightmares. The town was crawling with them. He arrived, parked beneath the edge of an elm and behind another car that was in front of the house.

As he went up the walkway the door opened and out came the young defense lawyer, Charlie Young, carrying a briefcase. Next to him in the doorway stood Margaret Masters. Young said something to her as Thomas approached, then the lawyer stepped to the middle of the flagstone path, blocking Thomas's way.

"I'm advising my client not to speak to the press at this time," he said.

"I'm not here to interview Ms. Masters," Thomas told him. "And I assure you I won't write anything I'm told in confidence. I think Ms. Masters can tell you I'm dependable in that respect."

Thomas glanced past him and gave the teacher a pointed look.

The lawyer shook his head. "Any information you want . . ." he started to say, but she cut him off.

"That's all right, Charlie. I think we can trust Mr. Thomas. He's been discreet so far." So she had found out that it wasn't Thomas who had reported seeing her.

Young frowned at her, then at Thomas, not knowing what she meant. He told her he would speak to her the next day and continued down the path to his car.

Margaret closed the door behind Thomas. Lying on the floor of the foyer were three books, all of which had been set fire to, and which were charred, largely destroyed.

"I found these on my doorstep a while ago. A little calling card. One is *The Sound and the Fury* by Faulkner. Isn't it incredible?" She looked genuinely appalled. Thomas glanced at them, then he followed her to a shaded porch at the back of the house that looked out on a garden of wildflowers. She waved him to a rocking chair.

"Can I offer you a coffee? It's early for anything else."

Thomas declined, and she sat down across from him with a cup of her own. He noticed that she looked much better than she had in the courtroom. Not quite as pale.

"I need to know a few things," Thomas said, "beginning with what happened Friday night and Saturday morning."

She sipped her coffee and nodded. There was nothing in her manner to suggest she was accused of murder. She looked at him several moments as if deciding if, in fact, Thomas was worthy of trust.

"The Reverend Sam Dash came to see me," she said finally.

"What time was that?"

She thought a moment. "Maybe ten o'clock."

"Why did he come to see you?"

She sipped her coffee, put it down. "He's quite a character, Sam Dash," she said. "He came here to tell me I was going to lose my job. He said Jack Eames had decided against me. He also said he was worried about my state of mind. That's why he was paying me the visit." She smirked. "That's quite a twist, isn't it? And it took quite a twisted mind to think of coming here, didn't it?"

"What else did he say to you?"

She shook her head. "Just lots of proselytizing. He told me it seemed things looked dark, but they really weren't. Here he is ruining my life and telling me to be content about it. He also went over my personal history with me, starting with my mother, explaining how my current situation was inevitable. It was in the cards."

"Did you try to call Eames to verify what he told you?"

"Yes, after Dash left."

"What time was that?"

"About eleven."

"And?"

"The line was busy. In fact, it was busy until after midnight and I stopped trying."

"It was probably off the hook."

She nodded. "It was."

"How do you know that for sure?" But he didn't give her a chance to answer. "Because you went there."

She nodded.

"What time?"

"About six-thirty in the morning," she said. "I sat here all night, not sleeping. Finally, when the sun came up I decided to call him again. I knew he always woke early. But when I called, the line was still busy, so I decided to go see him. I couldn't take it anymore. He had my life in his hands."

"Did you walk over there?"

"Yes."

"Why? Why didn't you drive?"

She answered readily. "Because I wanted to give myself time to think, to calm down some. And also I didn't want anyone to see my car there. At that hour, and given my already sullied reputation, people would reach the wrong conclusions."

"So you didn't leave the car behind because you were planning to kill him and didn't want people to see it? That's what the assistant district attorney is going to say."

She looked at him sharply. "I know that as I was walking over there I was thinking about what I would do if what Sam Dash said was true."

"And what did you decide?"

"I thought I'd kill him." She said it matter-of-factly without a hint of emotion. "I knew he kept his pistol in a drawer next to the bed. The same bed we had shared for two years. And this man was going to have me dismissed for immorality."

"What happened when you got there?"

"I found the front door open part way. I called out but I didn't hear anything so I went in. I walked back to the bedroom and there he was, lying face up on the bed. He had blood flowing down from the side of his head and a gun was on the floor maybe six feet away. The phone on the night table was off the hook."

"Was there a black duffel bag lying there too, right next to the bed?"

Margaret Masters thought back, then shook her head.

"No, there was nothing. Just Jack and the gun."

"You're sure?"

She nodded.

"Then what happened? How did your fingerprints get on the gun?"

"I heard something. I thought it was someone still in the house. I got scared and picked up the gun."

Her hand closed in recollection. "That was my fatal error," she said sardonically.

"Was anyone still in the house?"

"No. I guess it was the wind or the beginning of the hail. Then it got louder. I was stuck there with him and all I wanted to do was get out, get away, but I couldn't. I went to the front door but the hail was coming down too hard. And then when it stopped I saw the tornado coming."

"What did you do?"

"I did what they tell you to do. I went into the bathroom and got into the tub. I did it automatically, hardly thinking. When the tornado hit, one wall came down but the sides of the tub protected me. I was hit in the face with some shingle, but not badly." Her hand went to her cheek.

"And when it passed, you headed for your house."

"I guess, but I don't remember walking."

"I saw you."

"And you didn't tell anyone. I thought you had, but it turned out to be someone else."

She fixed on him with her frank, almost black eyes. "Why didn't you tell?"

"I don't know. Maybe I just wanted to get your side of the story first."

Her expression now reminded him of the one she had worn when she had told him about her past and her mother's life. It was more than frank. It was naked.

"Do you think Dash was telling you the truth about what Eames had decided?"

She shrugged. "I don't know."

"Dan Oates has his doubts and Jack Eames isn't here to recount it for us."

"The plot thickens."

"It isn't a joke."

"No, but it's my destiny, Mr. Thomas. It was inevitable, given my character, my background, and given this town. Inevitable that my fingerprints would end up on that gun. They'll probably find me guilty of murder."

"So you're resigned."

She shruggd again. "You give me another scenario."

"Maybe Eames decided to back you and not sell you out and that's what they talked about. That's possible, no matter how you felt about him." She cocked her head, listening.

"Maybe what he wanted to discuss with Dash was not

you at all. Maybe what he wanted to talk about was drugs. Because it's known that shortly after Sam Dash found God and returned to Paradise, the drug drops started outside town. And now one of his old drug buddies has shown up in town and Eames was seen talking to him. Maybe that's what the county attorney wanted to talk to Dash about and not you at all. And the sheriff knows that."

"So you're saying that Sam Dash killed Jack Eames. Then he came and lied to me. He might even have known that I would try to talk to Jack and took the phone off the hook, deliberately setting it up so I would have to go see him. Then they would say I killed Jack Eames."

"I wouldn't take it that far," Thomas said. "But he knew by coming here and telling you what he did he was giving you a motive for murder."

She looked at Thomas, her eyebrows raised in disbelief.

"You don't think Dash is capable of it?" he asked.

"Oh, I think he's capable of anything. You forget I knew him back when. He was a bad boy. He's always been a schemer and a plotter. Now he's put all his energy into the scheme of ruining my life. But you're asking the sheriff to believe an awful lot."

"Let's move to the chapter on Sam Cain," he said. "You called him the day before he died, is that right?"

"Yes. I asked him to defend me before the school board and he said he couldn't. That he didn't have the time." She shook her head. "Of course, that wasn't true. What he didn't have was the moral courage."

"Why did you go to Cain? Was he another old friend of your mother's?"

"Not at all. My mother could never stomach Cain. She knew him since the thirties and knew his history. She said he was a toady for the big ranchers, especially the Turners. She didn't like him."

"So why did you go to him?"

"For just that reason, because he had power and influ- ence here and it was known he didn't like Sam Dash and his people. He had told me that much. But then Sam Dash and his followers aren't bigwigs. I'm not either and maybe that's another reason he wouldn't defend me."

"Did you go to the hospital to see him Sunday?"

"No. I went to see the mother of a friend of mine who teaches art at the high school. She's been in the hospital since before the tornado. I talked with her for half an hour. You can check that."

"And then?"

"Sam Cain was on the same wing. The woman mentioned that to me. He was unconscious, but as I was leaving I stopped at his room, just to look in on him. He was lying there with an oxygen mask on. His head was all bandaged and he was hooked to one of those heart machines. I watched him for a half a minute. Then I left."

"What time was that?"

"Ten-thirty or so."

"So he was alive then."

"That's right. Not very alive, but alive."

"Did you see anybody else near the room you recognized?"

She thought and shook her head.

"Just hospital personnel," she began, then stopped. "And Sam Dash. I saw him walking down the hallway. He was carrying a Bible."

"Did you see him go into Cain's room?"

"No. I only saw him walk by."

"And then you went home?"

"Yes, and a while later the police came to arrest me. Then this morning they let me out and here we are."

She said it as if she were ending a fairy tale. He told her so.

"Well, I have a knight in shining armor, but it doesn't look like he's going to be able to save the damsel in distress."

"We'll see." And he got up.

"I want to thank you for being my knight in slightly dented armor," she said.

"I haven't done much."

"You believed me. You could have told the sheriff about seeing me at the house, but you didn't."

They were standing inches apart and she put a hand on his chest. He looked down at her and she lifted toward him. She didn't give him a chance to pull away, even if he'd wanted to. He hadn't touched a woman in two months. Her full lips opened and closed on his and her body pressed against him. His hand went to her back and he felt her trembling. In a moment she had gone from wariness to abandon. It took him by surprise.

Thomas opened his eyes and found that she was staring at him in an oddly detached way. Suddenly he realized that he might be wrong; that maybe she *had* killed Jack Eames and Sam Cain. Maybe she had played on his natural sympathy for her as a victim of fanaticism, a person fighting for the freedom to think. Of course a journalist would support her and of course he would be attracted to her. Maybe she was playing on that.

They stood looking into each other's eyes. Then a smile tugged at her lips.

"This is what is called in literature a sudden flight of passion, followed by a pregnant pause."

Thomas took his arms from around her and went to the front door. She opened it for him.

"Goodbye, Quijote," she said with a sad smile.

Chapter 18

*T*homas drove back through that landscape of destruction and wandering doom prophets to the motel and got on the phone. The night before, after going back to bed and fighting off nightmares, he had suddenly remembered Marshall Mundy and his question about the dark night of the soul. Thomas hadn't checked in with the editor of *Epoch* since arriving in Paradise, but maybe Mundy had tried to reach him after the tornado, before phone service had been renewed. Thomas got through to the desk clerk at the switchboard of the motel and put in a collect call to the editorial offices of the magazine.

After a minute he heard him come on the line. Mundy didn't bother with niceties.

"What do you have for me, Edward?"

In the background, Thomas could hear the gabble of television news programs and the chatter of a teletype. He could see Mundy with his running shoes up on the desk.

"I have the fact that I'm alive," Thomas said.

There was a brief pause. "That's not news, Edward. That's dog bites man," Mundy said dryly. "Where are you?"

"Paradise."

"Now you're confusing me."

"Paradise, Texas. There was a good-sized tornado here several days ago, Marshall. If you didn't know."

"Was there? Lots of news out of Moscow these days. Nothing else is getting any play up here."

Thomas told him about riding out the tornado in the culvert. "It almost took me up to heaven."

"It sounds hellacious," Mundy said, "but it'll make great copy. How about the Devil? Have you found him down there in the wreckage?"

"He's here all right and he's been busy." He gave Mundy the background on the deaths of Cain and Eames. He analyzed the political/religious situation in Paradise, the Revelation Temple campaign on the streets, told him of Margaret Masters's arrest and his interview with the Reverend Dash.

"My God, it sounds like he is down there," the publisher said with sudden enthusiasm. "The Devil, that is. And we have it all to ourselves. Is that right?"

"There were some state television and newspaper people in after the storm, but no one national."

"Wonderful. Real Texas Gothic. You're blessed with a wonderful nose for a story, Edward. And you'll be back here in the office by Monday to start coughing it up."

Thomas protested. "I don't know if it'll be resolved by then."

"Don't argue, Edward. I gave you my deadline and I just had another worthless writer cave in and leave me with a hole in the next number. You have enough to go with and we'll give it good play. Satan roaming the range."

There was a buzzing noise in the background. "I have

to go, Edward. Be here Friday and be careful. Don't die
with your boots on, or any other way."

Then the line went dead and Thomas hung up. It was
Tuesday. That gave him two days to finish in Paradise and
get back to New York. He had to start moving. He stared
into the beam of sunlight that slanted through the window
like a message from the heavens, except that dust floated
in it, impurities. He would start by going to see the Reverend Sam Dash, a messenger from God who also had his
defects. Thomas wanted to ask him what he was doing
near Sam Cain's hospital room about the time he died, and
other questions about drugs and death.

He drove to the Paradise Revelation Temple and found
several cars outside baking in the sun. The big wooden
front door was ajar and he stepped in. The murals looked
even more lurid now. He saw Sam Dash, Lloyd Haynes,
and several other men sitting on folding chairs in a circle
on the stage in front of the neon cross. It appeared to be
a prayer meeting, or maybe a strategy session for their new
offensive against sin in Paradise.

Dash looked up, saw Thomas and smiled the length of
the church.

"Good afternoon, Mr. Thomas, or shall I call you Reverend Thomas. I understand you've been doin' some
preachin' on the streets of Paradise."

Thomas walked up the aisle to the foot of the stage.

"Just a bit, but then everyone else is."

"Deacon Haynes says you have quite a talent. I just hope
you're not one of those preachers we've been warned about
who show up in the last days. Those false prophets."

Thomas shook his head. "No, I always deal in the truth.
That is, if I can get it out of people." He glanced at Haynes,
who was scowling at him. "Sometimes it's difficult."

Dash beamed him a smile. "It's like we said the other
day. I bet we have different ideas about the truth."

"That's very likely, Reverend."

"Yes, it is. But there's always been that difference between journalists and church people, ain't there, Mr.

Thomas? Ever since St. Thomas hisself, who wouldn't believe unless the Lord let him stick his fingers where the
nails had been. I guess you'd call him the first journalist."

Dash stuck a finger into his own side and wiggled it.
The men around him smiled back and Dash got up and
addressed them expansively, as if they were his congregation.

"Yes, I was thinking just yesterday what it would have
been like if our so-called journalists of today had been
around in the Lord's time. When Jesus Christ Hisself
walked the earth. It woulda been somethin' ta behold." He
looked around at his listeners, tongue in rosy cheek, and
then stretched a hand out into the distance. "The Lord
walkin' on the water at the Sea of Galilee. Right next to
Him a boat fulla journalists, with their television cameras,
filmin' it up close." He closed one eye and turned the crank
of an ancient camera. Then he stopped and looked per-
plexed. "But what they're filmin' ain't the Lord, only the
water. 'Who dumped that sludge in the water?' they'd be
askin'. Because that's the only way anybody could walk on
it. Must be water pollution. Better go get the fellas who
did it. Put 'em in jail."

The other men chuckled, and Dash looked at Thomas,
eyes twinkling. "Or Jesus turnin' water inta wine at the
wedding feast. Except the headlines would say, 'Savior Has
Drinkin' Problem; Large Quantities Consumed.' And poor
Lazarus, they woulda had him in front of press conferences
until he died again just from answerin' questions. I'll betcha."

There were more chuckles, but Dash kept his twinkling
eyes fixed on Thomas. "Ya understand, brother, there are
different ways of seein' what's important, what the real
truth is."

Thomas nodded. "What I know is, Jack Eames wasn't
killed by God. The Lord doesn't handle a .38 I also know
you're telling people Eames had decided against Margaret
Masters. But you're the only one who knows that, because
you were the last one to see him alive."

The twinkle left Dash's eyes. "I was the last except for the person who shot him, brother. The last but one."

"You were also in the hospital when Sam Cain died. In fact, you were seen right outside his room around the time he died." Thomas didn't say it was Margaret Masters who had seen him.

Dash nodded. "That's right. I was visitin' the sick and injured; my Christian duty and my work as a pastor."

The group had gone silent and tense.

"Then there's the whole Johnny Campos affair several years back," Thomas said. "Were you performing your Christian duty back then? You were a good friend of Johnny's, weren't you?"

Dash's voice went lifeless. "For a while we shared the same path, the road to damnation. Johnny died on that road."

"I understand what you shared was a taste for drugs. Except that you had more of a taste than he did."

Dash nodded. "That ain't no secret, brother. Back then I was lookin' for salvation in a bottle and a needle. Before I got high on the Lord."

He looked down on Thomas and searched his eyes.

"I'm not the only one who's done that, now, am I? I bet you known other folks who did that. I bet you've looked there yourself from time ta time. Ain't I right?"

Thomas met his stare but said nothing.

"I'll betcha I'm right." He was nodding as if he could read Thomas's life on the lines of his face. "You seen a lotta reality, haven't you, Mr. Thomas? A lotta the truth, as you call it. Enough so that you know why some people start lookin' for somethin' else. Why they decide it's time to turn to the Lord. Because reality ain't no comfort, is it? It ain't nothin' but pain in the end. It ain't nothin' but confusion and craziness. Until ya find the Lord. And once you find Him what your version of reality is don't matter. All your speculations and questions don't amount ta nothin', brother, and that's the truth. Because in the Lord you find the answers to all the issues."

He was smiling benignly now. He was saving Thomas's soul, not his own skin. Or at least that was what he expected those around him to believe.

"In my version of reality, there's a man in Paradise named Guillermo Vega," Thomas said. "He's an old friend of yours and of Johnny Campos too. An old drug buddy. Somebody who might know more about how Johnny really did die. And maybe he has something to do with those drug flights."

Dash's smile disappeared in a moment and he frowned. Thomas kept on him.

"You remember Guillermo Vega, don't you?"

Dash nodded cautiously. "Yes, I do."

"Have you seen him?"

"No, I haven't."

"He's wanted for questioning in the death of Jack Eames."

There were wheels turning behind Sam Dash's eyes now. Haynes had certainly told him about Thomas dropping Vega's name, but the preacher seemed genuinely surprised to hear that Vega was in town. He also seemed genuinely worried. His eyes had narrowed until all that was left were the cold slits of a scammer.

"Vega was seen talking to Jack Eames Friday night not too long before he died," Thomas went on. "I wonder what they were talking about."

Dash shook his head and his voice sounded hollow now. "I wouldn't know, brother. I haven't seen that man Vega in years."

"Is that right?"

"Yes, it is."

"Are you sure?" Thomas glanced at the Bible in Dash's hand and pointed at it. "Will you swear to that?"

Dash squinted suspiciously at Thomas. The other men had their eyes glued to the preacher. Haynes watched nervously. Dash stared at the Bible and then put his right hand on it, as if he were laying it on a griddle.

"I swear it," he said. "Now you'll have to excuse us. We have church business to take care of."

Thomas looked from one man to the other and then turned and walked toward the door. He could feel their eyes on him, especially Dash's. He hadn't gotten the truth out of Sam Dash, but one thing was sure. He had put something like the fear of God into him.

Chapter 19

*I*t was just after sunset when Thomas drove up to the Ralph R. Box and Sons Funeral Home. It was a one-story white stucco building with a high, arched portal outside like the gates of heaven. It was located just two blocks from the hospital. Most of the sidewalk prophets had retired for the evening, although a few still roamed the darkness.

A man with a name like Box must have felt fated for the mortuary business, Thomas thought as he walked up the path. On the plaque, beneath the name, it said the business had been founded in 1938, the same year as the first boom. While everyone else was drilling for oil, Mr. Box had been digging holes to bury the drillers. He too had found his fortune in the bowels of the earth.

On the wall in the foyer was an inexpertly done oil painting showing a vast prairie and a saddled but riderless horse,
a symbol of death and the afterlife. The last roundup. Next
to it stood a sign: Services for John J. Eames.

In the reception foyer he saw several persons he recognized: Arthur Layton and Deputy Harvey Abrams were
talking near the chapel door with Landon Turner. In a
group of women next to them he spotted Laurel Davis,
now wearing a long gray dress and clutching her Bible.
Esperanza Clark, the civil-defense nurse, stood near the
entrance with another middle-aged woman. The nurse
looked up at Thomas with that same fearful expression
she wore whenever she saw him. She reached out and took
him by the wrist as he approached.

"What's happening to this town, do you know?" she
asked him. He thought she was referring to the doomsday
patrols.

"I'm just hearing about Sam Cain," she said. "Somebody
killed him too."

"Yes, I know."

Esperanza gestured toward the other woman. "This is
Viola Buffet, Mr. Cain's secretary. She found the body."
She said it with a tremor in her voice. She introduced
Thomas and stepped away, clearly unwilling to hear the
story again.

The other woman, meanwhile, looked unruffled. She
was neatly coiffed, square-shouldered, about fifty, in a gray
suit and a lace-collared blouse. Glasses hung from her neck
by a chain. She inspected Thomas's face carefully as if she
were checking it for a typing error.

"So you found Mr. Cain?"

She nodded. "That's right. I walked into his office and
didn't see him at his desk the way he usually was. I looked
around, noticed the bathroom door closed and a small
puddle of blood just under the edge of it. I pushed open
the door and there he was."

"I guess the sheriff has talked to you?"

"Yes. I typed him an account of Mr. Cain's activities and appointments over his last several days and answered his questions."

"Anything unusual or suspicious?"

She lifted her pencil-thin eyebrows. "Margaret Masters called," she said. "That was unusual because she had never called him before. And given her circumstances and what eventually happened to Mr. Cain, some people would call it suspicious."

"He told you about the call?"

"He told me she asked him to defend her before the school board and he said no. That was all."

"Did he say how she reacted?"

"He said she wasn't happy about it. But he told her he was busy."

"What was he busy with?"

She leaned toward him with the expertise of a longtime office gossip. "The truth is, not much. I'd say he just didn't want to get mixed up in that can of worms. He had a case or two and then he was involved in a land deal."

"The section he'd gotten from Landon Turner? The one Walt Gamble was working on?"

"Yes," she said, obviously surprised that Thomas knew so much. "In fact, he said he would be tied up with that matter the next morning, that he was meeting with Gamble."

"Did he say what exactly he had to discuss with Gamble?"

"God only knows. It's like Mr. Cain himself said. Walt Gamble is *non compos mentis*. That means he's crazy."

"That was all he said?"

"Yes, that was all." She punctuated her answer with a final nod and walked away. Esperanza Clark came over again now that the secretary was gone.

"That poor woman. On top of eveything else, now she's out of work. Like almost everybody."

Thomas looked into the chapel. "Have you seen the body yet?"

"Yes, I've seen it and I'll be going now. I have to get

home to my kids. Paradise is getting too frightening to leave them alone."

"You haven't heard anything about this man Vega, have you?"

She shook her head. "People say they've seen men around, guys they don't know. But they just come in here for a day looking for work, don't find any, and leave. That's probably what happened to that one."

"Not this one." Thomas told her about seeing the Mexican and the foot race. "This guy is from here or at least spent time here some years back. He was apparently a friend of Sam Dash back when. And of Johnny Campos too, the one who died from drugs."

"I knew him."

"Some people say he didn't die the way the police said he died."

She looked around carefully, afraid she'd be overheard. "Lots of people think that, including me. I knew him a little. Johnny wasn't a good boy, but he wasn't any kind of heroin user."

"But you didn't know this boy Vega?"

She shook her head pensively. "There are lots of Vegas. But now that you know he was a friend of Johnny Campos that will help. I'll ask around."

Thomas told her he was still at the Range Motel, and she left.

He turned on his way to see the body and when he did he bumped right into Laurel Davis. Her bosom caught him in the upper stomach. He glanced down at it and then back up at her hazel eyes.

"Excuse me, Ms. Davis."

"Good evening, Mr. Thomas," she said, bringing the Bible to her breast. "I'm surprised to see you here. I didn't think you knew Jack Eames."

"I didn't," Thomas said." I only saw him once alive, at my motel, and not to talk to. And then I found the body."

"I read that in the newspaper. That must have been terrible," she said without much feeling. She looked away toward the chapel, where Viola Buffet was standing at the coffin, and then back at him. "I couldn't help but overhear you talking to Miss Buffet. About how Margaret Masters called Sam Cain just before he was attacked."

Thomas watched her. She couldn't have helped hearing because she had positioned herself right next to the conversation as soon as she'd seen him walk in. Then she had blocked his way as he had tried to walk away.

"Yes, she called him," Thomas said, "but then lots of people in Paradise had dealings with attorney Sam Cain. I understand you did at one time, when he represented your husband in divorce proceedings."

Her cat's eyes narrowed. "My husband was a man whose reason was altered by alcohol and he was also an adulterer, Mr. Thomas. I had no choice but to end the marriage."

Thomas found himself looking for blemishes in her smooth, honey-colored skin. There were none.

"I'm sure if he ran around on someone like you, Ms. Davis, his reason must have been impaired." She almost smiled then, but instead she bit her full bottom lip.

"Have you had dealings with Sam Cain since then?" he asked.

"Unfortunately yes. I had to deal with him regularly."

Thomas frowned. "Why 'unfortunately'?"

"Because my ex-husband, who lives in Houston now, is always behind in his alimony and support payments for the children. I had to go see Sam Cain almost every month and threaten to put my husband in jail. Mr. Cain called him and got him to send the money, which wasn't as much as it should be anyway."

"Sam Cain did a good job for him, I take it. He kept the payments down."

She nodded. "Sam Cain had a lot of influence with the courts and officials in Paradise. That's another thing the Reverend Dash is right about. Those things have to change."

Thomas looked into her eyes again and thought he found another reason hidden back there. "Or did Sam

Cain bring up your affair with Jack Eames? Did he threaten to bring it out in court? Was that his tactic?"

Her chin came up haughtily, but she didn't answer. She didn't have to.

"When was the last time you saw Cain to complain about the payments?"

"It was last week."

"What day?"

She hesitated. "Monday."

"The day before he was attacked."

Now it was Laurel Davis who looked suspiciously beyond Thomas's gaze. "You're having evil thoughts, Mr. Thomas."

"Yes, I am. I'm thinking that Margaret Masters isn't the only one who had reason to dislike Sam Cain, is she? And not the only one who had contact with him soon before he died."

Piety suffused and stiffened her. "If you're saying I would turn my hand against my fellow man, you're much mistaken. I have the Lord to avenge and protect me. I don't need to raise a hand against anyone."

"It looks like He did avenge you, Ms. Davis, with both Cain and Eames."

She shook her head. "It wasn't the Lord who did those things, at least not directly."

"Who was it, then?" She didn't answer and Thomas nodded. "I forgot. You're convinced it was Margaret Masters."

She didn't deny it this time because she didn't have a chance. She was staring at something beyond him, and when Thomas turned he saw Margaret Masters standing in the doorway. She was wearing a modest black dress and carrying a black purse. As usual she wore little or no makeup. She stopped in the doorway and the talking in the lobby quieted immediately. She looked as if she might duck out again, but then she scanned the people before her and her eyes fell on Thomas. That seemed to gird her.

She let the door close behind her and walked through the lobby without glancing at anyone and into the chapel.

Two elderly women near the coffin stepped aside as she approached. She stood motionless beside the casket for a minute during which the building was as quiet as death. Then she turned and, again not looking at a soul, walked through the lobby and out. Thomas went to the door and watched her get in her car in the parking lot and drive away. It had been a gutsy performance.

Laurel Davis had come out as well to watch the teacher make her exit. She cast a caustic glance at Thomas and walked to her car.

He went back inside, looking to speak with Landon Turner, but the rancher had already left. The people who were still there were whispering away again, almost certainly about Margaret Masters. Thomas's stomach was growling but he took a last minute to see the body.

It was lying in a coffin made of real wood and lined with white silk. The left side of Eames's head, where he had been hit by the bullet, was turned away from Thomas. There was no other mark on his face—surprising, since the roof had fallen on him. Either that or Mr. Box had done a very good job. Thomas remembered the face he had seen at the motel talking to the Mexican. He wanted to ask him now just what they had been talking about. Was it Sam Dash? Had the black duffel bag been in the house? He wanted to know what Landon Turner had wanted with him. And what had transpired that last night with Dash and Margaret Masters. But Eames wasn't talking.

Thomas left the hamburger stand a little after nine. He was tempted to go right next door to his room and get into bed, but he had work to do. He knew now that old Walt Gamble had talked to Sam Cain the day before he'd been beaten unconscious, meaning the old wildcatter was one of the last to speak to him. He'd also had an appointment to see him the very morning of the attack. Gamble hadn't mentioned that. Maybe he had forgotten, or it was an aspect of his craziness. Then again, maybe not.

Thomas turned onto the state road and drove west. As

the road left the town, the streetlights gave way and it was just his headlights cutting into the darkness of the prairie. The dark land and the night were seamless so that the range appeared to go on forever without a horizon. The high beams hit the brush along the side of the road and illuminated a pair of bright green eyes, maybe a jackrabbit or a coyote.

Thomas passed the entrance to the Buckknife Ranch and then he started passing pumpjacks. In the dark they appeared even more like prehistoric creatures. They gave the night landscape the ambiance of another world. A gust of wind blew dust across the road, clouding his view, and as it passed he saw the trailer on the side of the road as alone as a space station on another planet. He pulled in and noticed a car abandoned on the side of the road just past the entrance. He saw lights on in the trailer and Gamble's old gold Cadillac parked in the shadows next to it.

He got out and slipped through a space between the gate and the fencing. He heard television on inside, but he also saw something on the ground in front of the door. At first it looked like a shadow cast by a man standing inside the trailer, but as Thomas approached, he saw the shadow was strangely, unnaturally still.

Thomas walked up and found Walt Gamble lying on the ground, face up, one arm crossed over his throat as if he were protecting himself. He was still because he was dead. One side of his head had been crushed and the other side also seeped blood. Around the body lay several large granite-colored rocks like the ones Thomas had seen last time he was here. Walt Gamble had been stoned to death with them.

Even in death Gamble had a mad glint in his eye. That glint hadn't dried yet and the blood was still running from the gash in his head. Thomas crouched down and felt Gamble's face. It was still warm. Just to make sure, he put his ear to the man's chest. But there was nothing. The quiet of the prairie had occupied the body.

Then he heard a noise behind him, a shoe scraping the

dust. He turned, but he wasn't fast enough. The rock caught him on the side of the head and knocked him over on his side, where he lay with his skull ringing. He tried to climb to his feet, but another rock hit him, grazing the other side of his head and hitting his shoulder. Pain ran all the way down one side of his body and he felt light-headed. He fell on his face and felt the ground still warm from the daytime.

If he lost consciousness at all, it was only for moments. In that nether world of semiconsciousness, he heard foot-steps, then a motor starting and a car pulling away. Thomas rolled over and sat up. The car had been swal-lowed by the darkness, only two dimming taillights still visible speeding back toward Paradise.

He felt himself start to sway, held the ground and looked at the body. If he had arrived a few minutes earlier he might have saved Gamble. Whoever had hit him had been hiding behind the mobile home. The car Thomas had thought abandoned had been theirs. He hadn't seen it clearly enough to identify it, even to know its color.

His head was still ringing. He reached up, touched his scalp, and found he was bleeding. He heard a coyote howl. Maybe it smelled the blood. Maybe his would-be killer would smell it as well and come back to finish him off.

Thomas struggled to his feet, leaned against the mobile home, opened the door, and went in. The Persian rug was still on the floor and the gold mirror on the wall. He went into the cramped bedroom. The bed was unmade and clothes lay about, but there was no sign the place had been searched or anything stolen. In the top drawer of a dresser he found a money clip with a bit over a hundred dollars in it. Whoever had killed Gamble had done it not for his worldly possessions, but for some other reason. Maybe something he knew. Maybe revenge.

Thomas took a sheet from the bed and went back out. He thought of dragging Gamble into the trailer to keep him safe from the coyote. But in doing so he might disturb evidence.

He covered the body with the sheet. Just then a dust devil kicked up next to it. It disturbed the dirt a bit, then swept over the dead man, ruffling the sheet, dropped off him, and swerved across the ground into the shadows. They said the soul didn't leave the body until a few minutes after death. Maybe that was it. Just then the coyote howled again. Thomas turned and stumbled toward his car.

Chapter 20

*I*t was midnight by the time Thomas was released from the emergency room at Paradise Hospital. He got five stitches on one side of his head and four on the other, so that his skull resembled a baseball. The doctor had wanted him to check in for twenty-four hours of observation, but he had declined.

Thomas had driven himself to the hospital, advised the emergency-room staff to call the police, and a few minutes later deputy Harvey Abrams had arrived. Thomas told him about finding Gamble and being hit himself, and Abrams had left, siren fading into the distance. Now he came out of the emergency room expecting to find more police waiting to question him, but there was no one. Only moths battering themselves against the globe lights. He crossed to his car and headed for the motel. Halfway there he changed his mind, turned down State Street, and went to Margaret Masters's place.

The house was dark, but Thomas parked in front anyway, walked to the door, was about to knock, but stopped. He went around the house to the car port and felt the hood of the car. It was cool, but then the attack on Walt Gamble had occurred more than two hours ago.

He went back to the door and used the knocker. In a few seconds a light went on in the foyer and Margaret Masters's face appeared at the window next to the door. She opened it and let him in. She was wearing a long white nightgown, but he couldn't tell from her face if she had been asleep. She closed the door and leaned against it. The foyer still smelled of the charred books.

"I thought it was the sheriff," she said.

"Why was that?"

She was frowning at the patches on his head.

"The way my affairs are going what else should I think? What happened to you?"

Thomas tried to see behind those black eyes. It wasn't as easy as it was with Laurel Davis.

"There was someone else killed tonight, an old man named Walt Gamble." The surprise and distress on her face seemed genuine. "I found him at his mobile home out on the state road. Someone broke his skull with stones. Then they tried to break mine."

He gave her a few more details. Her expression turned to incredulity as she listened. But then she got that suspicious squint.

"That's why you've come here, isn't it? I thought maybe you'd come to see me for another reason, but that wasn't it, was it? Did you expect to find me with blood on my hands?"

He didn't answer.

"Is that it? You expected to get an exclusive interview with a triple murderess?"

"Where have you been tonight?"

She pointed at the chair just inside the study.

"I was reading. Then I went to bed."

On the arm of the chair sat a copy of *The Scarlet Letter*. She watched him read the title on the spine.

"I've been trying to read up on what it's like to be branded a scarlet woman," she said. "You've come to that opinion of me as well, haven't you, Don Quijote?" She looked down her sharp nose at him and her gravelly voice dripped with contempt. "My, how flimsy our modern heroes are."

Thomas bridled.

"You forgot I saw you walking down the street with blood on you, maybe Jack Eames's blood."

"Most likely my own since I had been in a house that had just been destroyed," she said. "But now you're wondering, because of what everyone else in this town is saying. You're wondering whether you should have turned me over to the mob. Why? Because I'm not the poor, defenseless schoolmarm you wanted me to be?" She laid a hand over her breast and looked demure. "Or is it a better story for you if the schoolteacher really is the town murderess?"

She walked into the study, turned on the light, shook a cigarette from a pack on the desk, lit it, and leaned against the desk.

"Well, I'm sorry to disappoint you on both counts, Mr. Thomas. I won't play the old-maid schoolteacher because I'm not a maiden. Ask anyone in town. Not only am I not a maiden, I'm an adulteress in the classical sense of the word; a woman who has joined in sex outside of matrimony. I'm also a divorcee. And even without those obvious blemishes on my record, I couldn't have played the maiden convincingly. I don't fit the type, do I?"

She put the cigarette to her mouth and exhaled languorously.

"No, you don't," Thomas said.

She shook her head. "No, I decided a long time ago not to play that part, Mr. Thomas. When you grow up the way I did, you make a decision early on. Whether or not to give a damn what people think. Whether to walk the street as if you were a whore, a fallen woman." She gestured at the book on the arm of the chair. "To have them treat you the way they treated my friend Hester Prynne. To let them brand you."

She drew on her cigarette, exhaled, and stared into her own smoke.

"It's that or you make your own rules about civility and integrity. You make sure you do your job well and that it be of some service to the community. If that sounds self-righteous, so be it. And knowing that in your personal life you'll never be able to please people because they already have you pegged as a bad apple, you decide to follow the dictates of your heart and nothing else.

"Some people in this town will tell you that I've followed other, baser instincts in running my private affairs, but that's not true. My first husband was a bit of a drinker and a carouser, an oilman who had a reputation for going around oiled, as they say. But I loved him. He was a man who didn't give a damn about public opinion and he loved me, in the beginning at least."

"You said your work took too much of your time," Thomas said. "That's why it broke up."

"There was that, and the fact I couldn't have children. Maybe that's why I've devoted so much of my time to my students." She looked Thomas in the eye. "There was no other reason for our divorce, although at the time there were rumors to the contrary. I loved my husband because he was willing to buck the tide. I loved his spirit."

"How about Jack Eames?"

"Jack was a different story. I loved him too, as unlikely as that sounds now. His character was completely different from that of my husband. He wasn't a good ol' boy, and he certainly did care about what people thought. But he had a respect for my intelligence, as much of it as there is. He appreciated the fact that I'd read a book or two. He also had some knowledge of the world outside here and a desire maybe to get out, something I'd thought of myself.

He even talked about one day running for Congress, getting away to Washington." She shrugged. "Of course, in
order to get there he had to get rid of me first. I didn't
know that at the time."

She looked at him boldly.

"That doesn't sound like a basis for love, does it? Want-
ing to get away. But at the time it was liberating. Maybe it
was also that he was one of the up-and-coming men in the
town and he wanted to spend his time with the daughter
of a saloon keeper, even if it was on the sly. That turned
my head too."

"Why didn't you go to the school board when this case
came up? Why didn't you tell them about his conflict of
interest?"

She cocked her head.

"Because that would be confessing adultery, wouldn't it?
It would be a public confession, like Hester Prynne standing on that scaffold in the middle of town with that crimson
A on her chest. I wouldn't give anyone that kind of satisfaction. As if I were trying to use what had happened
between Jack Eames and me as a kind of bargaining chip,
as a way of gaining leverage. No, I decided I would plead
my case on the basis of fairness, on my constitutional rights
of expression. I'd appeal to the town's sense of justice."
She shook her head. "Of course, a felon, a murderess, loses
lots of those rights, doesn't she?" She said it mischievously,
playing with him.

"Are you a murderess?"

She shook her head. "No, only your run-of-the-mill adulteress. I'm sorry to disappoint you and your magazine."

"There must be other people in this town who are on
your side besides Dan Oates."

"I'm sure there are, but they won't stand up now. Not
the way matters are in Paradise. Not now that the heavens
are about to rip open from horizon to horizon and the
dead are about to walk. Before the tornado things were
bad enough. Now that the Reverend Dash has been confirmed in his worst predictions, matters are worse. People

not only are still reeling from the storm, believing that the end is coming, but they've become more incensed with me. I can tell from those books on my steps and the phone calls I'm getting."

"Are they threatening you?"

She looked at him, but said nothing.

"They are, aren't they?" Thomas told her about Sam Dash's sermon after the storm and his receptive congregation. "You should be careful. You don't know what they might do. You should talk to the sheriff, ask him for protection, or maybe get out altogether."

"No, I won't run. I won't give the Reverend Dash that satisfaction. Anyway, I can't. I'm out on bail with the provision that I not leave Paradise."

"Then you should stay with someone else or have your housekeeper stay with you. You shouldn't be here alone."

She looked him in the eye. Thomas said nothing, but didn't make a move to leave. The clock marked the half hour. They stood studying each other. Then she turned off the light in the study and walked to the foyer, brushing by him. Thomas stopped her with a hand on her arm and brought her to him. This time it was his arms that enveloped her and he who found her mouth, this woman who just minutes before he had thought was a murderer. The notion didn't enter his mind now.

They stood that way for a minute. Then she pushed away and reached around him to lock the front door. The light went off and he felt her hand on his arm leading him toward the back of the house.

He woke the next morning as the first light came through the blinds. She lay asleep, looking not like the witch she proclaimed herself to be, but like an angel. Her hair, which she had taken down, lay spread across the pillow like a fine fan. Her face was composed, peaceful.

He got up and studied her as he dressed. If she were a murderess, she was one with an untroubled conscience. At least she had shown no sign of one the night before, nor did she at the moment. He leaned over and gave her a kiss on the forehead.

Thomas let himself out quietly and drove to the motel. It too was covered with blood red graffiti. He shaved and showered quickly and was on his way back out when he ran into the motel clerk, Robert, waiting next to his car. He looked even more spooked than usual.

"The sheriff was here late last night lookin' for you. He woke me up at two A.M. and had me open your door. I think he was afraid you were lyin' dead in there. When he didn't find you he wondered where you were."

Robert wanted to know too.

"Well, if he comes back you tell him I'm not dead." Thomas got in the car.

"There's a matter of the room rate," Robert said, holding onto the door. Maybe he was afraid Thomas would be dead soon, given his activities, and he'd better collect when he had the chance. Thomas took out three twenties and handed them over.

"Put that against what I owe you." Then he glanced at number three. "How about the Mexican? Has he shown up?"

Robert shook his head unhappily. 'No. He still owes me two days and the sheriff took his things so I have nothing to hold until he pays."

Thomas would have bet that the Mexican would never come back to claim his belongings. He pulled away, leaving Robert in the parking lot.

He took the west road out of town driving toward the horizon, which was clear and flat in the distance. He turned onto the dirt road that led to the Buckknife Ranch. As he reached the first complex of buildings he heard a motor, then a chopping sound. This time it wasn't Vachel Niles on his lawn tractor. It was a helicopter, a small two-seater, and it was flying low and fast, heading toward a bunch of white-faced cattle standing near the fence. As it approached them it dipped suddenly, falling to twenty feet off the ground. The steers grew wide-eyed and started to run along the fence toward the old ranch where Landon Turner lived. The helicopter swept back up, turned sharply, and followed them. It was as Niles had said, a bit of Vietnam.

Farther up the road, he saw two cowhands on horseback, probably hired for the day, as Niles had explained. They took over from the copter and drove the cattle toward the ranch headquarters. Thomas found Turner and Niles in the corral working on several young steers and heifers. Niles was dressed as he had been the other day but now he also wore long leather chaps. As Thomas approached, the old cowboy was swinging a lasso at his hip, then flicked it out and deftly caught one of the skittish animals around a back leg. He pulled the rope taut, then started reeling in the steer, hand over hand. When he was close to it, he quickly wrapped the rope around both back legs, then the forelegs and threw it to the ground. Turner walked up with a branding iron. He had been warming it over a flame from a butane cylinder. He placed it firmly on the flank. There was smoke and the animal thrashed and grunted. Then there was the smell of seared hair and burned flesh.

Thomas watched the two men as Turner injected the steer with what looked like a combination pistol and syringe. Apart from the Stetsons they looked like men out of different eras; Turner from the late twentieth century, but Niles right out of the nineteenth, with all the attendant differences in style and in values, Thomas thought.

Niles saw Thomas and waved, but it was Turner who came over. He held the hot branding iron in his hand and he didn't look as friendly as Niles.

"What can I do for you?"

Thomas glanced at the hot iron and back up at Turner.

"I just wanted to ask you a few questions about your neighbor, Walt Gamble."

Turner grimaced. "He wasn't my neighbor. He was just an old desert rat. The sheriff was here asking questions about him half the night."

"When was the last time you saw Gamble?"

"I'll tell you the same thing I told the sheriff. Old Gamble came to see me yesterday afternoon."

"Here to the ranch?"

"That's right." He pointed at the ranch house. "I was sitting at the desk and the next thing I knew he was standing next to me. Didn't knock, just walked in. Crazy as a loon."

"What did he want?"

"He told me the same fool thing you said: that I'd been swindled out of that land by Sam Cain. When he took it in payment for his legal services, he knew it was worth a fortune. He knew there was something on there I didn't know about. He said he was gonna do me a favor, that he was gonna make me rich. He talked as if he had walked in carryin' bags of money."

"Just like he was going to make Sam Cain rich," Thomas said.

"And look what happened to Sam Cain," Turner replied ominously. "He told me he'd found the seven cities of gold or something just as good. He said I'd make everything I lost and more ten times over and he said he'd found it on that piece of scrubland out there."

"What was he talking about?"

Turner scowled. "He said it was some mineral—borililim or beridium, somethin' like that. They use it in spaceships. That's what he claimed."

"What did you tell him?"

"What do you think I told him? I said he was a crazy old man and not to bother me. That I'd already gone broke investin' in spaceships and other fool things. I told him to go away."

"That was it?"

Turner shook his head, still scowling. "Then the other guy with him started working on me."

"Which guy?"

"I forget his name. He was wearing a ratty old Panama hat, some phoney jewelry and he did a lot of fast talking."

Surprise lit up Thomas's face. "Claude Denison? He was here with Gamble?"

Turner looked at Thomas suspciously just for knowing who Denison was. "That's right. He started telling me how he knew my daddy years back." His face twisted in disgust. "Everybody knew my daddy and almost all of them tried to cheat him."

"What else did he say?"

"He told me he knew Gamble was kinda crazy, but that this time he thought he might be right. This one scarecrow telling me the other scarecrow is right, when some of the best geologists in the world have been digging under this land for years and never found what they were talking about."

"That's all Denison said?"

"That's all I listened to. I said I didn't have anymore time for them."

"And they left?"

"They went out together and they got into an argument right out here in the ranch yard. I saw that Denison man get in his car and drive off. Left Walt Gamble standing there. Then Gamble walked off down the road. I told Vachel to pick him up in the truck and take him back to his trailer before he collapsed from the heat, the crazy old bastard."

"Did you see him last night?"

Turner shook his head. "Why would I see him?"

"So you still say he and Cain didn't swindle you out of anything?"

"That land's worthless," Turner said disgustedly.

"Because if they did cheat you, then you have reason to have killed both of them, don't you? If Jack Eames found out, somehow, that you'd killed Sam Cain, then you had reason to kill him. Maybe that's why you were going to his house that night. I think you say you weren't swindled so that you won't have a motive for murder, Mr. Turner."

Turner's puffy face stormed over. "Walt Gamble couldn't swindle a five-year-old child."

"But Sam Cain could."

Suddenly, Turner turned on Thomas as if he would hit him with the branding iron, but he stopped. He threw the branding iron down and stalked off toward the ranch house. Thomas watched him slam the screen door behind him.

Vachel Niles wandered over. He was sweating, the moisture filling the cracks of his face.

"Landon looks riled up," he said, "but he got like that last time you were here too."

"He doesn't like to talk about the fact that he got swindled, like you told me."

Niles frowned at the ranch house but said nothing.

Thomas watched him. He was sure Niles was holding something back and now he was also certain that it was the old cowboy he had seen on horseback near the motel the night after the tornado.

"Done any riding lately, Mr. Niles?"

Niles nodded innocently. "Oh, I still get on a horse from time to time."

"I saw you riding along the road the other day and also over near town, Saturday night."

The other man became as still as a deer caught in headlights.

"That's when the roads were blocked," Thomas said, "and nobody was supposedly allowed in or out of town."

"Nobody told me that. I wanted to see what the tornado did to the town, that was all."

"So you went over near the motel and near Jack Eames's house."

"That's the first part of town the horse and I came to. Anyway, if you know a man got killed there, you wanna see the place."

"Strange time to go—almost midnight, all the lights out."

"Like I said, I got curious."

"Or was it that Landon Turner had had some trouble with Jack Eames, and you wanted to make sure he hadn't left behind any evidence? Is that what you were worried about? That Landon had killed Eames?"

Niles was shaking his head, but Thomas didn't give him a chance to deny it.

"Were you afraid Landon had strayed too far this time, that he'd done something to get himself hung?"

Niles looked away, his gaze falling on the branding iron lying on the ground where Turner had left it. Thomas figured if you looked over Vachel Niles, somewhere on his hide you'd find that brand. He belonged to the Turner Ranch and the family the way the steers did.

"Old Coy Turner was your friend. You drove cattle together. But being a loyal hand and friend doesn't mean covering up for a killer, even if it is his son."

"I've known Landon since he was boy. He wouldn't kill nobody."

"He isn't a boy anymore, Niles. He's roamed far off the range and he's developed some expensive tastes. Maybe he developed reasons to kill you don't understand."

Niles kept shaking his head, but said nothing.

"Well, if Landon didn't kill them, maybe you did," Thomas said suddenly.

Niles looked at him, more with surprise than irritation. It was a possibility he hadn't considered before. He chewed it over a moment, then nodded.

"Yeah, maybe I did at that."

He met Thomas's gaze, his blue eyes without guile, but full of sacrifice, of dumb loyalty. He was ready to take the rap to save Turner. There was no sense pressing him on it.

"When you drove Walt Gamble back to his place yesterday, what did he say to you?"

Niles grimaced. "Walt Gamble only talked about putting holes in the ground and making money. I never listened to him."

"Did he say he'd told Landon about the swindle?"

"No."

"Was the man who came here with him, Denison, at the
trailer when you dropped him off?"

"I didn't see nobody there."

"He didn't say he was worried that someone wanted to
kill him?"

"That old man was too crazy to be worried."

The helicopter came over then about fifty feet up. Niles
glanced up at it, as if it were hunting him, a man caught
out of his epoch. The cattle in the corral stirred uneasily.
He turned away from Thomas and went back to the animals, which he understood in a way he didn't comprehend
the modern world.

Chapter 21

*T*homas drove back to the motel and found a sheriff's-department cruiser parked outside room number five with the door open. He pulled up, got out and saw Jim West sitting on the bed, six-shooter and all.

Thomas stopped in the doorway. "You get lost, Sheriff? This is *my* room."

West shook his head. "I'm not lost. It seems you're the one who disappeared from the hospital."

Thomas sidled into the room just as Deputy Harvey Abrams came out of the bathroom, where he'd apparently been looking around. Thomas glanced at him and back at West.

"I understand you came looking for me at two in the morning."

"Yes, but I didn't find you, at least not here."

Thomas didn't offer any information.

"I was worried too," West went on. "With three people already dead and you sticking your nose in all over town. I didn't want to think you were the fourth. So I got the tag number for your car off the registration card here at the motel. Then I had my patrol cars look for you. It didn't take them long to find you."

He spoke in the same barely inflected, emotionless voice Thomas had heard on first meeting him at the hospital.

"One of my men found your car. It was parked on the street outside 95 Houston Road. I went over there myself and saw it at three A.M."

Thomas leaned against the dresser.

"I was there talking to Ms. Masters."

West allowed himself a smile, or at least the ends of his lips moved.

"Well, you're the first journalist I've met who does his interviews at that hour and in total darkness. Those must be fairly intimate questions you ask."

Harvey Abrams chuckled. Thomas didn't.

"What article of law did I violate by being there?"

West shook his head. "Not any that we enforce. If there was, you'd be in jail. But still it makes me wonder." He stared at the toes of his cowboy boots. "There've been three murders and in two cases you found the body. You got to Jack Eames's house just minutes after it fell. A neighbor said she saw Margaret Masters walking away from the house just about then. You knew who she was, you'd talked to her the night before. You should have seen her and recognized her."

He looked up from his boots, but he didn't get an answer from Thomas.

"Then you find Walt Gamble dead and later that night a patrol car finds you at the house of a suspect at three in the morning."

"I suppose I also snuck into town a couple of days early

and hit Sam Cain over the head or helped her do it, an old man I'd never seen or heard of before. I also killed Gamble, or helped her do it, and then hit myself over the head with a rock so that it almost cracked my skull."

West shrugged. "You showed up at the hospital with your scalp bleeding, but nobody saw how it happened to you. Nobody except maybe a dead man."

Thomas scowled. "Come on . . ."

"No, you come on," West said, cutting him off, his voice cold as ice. "I want to know what your relationship is to the evidence in this case. Just what your knowledge is of the facts. You have what appears to be an intimate relationship with the prime suspect in the case and I wonder about you not seeing her at a place where other people did."

"If I thought Margaret Masters killed those people I might take all this seriously, but she didn't."

West crooked an eyebrow. "You're sure, are you? Her fingerprints were found on a gun that caused the death of Jack Eames and she had motive to kill Sam Cain."

"And Walt Gamble?"

"I don't know that Gamble's death has anything to do with the other two. We're looking for someone else in connection with his death."

"Denison?" West looked at him sharply and Thomas explained that he had been to the Buckknife Ranch that morning and heard about Denison being there.

The sheriff nodded. "They were seen arguin' and then Gamble shows up dead. I don't think this one has anything to do with the other two."

"But why would Denison bother to break Gamble's skull with rocks? Why would he take a page out of the Bible to kill someone? Why add to the madness you already have here?"

West shrugged. "Maybe that's all he had at hand. Or maybe to throw us off."

"I don't think the law of probabilities is on your side,

Sheriff. All of a sudden you have two murderers in town? I don't believe it. Especially since Gamble was involved in some shady business with Sam Cain."

West nodded curtly. "I've heard that too, but it doesn't appear there was any shady business. I've talked to Landon Turner."

"Turner tells you nobody did anything to him, so he has no motive for murder."

West's gaze went cold again. "Sam Cain wasn't known as a swindler and Landon Turner isn't known as a murderer. Why should I let you, a stranger, ruin the reputations of people who've been here all their lives and stayed within the law?"

"You yourself said it, Sheriff. In Paradise, anybody could be twisted by greed."

West looked hard into Thomas's eyes. "And a man anywhere can get turned around by a woman." He let the words sink in. Then he got up and went to the door. "Your suspicions don't interest me much, except for that Mexican man you supposedly saw speaking with Jack Eames. If you see him, I'd like to talk to him. And if I learn you've withheld evidence or obstructed justice in any way, you'll go to jail. I promise."

Even if West's voice was steady, Thomas could see the wear around his eyes. West was responsible for a town that was suffering a communal breakdown: destruction, fear, religious frenzy, murder. It had gotten to him.

West and Abrams went out then, got in the cruiser, and pulled away. Thomas closed his door and headed for the *Chronicle.* He wanted to ask Oates where he could look for William Vega, if Vega was still in town. The Mexican had stuck around after the tornado and after the death of Eames, as if he had business to finish, so there was a chance he was. It seemed to him that finding the Mexican was Margaret Masters's only hope.

When he got to the newspaper the Bronco wasn't in front and the office was closed. A note said Oates would be back later in the afternoon. The latest editon of the newspaper had come out that morning and he put a quarter in the machine just outside the door and took out a copy. The editorial Oates had been writing the day before appeared on page one. It was entitled "They Know Not What They Do." It was long for an editorial and laid out the history of the Margaret Masters case, including her recent arrest for murder. Near the end, Oates took his stand. He called for adherence to First Amendment principles.

Those who look to proscribe in a sweeping way what their children may read and may learn do nothing to protect those children. Instead they put them more at risk in our complex world. Ignorance will not serve them in the fight against evil. And those who look to trample on the rights of others to due process can only expect that same treatment for themselves and their own down the line. If there is a prayer from the good book that applies today in Paradise, it is Christ's prayer on the cross. "Forgive them, Father, they know not what they do."

It was a hard-hitting piece of work by Oates, a clear stand that was sure to anger segments of the population. That agitation was already visible. The proselytizers from the Paradise Revelation Temple were out in force on Main Street. They paced the sidewalks, waving the Bible, even more active than before, like bees who had been provoked. One rail-thin woman in a black dress, with her hair pulled in a tight bun, appeared suddenly at the window of his car, Bible in hand.

" 'And the kings of the earth who have committed fornication and lived deliciously with her shall lament for her when they shall see the smoke of her burning.' Revelation, Chapter Eighteen."

She hissed the words right at Thomas's eyes as if she knew what had happened between him and Margaret Masters; then she moved away. Other sidewalk preachers yelled at him to repent and warned him of the day of

reckoning. He sat there a few more minutes. Then he put
the car in gear and began to cruise the streets, looking for
the Mexican.

He went up State Street until the houses gave out,
turned the corner and came back on the next block. He
drove slowly, crawling like a patrol car. Many of the
houses were empty and Vega could have been hiding in
any of them. When he saw people in their yards, the few
there were, he stopped, got out and asked them. But he
didn't have much to ask. Had they seen a heavy-set Latin
man, a stranger, with a tattoo on his arm? If he had the
tattoo covered he would look like countless other Latin
men.

He went through the section of town hit by the twister.
He saw the ruined houses and the residents, some of them
still picking through the rubble and looking lost. It was
the wreckage not only of their homes, but of their lives,
many of them having lived all their days in those houses.
What had been destroyed wasn't just buildings, but touch-
stones, landmarks in their psyches. He didn't stop to ask
them about Vega. They already had enough troubles.

And everywhere he saw the red splashes of paint, like
blood, and the proselytizers, especially in the areas where
there was damage. Men, women, near children, all with
the same mad glint in their eyes. They stalked the wreckage, not with sorrow, but in a frenzy as if destruction and
desolation were their natural elements.

Thomas saw them, but he didn't see Vega, the one who
if found, might defuse that tension. He drove the streets
methodically and near sunset he crossed over into a neighborhood that was predominantly Latin. There were fewer
of the doomsayers here, the neighborhood being cut off
from the rest of Paradise by rusty, unused railroad tracks.
It was where he should have started, he thought, although
it would be no trick for Vega to get lost in that population.
The houses were one story, small, weathered, and desolate;
they seemed to be hugging the ground, cowed by the im-
mense sky. The trees were dust-covered. He stopped and

asked an older, nut-brown woman in a floral housedress
who was sweeping bravely at the dust on her walk if she
knew of a William Vega. He was told the same thing the
sheriff had said: the town was full of Vegas. But she di-
rected him to a bar on the next street, where he might ask.

The Cantina was in an old, small, unadorned adobe
building that looked as if it had been there longer than
the town. Some of the red tiles in its roof were broken and
its white stucco walls were cracked and stained. Thomas
parked next to two beat-up pickups. Inside, the place was
dark and surprisingly cool after the heat outside. A few
old tin tables surrounded by folding chairs took up one
side of the room. A bullfight poster barely visible in the
shadows, was tacked to one wall. On the other side of the
room was a bar, some bottles on shelves, and, in the middle
of that wall, a small shrine, including a picture of the Virgin
of Guadalupe and two votive candles burning in red glass
holders on either side. A siren sounded in the distance as
Thomas walked in.

The bartender was a tall, older Latin man with very
broad shoulders and muscular arms. He looked as if he
had put in time working in the oil fields before going
behind the bar. Maybe it was there he'd gotten the scar on
his face; it ran horizontally an inch below his eyes and
crossed over his nose. It made him look as if he were
peering over a fence. Right then, he was looking warily at
Thomas. There were a handful of other men drinking beer
at the tin tables. There was a chance that some of them
were illegal and he was worried that Thomas was an im-
migration agent. Or maybe he was just worried.

Thomas went to the bar and ordered a Coke, told the
bartender who he was, showed him a press card, and explained who he was looking for.

The bartender slid the Coke in front of him. "I haven't
seen nobody like that," he said.

"Maybe you've seen him in the past. He used to live here
and he was a friend of Johnny Campos, the boy who died
a few years back from drugs."

The man glanced past Thomas to the other men, then started to wipe the bar.

"Johnny didn't die of no drugs." ·

"I've heard that too," Thomas said. "I've heard maybe he was killed."

The big man shrugged, but said nothing.

"I'm not a policeman," Thomas told him. "I just want to ask Vega some questions. I don't think he's responsible for the killings either."

"Like they asked Johnny Campos some questions. Like they sometimes ask Mexicans some *extra* questions."

Thomas sipped his Coke. "You think Johnny was killed because of racial prejudice?"

The bartender peered over his fence at Thomas, as if he were looking at someone hopelessly naive.

"I'll tell you what happens in this town, mister. When the boom is on everybody does all right. Nobody cares where you come from or what you look like. Everybody has work. They even open up the jails and give the cons work at ten dollars an hour. But when things get bad, when people lose their jobs, then we start having problems here again. Then all of a sudden, to some people, this is a white man's town again."

"People like Lloyd Haynes?" Thomas asked. "I've heard Lloyd Haynes didn't love Mexicans to begin with."

The mention of the deacon's name made the other man look at Thomas differently. He leaned toward him and his voice dropped.

"Johnny died because he knew too much about Lloyd Haynes, that's what I think."

Thomas frowned. "Too much about what?"

The man peered slyly over his fence with his muddy brown eyes. Then he held his hand in front of Thomas and rubbed his two fingers together.

"Money, amigo."

"What money?"

He shook his head and went back to polishing his scarred bar. "You should ask Lloyd Haynes about it."

"About what?" Thomas looked into the other man's blank face. "Was he being paid off by someone?"

The bartender shrugged. "Ask Haynes, or maybe Sam Dash if he knows."

"You mean Haynes was paid off by Sam Dash when he was dealing drugs back then?"

A customer at one of the tin tables asked for another beer and the bartender gave Thomas a last pointed look and shuffled away. He left Thomas staring at the Virgin of Guadalupe and her shrine. Just then another siren sounded, an urgent wailing. Thomas drained his Coke, threw some money on the bar, and went out. The sun had disappeared by that time, but as Thomas went out he thought it was still setting. In the direction of downtown there was an orange glow in the sky. It danced in the darkness like fire. He knew right away what it was the moment he saw it: the *Chronicle*.

Chapter 22

A mushroom cloud of thick black smoke billowed into the sky as Thomas raced to the downtown area. It wasn't until he turned onto Main Street that he saw flames. They were licking at the *Chronicle* offices, less so at the two adjacent buildings. Sirens sounded everywhere. Two trucks from the Paradise Volunteer Fire Department blocked the street, pumping arcs of water at the fire. Sheriff Department cars, their roof lights turning, painted the scene in red.

Thomas jumped out of his car and ran the last hundred yards along the sidewalk. Already a large crowd had gathered along the opposite curb, their faces lighted by what was left of the blaze. Among the onlookers Thomas saw some of the proselytizers, Bibles in hand, including Sam

Dash and Lloyd Haynes. A drizzle of live embers fell around them, but they didn't move.

He found Oates standing next to one of the fire trucks. He looked like he'd just walked out of hell. His face and clothes were black with soot, although he didn't look hurt. He held a charred briefcase in one hand, and in the other, copies of the *Chronicle*. He was staring with a lost expression into the offices of his newspaper, or what was left of them. The firemen had blown out the front window with its archaic gold lettering and shone a spotlight inside. Thomas could see the charred metal desks, and a computer terminal, blackened and exploded, lying on the floor. Beyond them he saw the *Chronicle* files, which had been consumed by the fire, as if the memory of the town had been burned out of its mind. Water seeped down into the ruins. The red police lights made it look like blood, the rain of blood described in Revelation.

Thomas glanced up at Oates. "Were you in there when it started?"

The big man shook his head without looking at him. "I got here just after. I managed to run in and get a few things."

"You didn't see how it might have started? Who might have done it?" It was clear to both of them that someone had set it off because of the editorial.

Oates shook his head again, a brooding anger in him. "I didn't see, but I didn't have to see."

Within five minutes, the firemen had extinguished all the flames. The adjacent buildings, a clothing store on one side and a boarded-up storefront on the other, had suffered only slight damage, but the *Chronicle* was gutted. Firemen were picking through the damage in the front room. They tried to stop Oates from going in, but he brushed by them. Thomas followed.

The room was still hot and the last smoke rose from the charred surfaces and made Thomas's eyes run. The old framed *Chronicle* headlines had all fallen from the walls and had been destroyed by the fire. The flames had not reached the expensive computer equipment in the back room or the press, although they had taken some smoke and water damage. But it was the files that most concerned Oates. The blackened metal of the cabinets was buckled and too hot to touch, but he and Thomas pried open a drawer with a splintered board. Some of the files were already black and in ashes. Other envelopes of yellowed clippings appeared to be intact. But when Oates picked up one of the articles, it disintegrated in his fingers and fell like confetti. Oates stared at it and a sound of pain escaped him. He took out another envelope and the same thing happened. He watched the brittle, desiccated paper fall as if he were watching his own life crumble in his hands. Chronicled by his father to begin with and then himself, it was, in fact, his history, his identity.

Then the big man lost it altogether. He picked up the splintered board and began to beat at the charred file cabinets in a rage. One of the firemen tried to grab him, but Oates swung his large arm around and knocked the man down. Then he saw something outside that made him even crazier and went stumbling over the wreckage, headed for the street. He was charging right at the line of people across the street where Sam Dash was standing. Thomas yelled and scrambled after him. Out of the corner of an eye he saw Jim West in his Stetson and another deputy cutting through the tangle of hoses and the whirling red lights of his own sheriff's cars to head off Oates.

West didn't get there in time. Oates had busted through the crowd and had Dash by the throat by the time two deputies grabbed him and dragged him off the preacher. Women screamed and men were shouting. It took three people to hold him down. Oates, his face soot-covered, was struggling with them. A man of moderation, he'd been driven over the edge.

Dash, dressed in a black suit and white shirt, looked at Jim West, and rubbed his throat where the editor had grabbed him.

"You better arrest that man, Sheriff," he said, his voice

quavering. "He's a danger to the community . . . in more ways than one."

The deputies had Oates on his feet, holding him back. Jim West stepped close to Dash, staring into his face.

"The only one who's going to be arrested here is the one responsible for this fire." His voice was as steely as the pistol in his holster.

Dash didn't blink. Haynes, standing beside him, shook with agitation.

"We had nothing to with this," Haynes said.

"You had everything to do with it," West said. He kept his eyes on Dash. "We're going to investigate it and I guarantee you, everyone connected with it will go to jail, no matter who they are. Those who started the fire and those who instigated it." His voice dropped and grew ominous. "Along the way we're gonna look into some other crimes that might have been committed in the past. We're gonna clear those up as well."

Haynes went quiet and pale, but Dash's gaze remained steady.

"The Lord sent this municipality a sign," Dash said, waving his Bible and speaking so that he could be heard by those around him. "He sent that tornada to warn us. It was a message and the people of Paradise ain't gonna let so-called town leaders or newspapers ignore that summons. We won't let it happen again to us. You follow the laws of the Lord or we won't follow your laws."

West stiffened and glowered at the preacher. "And I won't let you lead this town into anarchy, no matter who you make believe you are." He stepped back and addressed the crowd. "Now I want all you folks to go home, but first I want you to look at this," he said, pointing at the burned-out husk of the *Chronicle* where smoke still rose. "I want you to realize what's happening here in Paradise and decide that this madness can't go on. You're driving yourselves crazy and you're destroying this town. It's gone too far already. Any more of it and this municipality will cease to exist, not by God's hand but by your own, and when you wake up out of this nightmare you're in, you'll have nobody to blame but yourselves." The proselytizers watched him warily, but they listened. West was one of them. "And I want anybody who knows anything about this crime to come forward before it's too late."

He met Dash's gaze again and held it: the temporal and the divine leaders of the town in a standoff. It lasted only a few seconds, then the preacher turned and pushed his way through the crowd and stalked off. Haynes continued to blink nervously at West, looking as though he might fall apart right there. Then he slunk off as well. The others began to move away through that burned-out and boarded-up downtown. It looked like a ghost town and they like shades.

The rotating roof lights of the police cars still played over the scene and caught the street in a smokey, chaotic, dizzying gyre. Oates stood in the midst of it, smoldering with anger. A deputy told him the sheriff's department would guard the office during the next days and nights and offered him a ride home. Thomas retrieved the briefcase and the copies of the *Chronicle* that carried the editorial.

"This will work out," he told the big man. "We'll build it again."

"Did you find out anything else?" Oates asked tiredly. "Have you seen the Mexican?" Maybe Oates figured that the Mexican could finger whoever had burned his newspaper, that he could finger Sam Dash.

Thomas said he hadn't. "But what is this about Lloyd Haynes taking payoffs while he was in the sheriff's department," Thomas asked, "and Johnny Campos's death being tied to them?"

Oates nodded, staring into the gutted remains of his newspaper. "I heard that at the time. But it was just angry whispers by the same people who questioned how Campos had died. Nobody had any proof. The only one besides Haynes who might have known about it was Sam Dash. He wasn't around and he wouldn't have talked anyway, since he was implicated too." He looked at Thomas. "But I know that by the time Lloyd Haynes had his accident, Jim West had become sheriff and he wasn't sorry that Lloyd was off the force. There was no love lost there. Maybe Jim suspected Haynes of being corrupt."

"Sam Dash never talked about it when he came back?"

Oates shook his head, bitterness twisting his lips. "Not to me. He said that was part of his past life, before he'd been saved."

Thomas's face was gripped by thought. "The other person who might have known was Vega. He was acquainted with them all. That's another reason to find him."

"He's probably long gone," Oates said.

"I don't know. He stayed after the tornado and after Eames died. I saw him. Maybe he's had a reason to stick around."

"This afternoon they picked up this man Denison, the one they think killed Walt Gamble," Oates said, "They stopped him in his car and took him in. That's where I was going when this happened. Maybe you should go see him."

Oates gave him the name of the duty officer at the sheriff's office. Then he went back into the charred wreckage of the *Chronicle* to see what he could salvage and Thomas walked to city hall.

He entered by a door on the side of the building marked Sheriff's Department, passed a dispatcher's station stacked with radio equipment, and found the brown-shirted duty officer at a desk next to a wall covered with grim faces on WANTED posters. Thomas explained who he was, that Oates had sent him, and he was escorted down a narrow hallway lined with clean, tiled cells which were empty except for the last one. There he saw Denison standing with his hairy fingers clutching the bars. The land man once again didn't recognize him.

"Are you a lawyer?" he barked. "If you are you've got yourself a case."

"No, I'm the writer," Thomas reminded him.

Denison nodded his grizzled face in recognition. "Then you should write about this," he said, trying to shake the bars. "These people are locking me up for no reason. I'm gonna sue them and it's going to be a big payday. You wait and see. They're all crazy around here."

"I understand you knew Walt Gamble."

Denison's face stormed over. "But I didn't have anything to do with killing him. I was in Odessa on a little business when Gamble got his. People there can tell you that, just like they'll tell this sheriff. I drive back into town a little while ago and they grab me. As soon as I get a lawyer they'll pay for it."

Thomas nodded. "I don't think you killed Walt Gamble. I just want to ask you a few questions."

Denison calmed, his beady eyes fixing on Thomas. "What's it worth to you?"

"That depends on what you tell me. How did you know Gamble?"

"I knew him for about forty years. We started around here together."

"When Gamble was a geologist for the oil companies?"

Denison nodded. "And I was a land man. He did studies of what was under the surface and I bought the rights. That's when people were drilling all over the county. Those were big-money days."

"You worked together?"

"A few times, but then I quit workin' for the oil companies," Denison said with distaste. "Like I told you, that was a sucker's game. You did the work but the real money went into somebody else's pocket. I started putting together my own deals. Gamble quit them, too, and he worked for me a few times."

"You were a promoter and he did the surveys for you?"

Denison nodded, still sour-faced. "Gamble wasn't much of a wildcatter or geologist, for that matter. He made too many mistakes."

"You mean he drilled too many dry wells?"

"After a while that was all he drilled. I raised money from investors and later they accused me of swindling them when the wells came in dry. But it was Gamble. He thought he saw oil everywhere."

"Was it Gamble who did the studies for that land where he was living?" Thomas asked. "The land Sam Cain owned?"

Denison shook his head. "No. That was somebody else's duster."

"Then how did he know, forty years later, that there was something in it worth money?"

"Because somebody told him. Somebody whose brother or father had worked on it. They had this big piece of rock, this mineral. Gamble saw it and they told him where it came from."

"Who told him?"

Denison shook his head. "Some Mexican name."

"Vega?"

Denison brightened, as much as he ever brightened. "That's right—Vega. That's where he got it."

Which meant that Vega had been in Paradise a few weeks back as well. That was entirely possible.

"Gamble showed me this rock," Denison said. "He said it was beryllium. And he showed me it in this book on minerals. They use it in space technology and they pay big bucks for it, that's what he said. When the hole was drilled forty years ago, there were no spaceships and nobody knew it was worth anything. You get it? They didn't find oil and they just plugged up the hole. Crossed it off. Now it's worth a bundle. That's what Gamble said."

"And he told Sam Cain, who acquired it from Landon Turner without telling him what was under there."

"I don't know anything about that," Denison said. "I haven't seen Sam Cain in years and I was right in this cell when he got his skull cracked. That was the first time they arrested me here. It was after I got out that I bumped into

Gamble and he told me about that mineral. He said if we could get some money together we might be able to buy the rights."

"So you went to Landon Turner, but he told you to get lost. Then you fought with Gamble."

Denison squeezed the bars hard again and scowled. "I didn't fight with him. I didn't lay a hand on him. I just told him I didn't want to be mixed up in it. Turner said there had been geologists all over this town in the last forty years and they hadn't found that stuff or if they had, it wasn't worth anything. It was Gamble seeing money where there wasn't any money, just like always. That's what I figured. I didn't want more of my time wasted. I left him there at the ranch and I drove to Odessa. I came back, just passin' through, and they grabbed me. I didn't even know Gamble was dead. And everybody in this town had gone insane."

"You didn't see Gamble again after Turner's place?"

Denison shook his head. "No."

Thomas looked into the washed-out green eyes, the color of old dollar bills, and believed Denison. It was the only time he had since he'd met him. He took out a twenty-dollar bill and passed it through the bars, explaining that it wasn't payment for information, but a humanitarian gesture.

Denison sneered at it. "Chicken feed," he complained.

Thomas left, thanked the duty officer, and walked back toward the *Chronicle*. The crowd had dispersed and a few firemen were still picking through the rubble. The destruction looked even worse now. Oates wasn't in sight. Maybe he just couldn't stand to look at it.

Thomas found his car but instead of going directly back to the motel, he drove up Houston Street. When he reached the corner before Margaret Masters's house, he stopped. He didn't see a light on in the house, but what he did see was a sheriff's-department car parked in front of it in the shadows of the elms. Jim West no doubt figured that if someone had been angry enough to set fire to the

Chronicle, they might go after Margaret directly. The sheriff could protect her tonight, Thomas thought. He turned away from the house and drove to the motel.

As he undressed, he glanced at the phone. He sat down and looked up the number in the phone book. She answered after about ten rings.

"Did I wake you?"

"No," she whispered. "I figured it would be one of my usual crank callers. Not you."

"Are you all right?"

"Yes, I'll be all right."

"Sleep well," he said and hung up.

Then he lay in bed thinking about the day. Vega had had something to do with that plot of land. He had something to do with everything: Jack Eames, Sam Cain, Johnny Campos, Dash, Haynes, Gamble. He was the missing piece at the center of the puzzle and Thomas had let him get away. Well, maybe he would show up at the motel again and maybe this time Thomas would be fast enough to catch him.

Chapter 23

*B*ut the Mexican didn't appear that night, at least not in reality.

Thomas woke the next day with the very tail end of a dream in his head that he thought involved Vega. Thomas was in the courtroom at the Paradise city hall. The only other person there, a murky figure whose face he never saw clearly, spoke to him urgently, explaining everything that had happened both before and since he'd arrived in Paradise. He thought it had to be the Mexican. The dream left behind that feeling of perfect comprehension, that crystal clarity dreams sometimes produced, although Thomas couldn't capture anything specific of what he was told, only the sense that everything came together. He lay staring at the ceiling, not moving for minutes, trying to bring back that information from the other side of sleep, even one shred of it, but it wouldn't come.

He looked at his watch and saw it was almost nine A.M. He had slept for a change, but it was no consolation. This was his last day in Paradise and he had only half a story. He lay for a long time thinking about what to do and again straining to remember the dream, but he couldn't. It had floated even farther away. His gaze drifted around the room and finally fell on the Bible that lay on the night table. He stared at it for some time and then he decided what to do.

He got up, prepared, looked up an address in the Paradise telephone book, grabbed a small tape recorder from his pile of equipment, put in a fresh tape, slipped it into his shirt pocket, and went out. The sun was rising in a cloudless sky and it would be another blazer. He drove west and turned into that same run-down neighborhood he had driven through on his way to the Reverend Dash's service his first night in Paradise. Although the proselytizers had been out pounding the sidewalks the last days, now there was no one to be seen. Maybe the sight of the *Chronicle* gutted and charred had scared them, that and the warning from Jim West. The streets were deserted.

Thomas found the address two blocks from the Revelation Temple. He pulled up in front of a small, white, badly weathered clapboard bungalow sitting in the middle of a yard of dried-out weeds. The roof was missing some of its green shingles and the screen door had a large rent in it. Thomas went up the walkway and knocked. The inner door was open and he looked into a small front room that held a ratty, faded sofa, losing its stuffing at one end, and a stuffed chair to match. An old throw rug lay twisted on a painted wood floor. The walls were water-stained and soiled, a plain wooden cross the only decoration, except for pamphlets and stacks of books, all of which looked like Bibles. They lay around the room in disorganized heaps. Thomas could see through to a back room and to the foot of an unmade, disheveled bed in another starkly empty room. A person who lived that way was better off thinking of the next world.

Then Lloyd Haynes came out of what must have been the kitchen. He scowled through the ripped screen. His hair was unkempt and his clothes were wrinkled as if he'd slept in them, except he didn't appear to have slept very much. He had dark circles around his brooding eyes. He looked even more ravaged than usual.

"What do you want?"

"Good morning, Deacon. You're up bright and early. We seem to be the only ones."

"The righteous always sleep well and rise early," Haynes answered despite his haggard appearance. "It's only sinners who have troubled sleep."

Thomas nodded. "I guess I must be a sinner," he said. "I didn't sleep well. But then I had somebody come see me in the night. Somebody you know. William Vega."

Haynes's eyes narrowed suspiciously, but he said nothing.

"Vega came to me last night," Thomas went on. "He knew I've been looking for him all over town to ask him some questions about certain things that have happened lately, but also about what happened a few years back. About his friend Johnny Campos."

Haynes scowled. "He's a delinquent and a liar just like that other one was."

"I don't think so, not after what he told me. I don't believe the sheriff will think so either. That's where he was going next. He said he was here to settle some matters once and for all. Something about some money that was paid."

Haynes's scowl deepened.

"Money Sam Dash paid to you that Johnny Campos must have caught on to," Thomas said. "The old crimes that the sheriff talked about."

The deacon showed his teeth. "You're bearing false witness. You're making it up."

"Call the Range Motel. He's checked in right across from me. I'm not lying."

That scared Haynes. He had been frazzled and unraveled the night before and after a sleepless night he was ready to crack. He glared through the damaged screen like an angry insect at the desolate houses across the street. He didn't say a word for almost a minute. There wasn't a sound anywhere.

"It don't matter anyhow," he said finally. "This town ain't gonna be here much longer. It's gonna disappear from the face of the earth. In fact, the whole planet is gonna be destroyed. The continents is gonna sink and the oceans dry up and all worldly possessions and all man's works are gonna turn to ashes in his mouth. The buildings, the cars, the trains, the bridges, everything. Because the end is comin'. It's almost here. The drowned'll float and the dead'll walk."

"Including Johnny Campos?" Thomas said. "What will he say when he rises? Will he say you killed him?"

Haynes looked bleakly into the middle distance, but didn't speak.

"Did he find out Sam Dash was paying you off?" Thomas asked. "If he did, he'd tell, wouldn't he, because you'd always been rough on Mexican boys. The question is how you did it. How did you get that needle in his arm?"

"Oh, it wasn't hard," Haynes told him. He stepped away from the door for a matter of seconds and when he came back to it he held a small black pistol in his hand which was aimed right at Thomas's stomach. He pushed the screen door open and stepped out, making Thomas draw back.

"I just pointed a gun at him. This same pistol right here."

Thomas looked into the eye of the gun. Haynes nodded.

"The Campos kid didn't like it either," he said with a twisted smile. "He got scared just like you and he did what I told him. He didn't know what was goin' on until that night. But he got there at the wrong moment and I couldn't let him leave."

A young woman, carrying a red-haired baby, came out the door of the next house just then. She froze in her tracks when she saw the pistol in Haynes's hand. The deacon didn't seem to notice her. She stood there a few moments and then carefully stepped back into her bungalow.

Thomas glanced at the gun again and back at Haynes, who was staring into the past.

"You told him to inject himself."

Haynes shook his head. "He wanted to be around drugs, he could do 'em." He shrugged and looked desolately at something Thomas couldn't see. "Then he died right there in front of us. He was better off that way. This world ain't no place to be. All it is is sufferin'.'"

He stared at nothing for at least a minute. Out of the corner of his eye, Thomas saw the sheriff's car come around the corner. It was going quickly, but then it skidded to a stop. He saw the brown shirts jump out and he held a hand out behind him so that they would take it slow. Haynes was oblivious to them.

"Sam Dash was there in that empty house," Thomas said. "He was the one who had the heroin and that's why he took off. That's what Vega said."

Haynes nodded. "And the Lord got his revenge on both of us."

His hand went up to his scarred cheek. Thomas could feel the sheriff's men close behind him on the sidewalk.

"How about Sam Cain, Eames, Gamble?"

"Somebody killed them, I suppose. It shows you how things are coming apart."

"But you didn't kill them?"

Haynes shrugged indifferently. "No. But it don't matter much that they're dead either. It's all gonna end anyway. There ain't gonna be no more evil or good, no more sufferin' or pleasure, no more light and dark. No more nothin'."

Then one of the deputies called Haynes's name. Thomas looked over his shoulder and saw two men with pistols in their hands. When he turned back he saw Haynes had put the gun to his own temple. The men behind him shouted, but Haynes didn't hear them.

"It don't matter, the end is here," he said.

Thomas started to move to him, but it was too late. The shot cracked the silence. Haynes's head snapped to one side and then his body toppled in the same direction. Thomas heard a cry from the next house as Haynes hit the dirt.

The two deputies ran by Thomas to the body. Thomas went as well, but he knew there was no hope. Lloyd Haynes lay staring into nothing, as he had in life, staring into eternity. Haynes had talked over and over about the end coming, maybe as a way of preparing himself for what he had just done. He had repented, but he hadn't been able to forget.

Down the block, people had come out of their houses and were approaching. Sirens sounded in the distance. Thomas went and sat on the curb.

The deputies nosed around the body a few minutes and talked to the woman next door who had made the call alerting them and who had heard much of Haynes's confession through her window. Then one of the deputies drifted over to Thomas.

"There was nothing I could do," Thomas said.

The deputy agreed with him. Thomas wanted out of there before West showed and accused him of being at yet another death site. Thomas told the deputy he would be at the motel later if there were more questions.

As he was walking away, Oates pulled up and jumped out of the Bronco. He took a look at Haynes's body and then approached Thomas.

"I'll give you a first-person account when I come back," Thomas said. "Right now I have to go find Sam Dash."

He drove to the Paradise Revelation Temple first, but it was closed. He went around to a side window and looked in, but no one was there, just empty chairs facing an empty stage. The neon cross was still burning. He walked back around to the small house next door and found the name Dash on the mailbox. He went to the door, knocked, and after a moment it was opened a crack by a thin, dry-skinned, brittle-haired woman, who had to be Dash's mother. She had the same dark eyes, except hers weren't wired. They were tired and worried as if she had been staring at failure and problems all her life. Her face was heavily lined, not so much from age as strife. She peered through the crack in the door at Thomas.

"He ain't here," she said in a thick Texas accent.

"Do you know where I can find him?"

She hesitated. "He went ta pray last night and hasn't come back. He's got somethin' weighin' on him."

Thomas looked into the eroded face. "What is it he has bothering him, Mrs. Dash?"

She shook her head, her expression troubled. "I don't know. I haven't seen 'im like this since he was in trouble before. He found the Lord, but he shouldn'ta come back here. He shoulda stayed away."

Thomas thanked her.

He got in his car, took the state road three miles west, turned off at the cattle guard, and went up the same dirt track he and Oates had driven the Sunday before. Now it wasn't filled with cars. Instead there was just one old white pickup at the side of the road. He parked behind it and walked to the tent. It was empty now as well, except for a lone lizard that apparently had come to pray. It took one look at Thomas and skittered for cover.

Thomas saw Dash sitting on the side of the raised mound of earth that served as the altar, looking out at the land that was flat and empty all the way to the horizon. The sun was so strong that the prairie looked white, drained of color. Dash didn't appear to be praying, just staring across the empty expanse with the Bible in his hand. He hadn't shaved, and with his burnished face and in his black suit he looked like a twentieth-century holy man stranded in the desert.

He glanced up at Thomas, who stopped a few feet away. "I came to tell you something," he said. "Lloyd Haynes is dead. He shot himself just a little while ago."

Dash cringed, as if he had been shot himself. He studied Thomas's face until he was sure he wasn't lying, then he looked away and shook his head. "He was falling apart, old Lloyd."

Thomas nodded. "From guilt, I guess. Before he did it, he confessed to having killed Johnny Campos. I heard it and so did at least one other person. He said you were there that night."

Dash stared out at the prairie before speaking. "Yes, I witnessed it."

"Haynes said you did more than witness it. He said it was your heroin that he made Campos shoot up with. That made you guilty of possession. He also said that you had paid him protection money to let you deal drugs in Paradise and that Johnny Campos found out about it."

Dash's eyes narrowed defensively.

"Like I said, someone else heard it as well," Thomas told him, "a neighbor of his." Thomas stood over him. "It was your heroin?"

Dash nodded pensively. "Yes, that's right. Johnny, he didn't do nothin' like that. I didn't either, not heroin, but I was gonna that night for the first time. I told Johnny to be there with me just in case somethin' went wrong. And somethin' did go wrong."

"Lloyd Haynes showed up looking for some payoff money."

"He did, and then Johnny came. Johnny didn't know nothin' about the money changin' hands, but he heard Lloyd and me talkin' and Lloyd freaked out. That was enough. He figured Johnny knew and he pulled his gun out. At first he thought of arresting us both, but since he'd taken money from me, he didn't want to do that. Not that it was any big amount of cash. I dealt a little speed and some pot. Me and Lloyd, we was both real small-time. But he didn't want me anywhere near the sheriff. I think he might have shot us, except Johnny and I didn't carry no guns or weapons and everybody knew that."

"So Haynes made Johnny shoot the heroin?"

Dash nodded. "I had it out before he came, gettin' it ready. Lloyd saw it and made me cook it up for Johnny. He said a boy with needle marks in his arm, heroin in his system, nobody would believe a thing he said. Especially if he was a Mexican." Dash shook his head. "But I think he wanted it ta kill Johnny right there. Lloyd was always crazy. He made us sit next to each other against the wall, kept the gun on us and made me cook it, and load it. Then he made Johnny put it in his arm. He found a vein and I saw some blood go up into the hypodermic and he shot it. I saw Johnny was scared as hell. The I saw his eyes go big all of a sudden." He glanced at Thomas, but his own eyes were glazed. "It was like he'd seen God, ya know? And then he just fell over. He started to shake. I didn't know if it had been an overdose or maybe he'd gotten a bubble in there. But he went out."

"And Haynes?"

"He stood there with the gun and didn't move. I don't know if Johnny died right away, but Lloyd didn't move and wouldn't let me move. Johnny stopped breathin' right there. Then I was afraid he'd kill me, since I seen it."

"Why didn't he?"

Dash shrugged. "He woulda had to shoot me right there and like I said, that coulda been hard to explain. He also didn't know who else I mighta told about the payoffs. On top of that, he knew nobody would believe me if I told that story about how Johnny died, especially since I was the one who had the heroin. I'd be riskin' my own skin. He knew I'd keep my mouth shut and do what I was told. I was a coward and nothin' else."

"He told you to get out of town."

"That's right. And I got out because I knew if I didn't he *would* kill me."

"How about William Vega, what did he know?"

"He was a buddy of ours. Later, after Haynes let me go, I met up with William and told 'im what had happened. He was scared too. We both knew nobody would ever believe us. He's Mexican and he figured he wouldn't last in Paradise."

"So he blew town too."

"That's right. William headed down to some folks he had in McAllen and I just started to drift."

"Until you found the Lord," Thomas said cynically.

Dash looked up at him now with a wounded expression.

"Oh, I did find the Lord, brother. Or He found me. Don'tcha bet against it. He chased me into the darkest corners of the earth, until I had veins fulla holes and a mind fulla pain. I won't tell ya the things I saw and did. But then the Lord dragged me up outa the filth. That's a true story."

Thomas frowned, not knowing whether to believe him.

"Then you came home and you brought Lloyd Haynes into the church with you. How was that?"

"He'd had the accident. It ruined his health and his mind. I went ta see him. I told him I was back and that what had happened to him had been a message from God, just like I'd gotten a message from the Lord. I told 'im we had the goods on each other, but it didn't matter. We'd leave all that behind. He could go straight like me. Straight to the Lord."

Thomas stood over him now.

"But you didn't go straight. You were still involved with drug drops over the ranch lands."

Dash looked up with big eyes.

"That ain't so, brother. I haven't touched drugs, either ta take them or ta sell them since the Lord chased me down. And if I'm lyin', let Him strike me right here." He lifted an arm into the sky like a lightning rod.

"Then what was William Vega doing here? He was here to see you about drug business."

Dash shook his head. "He was here in a way on drug business, but not with me."

"So you did see him?"

Dash nodded. "Yes, but only after you told me he was here. Only last night. I didn't bear false witness. I didn't lie to you. I hadn't seen 'im. Then last night he came ta see me after all the trouble downtown."

"What for?"

"He wanted to know if I had a gun."

Thomas frowned. "What for?"

"He said there was a person who owed him something here and they weren't paying up. But when I asked him about it, it turned out he was blackmailing someone, a man who he knew had become involved in smuggling. He said he heard about it down in McAllen after that smuggler was killed here a few months ago. That fella was from McAllen too. William said he talked to people he knew there and figured out who the contact person was up here. It turned out it was a man with lots of money, so he came up here to squeeze some of that money out of 'im. But the man was resisting and that's why William wanted the gun, to scare 'im."

"What did you do?"

Dash shook his head. "I didn't give 'im no gun. I don't have one and I wouldn'ta if I did. I told him he should stop right now. Get on his knees and turn to the Lord, just like I had. But he wouldn't listen. He had to do it anyway."

"Who was it he was blackmailing? Whom did he go to see?"

Dash gazed out further west of town.

"You go talk to Landon Turner. I went out there last night to warn him and to try to get him to come to the Lord. He told me it was too late."

"You told him Vega might be after him?"

Dash nodded.

Thomas had to get out of there, but there were a couple more things to set straight.

"Who set fire to the *Chronicle*?"

Dash shook his head. "I don't know, but I think it mighta

been Lloyd. I asked him and he just looked at me. He had that kinda madness in him."

"And why did you go after Margaret Masters the way you did? Why did you try to drive her out of Paradise, to ruin her life? Was that Lloyd's madness too?"

Dash frowned at him as if he didn't understand the question. "Because she's lost her way, brother," he said. "And she is leadin' the town that way too. Her sin is written all over 'er, just like the good book says: 'Mystery, Babylon the Great, the Mother of Harlots and Abominations of the Earth.'"

Dash's conversion was no act, no scam, not as far as Thomas could tell. He left the preacher sitting in his own private desert and headed for the Buckknife Ranch.

Chapter 24

*T*homas took the dirt track back to where it connected to the state road and then did seventy-five on that abandoned stretch until he reached the sign of the saw-toothed knife. Near the entrance, cattle had come through a hole in the fence and he had to slow down and inch his way through the milling steers. He got through them and headed for the old ranch house, a plume of dust rising behind him.

On either side of him the grazing lands of the ranch lay under the sun looking even drier and deader than they had before. Thomas left the brick complex behind and a minute later pulled up under the elms outside the original Turner ranch headquarters. The same two horses were in one corral and there were steers in the other. There was no one around and no noise. The helicopter was no longer clattering in the sky and the pickup truck was gone. Except for the pumpjack next to the house, it might have been sixty years ago.

Thomas found the door to the ranch office open. It was empty, but another door leading into the interior of the house was open and he stuck his head in. He found Landon Turner by himself in what had been the old sitting room. The room looked much as it must have sixty years before, too. The furniture was old American colonial. There were sepia photos of family members on the walls. Prominent among them were two men wearing Stetsons. Both men had rugged, lined faces, and both of them strongly resembled Landon Turner, except for the defeat in the eyes. They had to be his grandfather and father. There was also a stuffed wolf's head, probably one killed for bounty by the patriarch of the Turner family sixty years before. There was a marked resemblance between the wolf and the two portraits.

Also on the wall was a rifle rack that held three old repeater rifles, Remingtons or Winchesters, Thomas assumed, with beautiful filigreed metalwork. Another rifle was propped next to Turner, who sat on a couch. He was looking into the fireplace as if there were a fire there. Or maybe he was examining the ashes of his life. He hadn't shaved since the last time Thomas had seen him and again he smelled of liquor. He glanced up with a look much like that worn by his ancestors.

"You breakin' inta people's houses now, are ya?"

Thomas, feeling like a bounty hunter himself, walked farther into the room.

"I need to talk to you. It could mean saving your life."

The other man smirked. "My life ain't worth savin'. Don't bother."

Thomas moved closer. "William Vega may be on his way here and he may be armed."

Turner nodded. "Oh, he's been here already." He pointed at a side doorway which led out toward the old bunkhouse. The frame around the door was splintered where it apparently had been hit by something. On the floor beneath that scar there was what appeared to be blood. Thomas studied it.

"You shot Vega?"

Turner shrugged. "I didn't shoot him bad. I just grazed him." He sighed, his large, soft stomach rising and falling under his shirt. "I shoulda killed him given what he was tryin' to do to me, but I don't have the guts for it."

He sounded disappointed in himself that he was incapable of murder, if, in fact, he was.

"What happened to him?"

Turner pointed back over the ranch lands toward Paradise. "He staggered out that way. I assume he was goin' back to town."

"When was that?"

"Two hours ago."

"Was he blackmailing you?"

"He was tryin' to. He was preying on me, like a vulture. I'm almost dead and he was preying on me."

"Because you were smuggling drugs?"

Turner's expression went sour. "I didn't smuggle nothin'. I'm what they call an accessory. I wasn't even a smuggler."

"You were on the ground, the local contact."

"That's right. A man I met from Odessa knew I was havin' trouble and put me in touch with some fellas from down south Texas. They're in the business. All they needed they said was somebody who knew the ranch roads around here and had a reason for being out and around here at night. All I had to do was drive out to a prearranged place, blink my lights when I heard the plane and the guys with me picked up the bags when they fell to the ground."

"And they gave you a cut."

"Not that it amounted to much, not given what I owe."

"Vega found out about your involvement from someone down in McAllen."

"That's right, and he came up here ta bleed me."

"Did you pay him anything?"

Turner shook his head. "Like I said, I didn't have anything ta pay him. I told him that, but he didn't believe me. He said if I didn't come across with twenty thousand dollars, he'd go to the authorities here and give them everything he knew from his friends in McAllen."

"So what did you do?"

"I went to Sam Cain and confessed everything to him. I'd known Sam all my life. He was my daddy's lawyer. He told me I'd been stupid and that now I should go to Jack Eames, turn state's evidence, cooperate, and I might get off free. He said Jack would understand my situation."

"Is that what you did?"

Turner nodded. "First Sam talked to Jack. That was the day before he got attacked."

Thomas frowned. "Sam Cain's skull being cracked might have had something to do with that. Maybe your business partners caught on."

"Not that I can see," Turner said. "They had no way of knowing. Only me and Sam and Jack knew about it. I don't have any idea who did that to Sam or why."

"And then you saw Eames yourself?"

"That's right."

"When was that?"

"Friday, the day before the twister hit."

"When Dan Oates and I saw you at his house?"

"No. I already went ta see him earlier in the day. I told him everything and about this Vega trying to bleed me, too. I said I'd rather just see him run off. I didn't want no more scandal than necessary. Jack said he'd see what he could do."

Thomas nodded. "That was why he was at the motel talking to him Friday evening when I pulled in."

"When you saw me later outside Jack's house, that's when I was going back to see what had happened. To try and make sure it would all be done as quiet as possible."

"And the black bag with the drugs in it?"

"I handed that over to Jack earlier. I had it from the last drop they'd made. It got lost down in a ravine and I had to go back later and get it."

"So it was already in Eames's house when the twister hit," Thomas said. "Although it wasn't where the sheriff found it. Somebody tampered with it."

Thomas was convinced Turner had been telling the truth until that moment. Then ideas started skulking around behind his desolate, bloodshot eyes, the way they had the first two times they had talked.

"I don't know nothin' about that," he said.

"Did the sheriff know about this deal you'd cut with Jack Eames?" Turner shook his head.

"Then you're going to have to tell him all of this," Thomas said. "Maybe Layton will give you the immunity from prosecution that Jack Eames offered, maybe he won't."

Turner nodded tiredly. Thomas glanced at the rifle propped against the sofa. Turner followed his eyes and then looked back at him.

"Don't worry, I ain't gonna use it on myself. I don't have the courage for that either."

Thomas believed him. Landon Turner was a defeated man.

"Do you know where Vachel Niles is?"

"He's out on the ranch somewhere."

Thomas left him sitting there staring at the old photos of his ancestors and the stuffed wolf head.

He got into his car and took the dirt track that cut through the grazing lands, and passed stands of cattle on the almost grassless ranch lands. They watched him closely as he went by, as if they knew that he meant trouble for the Buckknife Ranch.

He saw the white horse tied underneath a small windmill, next to a large cement water trough. Cattle were grouped around the trough waiting to drink and he saw Vachel Niles up in the windmill, where he was apparently making repairs. Niles was just climbing down as Thomas pulled up. Thomas stroked the horse's flank.

"Quite a beauty," he said.

Niles wiped the sweat off his creased face with a blue bandanna. "He's as good a horse as there is around here."

"This is the horse you rode the night you went to town, isn't it? The night after the storm hit."

Niles moved to the other side of the horse, glancing at Thomas under the brim of his hat.

"That's right, it is."

Thomas held the bridle to keep the horse still.

"But you didn't just go to town. You went specifically to Jack Eames's house and you didn't just go to look, did you? You went to make sure there was nothing in the ruins of Eames's house that would incriminate Landon Turner."

Niles's sky-blue eyes stormed over, but he said nothing.

"You don't have to worry, Turner told me everything. I know about the drug drops. I know he was trying to make money to pay his debts."

Niles looked past him, back toward the ranch house.

"You went to make sure there was nothing to tie Landon Turner to those drugs or to that black bag he'd given Eames," Thomas said. "Because you knew once Eames was dead there was no way of telling if the deal Landon had cut would stand up. Is that it?"

Niles shook his head sadly. "You put your whole life into a place and you can't stand to see it lost, especially the way this one was lost. And you put your whole life inta helpin' raise a boy and you don't wanna see him lost either. I told Coy Turner I'd help take care o' both of them, the ranch and the boy, and I didn't do a very good job."

"So you went, found that black bag, but you left it there. Why?"

Niles didn't look at Thomas, as if he were ashamed for having been mixed up with such things—the sins of the modern world.

"I found it under some tiles and I looked inta it ta make sure there was nothin' Jack Eames had put in there that identified Landon with it. He wasn't really a smuggler, ya know? He was just tryin' ta save the place, what was left of it. We'd run it the way we used ta. No helicopters."

"But you left it there."

"There was some National Guard close by and I was afraid they'd seen me. I didn't wanna be riding away from the place carryin' anything. I just left it there."

"So you knew all about it?"

Niles gazed sadly at the ranch lands. "I knew at first that he was disappearin' some nights and after a while I figured it out. He got hisself mixed up with rattlesnakes, because that's what those smugglers are. But by then it was too late. The day of the twister I saw 'im frettin' and got out of him that he'd given that bag to Jack Eames. And how he could be in a lotta trouble 'cause of it."

He looked at Thomas. "What's gonna happen to Landon now?"

"I don't know. Maybe he can cut the same deal he cut with Jack Eames."

"Da ya think he'll lose the place altogether? Old Coy'll see me in hell if that happens."

"I don't know."

Niles licked his dry lips and stared into the glaring sunlight.

"I knew somethin' like this would happen. I knew it when they first hit oil here, when the first derrick went up. I said ta myself, 'Another world is comin' here. It's all gonna change.' And I was right. The people who came here weren't cattle people. The land wasn't the same thing to them, just a place to put holes in. It didn't mean nothin to 'em. Just what was under it and how much money they could take out of it. Men didn't mean anything to 'em either. The way those men had worked and lived for years and years." He shook his head. "Now we hardly got any livestock. Nobody rides a horse. People from the other side o' the earth own it. Don't even know what it looks like. They don't know how to work it and they never tasted its dust."

Niles grimaced from the bitterness of the dust or his fate. Thomas left him there and headed back to town.

Chapter 25

*A*ll the way to town Thomas scanned the grazing land off the state road looking for William Vega, expecting to see him stumbling along or maybe collapsed, vultures circling overhead. He didn't see a sign of him.

Thomas saw Oates's Bronco parked outside the Sheriff's Department. He found the editor sitting on a wooden bench in the hallway, writing in a notebook.

"Composing the Lloyd Haynes story?" Thomas asked.

Oates looked up from his notebook. "I'm chronicling more of the terrible history of Paradise," the big man said somberly.

"You better hold off some. There's more to it."

Thomas sat down and told him of going to see Dash and

what he had learned about the death of Johnny Campos.
Then he related his visit to the Buckknife Ranch, his con-
versations with Turner and Niles, all about the smuggling
and about William Vega being on the loose.

Oates listened, his eyes narrowing and his wide shoulders slumping. He looked as though he were aging right
in front of Thomas's eyes. "Jim West left a while ago to
go talk to Dash," he said. "He'll probably get the same
story, go see Landon Turner, and be out looking for
Vega." He grimaced. "So Landon Turner not only risked
and lost his family's fortune, the whole empire, he lost
their reputation too."

"Depending on the deal he cuts with the new county
attorney," Thomas said.

Oates's expression hardened. "No, it doesn't depend on
that. Because I'm not gonna sweep it under the rug. If the
man wants to smuggle drugs, I'll print it, no matter what
kind of deal he cuts."

He glowered at the portraits of old sheriffs that lined
the hallway.

"You don't think it was him or his business partners from
down in McAllen who were responsible for the killing of
Jack Eames and of Sam Cain, do you?"

"No," Thomas said. "I believe Turner when he says he
doesn't have the ability to kill somebody. He's greedy and
foolish but not murderous. And if it had been his business
partners, they would have used more modern technology
to get rid of people, like assault rifles, not stones and
skulls."

"So who did kill those men?"

"The first question is why were they killed? If it wasn't
Turner and it didn't have to do with drugs, then why did
they die? What's the connection among Cain, Eames, and
Gamble? The first two were lawyers and politicians, but
the last was an old wildcatter. Cain and Gamble knew each
other from the thirties and had some kind of land deal
going, but what did that have to do with Eames? Unless

Cain and Gamble were involved in some swindle and Eames found out about it. Except Landon Turner still insists there was no swindle."

Oates's long body was bent over his notebook like a question mark as he thought. The sheriffs on the wall watched him and Thomas. Then the editor straightened up and looked down the corridor.

"You know, there is something else that connects them."

"What?"

Oates pointed down the hallway.

"I was here a few days ago, after the tornado, and I bumped into Mattie Archer, an old girl who works in the Land Records office. We started talking about the killings of Sam Cain and Jack Eames and she told me she felt spooked because both those men had been in her office looking at land records just last week."

Thomas raised his eyebrows and Oates shook his head.

"That wasn't anything too unusual. They're both lawyers and Sam Cain had clients with land and Jack would be here to look into tax cases."

"So why is it important?"

"The connection is that later that same day, while I was walking down that same corridor, I happened to glance into Mattie's office and I saw somebody in there. It was Walt Gamble. I didn't make anything of it at the time and I forgot all about it. But now Walt Gamble's dead, too, isn't he?"

"So all of them were in there in the past week?"

Oates nodded.

"Well, then maybe we should go talk to your friend Mattie Archer."

Oates led him down that corridor to another, then to the back of the building and entered an office marked Land Records. It was a room lined floor to ceiling with bookcases all filled with ledgers bound in red. Behind a long wooden counter like a judge's bench sat a woman with blued hair, wearing bifocal glasses. She looked through the top of them as the two men walked in.

"Good afternoon, Mattie."

"Hello, Dan."

She sat ramrod stiff, protecting her records. Oates introduced Thomas and began to explain why they'd come, but she cut him off.

"Oh, I know why you're here," she said. She reached under her bench and produced one of the red ledgers, a bookmark protruding from it. "I just became aware of it myself this morning. I was gonna tell the sheriff."

Oates's broad brow creased. "What was that?"

"About the three men, the men who were killed. They all came in here and they all looked at the same volume." She glanced down at it as if it were cursed. "I don't really keep track of what ledgers folks ask for, not in my head, but I happened to look at the user list and noticed it. When the men have died recently and all asked for the same ledger and same plot of land, that's quite a coincidence." Her face assumed a canny expression, making it clear she didn't think it was a coincidence at all.

Oates turned the ledger around and opened it. The first lined pages were yellowed with age and filled with entries written in faded blue ink. Each entry was made on one line running across the page: a name or names, dates, and then sets of letters that Thomas didn't understand.

"What is this about?"

"It's a record of any land transaction of any kind for each lot in Paradise County, going all the way back to the homestead days. Is that right, Mattie?"

"It's more than that," she said. "It tells ya not only who sold the land and bought it, and controlled it, but who paid taxes on it, who owned shares, who drilled on it and who made claims on it." She looked again through the tops of her bifocals at Thomas. "All respect to our local preachers, but this here is the Bible in Paradise."

She opened the ledger to the bookmark. "This is the lot all three of 'em wanted to know about."

The page started as the other had, with neat longhand entries in blue ink. At the top of the page it said Section

27, Lot 8. Thomas remembered now the small signpost near Walt Gamble's trailer.

Beneath the lot number came the first entry: from State of Texas, to Juan Jose Vega Mendez et al., July 7, 1910, then the letters AWD.

"What does that mean?"

Mattie tapped the entry with a long fingernail. "AWD stands for award. It means the state gave the Vega family that land as a homestead. That's how all the entries in these books start. This was one of the Vega sections."

Under the first entry came another: Juan Jose Vega Mendez, 9-13-13, to Pedro Vega Sanchez, AH.

"That AH is an affidavit of heirship. It means old man Vega died but left the land to this other man, probably his son. The second last name is different because the two men had different mothers, of course, and that's the name of the mother. Mendez changed to Sanchez, but it's the same family."

The next line read: Pedro Vega Sanchez to State of Texas, 6-21-34, OA., and under that, Payne Turner, AWD.

Mattie tapped the line. "This is where it changed ownership, changed families. OA stands for occupancy affidavit. It means somebody challenged the Vega family's right to the land. If you got a homestead you had to stay on it. But lots of people lost their land when the droughts hit and they went to work someplace else. This means the state took the land away from the Vegas and Payne Turner took it over. It was probably he who challenged the ownership. He did that with other folks."

Mattie Archer's voice had gone cold. She didn't like what Turner had done to the Vegas. Her finger went down the page.

"The Turners took over the land and here the next entry says OGL. That means oil and gas lease. That's where they sold the drilling rights. They made a lotta money there."

Further down Thomas saw the name Atty. Sam Houston Cain and next to it PA. He pointed at it.

"What's this?"

"It's where Sam Cain was given power of attorney to represent the Turners' interests," she said.

Below that line came a list of names of individuals. It filled that page and each of the next six pages of the ledger. In the middle of the list the entries started to be type-written. That was in the forties. Next to each name were the letters RD. Mattie turned the pages.

"These are all royalty deeds, RD, sold to investors from all over the country. These were people who invested twenty or fifty dollars or even five dollars. They invested in an oil well that got drilled on that lot. There were hundreds of these people, all of whom believed in the oil boom. They each got a fraction of one percent of the profits, if there were any."

Her finger went down a long list of entries that covered the rest of that page. Then she stopped and she tapped a line. It said: Pedro Vega Sanchez, 7-8-1939, CL.

"Here's the Vegas claiming the land is still theirs. CL stands for claim. The Turners had sold the drillin' rights and it was worth a lot of money."

She turned the next few pages, filled with the names of investors, the dates of renewed drilling leases, tax suits, and, regularly, challenges by the Vega family. Sam Cain's name always appeared in defense of the Turner interests. Mattie Archer stopped again at an entry: Coy Turner to Landon Turner, 10-2-80, AH. "That's where Coy died. He was the son of Payne Turner and left the ranch to Landon. That was ten years ago." She turned pages until she got to the end. The last entry was dated just a month before: Landon Turner to Sam Cain, WD. "That means warranty deed. It means it was sold by Landon to Sam Cain. Or at least Sam took over ownership of it. That was the last bit of business."

"So the Vega family always claimed that it was theirs."

Mattie nodded. "Unless they filed a quitclaim. Some-times an owner agreed to a settlement with people who made claims on their lands. Then those people would take the money and sign a quitclaim, which meant they gave up their claim."

She flipped back through the pages and shook her head. "I don't see one filed here, which means they never did give up their claim. Sometimes, real bad blood developed between families over those claims."

Thomas turned to Oates. "Maybe that's what William Vega meant when he told Sam Dash that somebody owed him something." He tapped the book. "Is there a William Vega listed as making a claim?"

Her finger went down the last page of typewritten entries and then stopped. "Here's the last claim on this lot. It was only two years ago." The line read: Landon Turner, 1-2-88, Maria Esperanza Sanchez Vega de Clark, CL."

Mattie Archer looked up at Oates.

"That's the girl who married Tom Clark, isn't it? The Clark who ran off."

Thomas looked at Oates. "William Vega and Esperanza Vega."

Then he followed the big man out the door.

Chapter 26

*T*homas and Oates walked the three blocks to the small civil-defense clinic at the corner of Alamo and State. The van with the red cross on it was parked outside the old ocher brick building. Although the hours posted said the facility was closed, Oates tried the door and found it open. As they walked in Thomas noticed dark spots on the floor. Oates saw them as well and stopped. It was blood.

They were still standing there when Esperanza Clark, dressed in her white nurse's uniform, came through a doorway into the reception area. She stopped halfway in the room and with those dark, soulful eyes of hers, looked up at Oates, who was almost twice her size, and then at Thomas.

"Good afternoon, Esperanza," the editor said.

She stood there several moments without answering, then picked up a package of cotton from the reception desk and went back through the doorway. Thomas and Oates followed her into another room and found William Vega lying on an examination table. His upper arm was wrapped in a bloodstained towel. There were more drops of blood on the floor beneath him. As they walked in he tried to sit up, but Esperanza put a hand on his chest.

"No, William. It's no good." She said it sternly into his frightened face and pushed him back down. Vega glared at the two journalists, but laid his head back on the table.

She took the towel off his arm and revealed an ugly wound in his bicep, just beneath the tattoo of the eagle with the snake in its claws. She took out the cotton and began to clean around the gash. On the walls were posters. One warning about the danger of leaving guns lying around in the reach of children. Another of an old Mexican cathedral. There was a paperweight on the desk, a rock like those Thomas had seen in Walt Gamble's trailer and also around the old man's body, rocks that had been used to kill him.

Thomas came up next to the examination table, Vega watching him suspiciously.

"Is William your brother, Esperanza?"

"No, he's my cousin," she said, daubing at the wound. "But he can't talk to you right now."

"It's not William we came to talk to," Thomas said. "It's you."

Vega's eyes shifted to her with alarm and then he tried to get up again. She put her arm across his chest, put her face to his, and told him to lie still. The younger man smoldered, looked up at Oates, who had come a step closer, and didn't move.

She went back to cleaning the wound. "What is it you want to know?"

"Was it you or William who tried to kill Sam Cain?"

Her head snapped around at him.

"William did nothing," she said. "Do you understand?"

The anger in her and the quality of the dejection in the face of Vega right then made Thomas believe it. He reached over and picked up the paperweight.

"Sam Cain kept your family from getting back its homestead," Thomas said. "That was the beginning, wasn't it?"

She put her foot on the pedal of the waste can, threw a piece of bloody cotton in, and let it slam closed.

"He stole it from us," she said flatly. "It was Cain who told old man Turner he should take that land from us. Because of the drought, Grandfather couldn't live off the ranch, couldn't feed his family. So he went to Amarillo to work for a couple of years, but he would come back from time to time to keep our claim to the land, Turner knew that and Cain knew it too, but they lied to the state. Turner just wanted more land for his cattle, more land just to have it. And because he was a powerful man, the law did what he and Cain wanted no matter what my grandfather said."

"Then they found oil around here."

She nodded. Vega was staring at the ceiling. He had heard the sad story many times before, Thomas figured.

"That's right," she said. "Instead of owning oil wells, my grandfather and his brothers and sons had to work on the oil fields as hired hands. They were Mexican and they didn't even get the good jobs. Sometimes they didn't work at all. The Turners could have given us back just a small piece of it and things would have been much easier. My grandfather asked them for that, but they wouldn't listen. The Turners were greedy and dishonest and Sam Cain did all their legal dirty work for them. I knew about Sam Cain from the time I was a baby. He was the villain in the fairy tales I knew when I was a kid."

Thomas hefted the rock in his hand.

"But why now, after fifty, sixty years? What did it have to do with that piece of land, with these rocks?"

She poured disinfectant on the wound and Vega flinched.

"Walt Gamble came here a couple of months ago to get a cut looked after. He saw that rock sitting on my desk and asked me where I'd gotten it. I told him that my father had taken it from a drilling site that he had worked on after World War II. That it was land our family had once owned." She looked up at Thomas. "You understand he had to break his back working on a rig on his own land, when he should have been sitting back pulling in the profits. He worked himself to death."

"Gamble knew something about this kind of rock?" Thomas asked. "He saw money in it?"

She nodded. "Yes, but he didn't tell me that. He just asked where it came from and I told him. I didn't think anything about it. Then I heard that after Landon Turner had his money problems, Sam Cain had gotten hold of that land and that maybe they were gonna drill for something on it. Walt Gamble was going around telling people it was worth a fortune.

"One day I bumped into Sam Cain on the street. He told me right out that they hoped there was something valuable on the land, a mineral that was used in space technology. He didn't even remember who I was and what my family had to do with the land, even though I'd continued making claims, even though he had stolen it from us."

"But you let him know?"

"Right there I told him, on the street. I told him Walt Gamble would never have known that mineral was on the land if it weren't for me. That the Turners would never have owned it if he hadn't stolen it from us. And he just walked away. He didn't care. He was nothing but a thief."

"When was it you talked to him?"

"Last Monday."

"And the next morning you went back to argue with him some more."

She shook her head. "I didn't even try to talk to him. It wouldn't have done any good." She glanced at the bloody cotton in her hand. "Things have been very rough these last few years. You have kids, your husband has run out on you, and you're having to scrape. You look at the man who could change all that, who could have changed your whole life. He was a bad man. There are lots of bad men around here." Her voice trailed off.

"How about Jack Eames?" Thomas asked, turning to Vega. "Was that you, William? I saw Eames talking to you outside the motel. Was he telling you that your attempt to blackmail Landon Turner was over and you should get out of Paradise?"

Esperanza was shaking her head. "I told you William didn't do anything to anyone. That money he was trying to get out of Turner was really ours to begin with. Any money he had was ours because of what they had stolen from us."

Thomas looked from Vega back to her.

"And William told Jack Eames that and maybe he even told him about the claims you had made on the land. Did Eames figure out that you had a motive to kill Sam Cain?" Vega turned his face away and Thomas knew he was right. "Did he go to see you?"

She was still daubing around the wound. She worked on her cousin's arm with the utmost gentleness, as she recalled her murders.

"He went to my house, but I wasn't there," she said. "I found out that night when I got back. I didn't want him coming to my house where my children were. So I went to see him, thinking he just wanted to talk to me about William and Turner." She looked at Oates and then back at Thomas. "But he was like you. He wanted to talk about me."

"He accused you of attacking Sam Cain?"

"He asked me about it. I explained to him everything that had happened between our two families. But it didn't matter to him either. He was going to take their side in it. It didn't matter what Sam Cain had done to me and my family."

"Where did you get a gun?"

She shrugged. "It was my husband's. He bought it from a guy here years ago."

"Unregistered," Thomas said.

She nodded. "Jack Eames saw it in my hand, ran out of the office and into the bedroom trying to get away. He was a bum, I knew what he'd done to Margaret and to Laurel Davis before her."

"You shot him and wiped the prints off it," Thomas said. "When the tornado hit the next morning, you went to see what happened when he was found. You saw me there and you saw him dead."

She nodded as she placed gauze over the wound in her cousin's arm.

"Then there was Walt Gamble. That night at the funeral home, Viola Buffet, Cain's secretary, told you that Gamble had talked to Cain and that they had an appointment for the next afternoon. When I came in you knew she would tell me the same thing and you figured I might go back and talk to Gamble and he would tell me about what was on the land and how he'd found out. You left the wake and drove to his mobile home and killed him."

"Walt Gamble was helping Sam Cain to cheat us. He got what he deserved. He was another one of the bums around here."

"In between killing Eames and Gamble, you had to make sure Sam Cain didn't wake up. After he died, staff at the hospital said that apart from Margaret Masters, nobody but hospital personnel had been in his room. But you worked in the hospital during the emergency after the storm. You were in your uniform and you went in and unplugged the respirator and walked out. No one noticed. You also left that lamb in the park, didn't you?"

She nodded avidly at Thomas. "Oh yes. I felt bad about Margaret. I didn't want to see her suffer more than she already had and I wasn't going to let her go to jail. If they had found her guilty I would have confessed."

Thomas believed her. She, unlike Landon Turner, could mount righteous anger, but she would not let the innocent suffer. She clipped the bandage in place over her cousin's arm and then went to the sink to wash the blood off her hands.

"I don't understand these men," she said, watching the blood come off and go down the drain. "They think you'll forget what's been done to you. They want to forget the bad they have done to you, and they want you to help them by forgetting it too.

"Like my husband. He was like that. He wanted to forget me and the children and he told me to forget him too. Even though I had known him all my adult life and even though he knew things would be real hard for us. How could I forget him?"

Thomas saw Oates stir. The big man was looking at her as if she were a bomb that might suddenly go off. Thomas read his mind.

"Where is your husband, Esperanza?" Thomas asked her. "What happened to him?"

She shook the water off her hands, grabbed a towel, and dried them. Her eyes fell on the rock that once again sat on the desk and then went from Oates to Thomas. She didn't say a word. She didn't have to.

Oates went out to use the phone on the reception desk to call the sheriff. Seconds later there was the sound of sirens approaching.

Chapter 27

*F*ive weeks later Thomas drove back into Paradise bringing copies of *Epoch* magazine in which his article appeared. It was the cover story for that issue and was illustrated by a drawing of a posse chasing the Devil across the prairies. Satan, horns and all, was on horseback wearing a Stetson, spurs, a six-shooter and a wicked grin. The leader of the posse, a gold star on his chest, looked not like Jim West but suspiciously like Marshall Mundy.

Thomas also brought with him a check from a journalists' organization in New York, a contribution toward the rebuilding of the *Chronicle*. He drove right to the newspaper office, where he found a new front wall had been constructed and a new window installed. But the inside was still smoke-stained, and Oates was having to work on

a typewriter at an old wooden desk. The big man greeted
Thomas as he always did.

"So where have you been?"

Thomas dropped a copy of *Epoch* on the desk. Oates
glanced at the cover suspiciously, but said nothing.

"I've been in New York," Thomas said, dropping into a
chair. He slid the check across the desk. "Here's a bit of
solidarity from the hacks back East." Oates picked it up
and read it. Thomas could see emotion rising in him.

"You'll tell me who to get in touch with to express my
thanks."

"Yes." Thomas leaned back in his chair. "Now tell me
what's gone on here in Paradise."

Oates filled him in. Esperanza Clark had confessed to
four counts of murder and was awaiting sentencing. The
sheriff's men had opened another dry well near the land
Sam Cain had acquired and had found the remains of Fred
Clark, her husband. He had been identified through dental
charts, and further tests established he had been dead
about five years, which coincided with his disappearance
from Paradise.

"She asked about you," Oates said. "She wanted you to
know she was sorry she'd hit you over the head. I think it
was really the only thing she was sorry about. The rest of
her victims were better off dead, as far as she was concerned."

Her cousin William had been detained on charges of
blackmail, but was later released when Landon Turner
refused to press charges. Vega insisted he had known nothing of the killings and Esperanza backed him up.

Turner himself had been arrested on drug charges, but
Oates said it appeared he was cooperating with the au-
thorities and would get off with a reduced sentence. Vachel
Niles was in charge of the Buckknife Ranch.

Claude Denison had not been seen since he had been
cleared of the death of Walt Gamble and released. Lloyd
Haynes had been buried the day after Thomas had left
town.

"And the Reverend Dash?"

"Oh, he's still in his church. The sheriff's men talked to him and he confessed all about what happened five years ago. But Jim West decided to leave him alone and not stir up more trouble. As it is, his congregation has shrunk quite a bit. Folks, it appears, got scared hearing themselves talk about the end of the world and got scared about what was happening around here." Oates looked around the charred office. "But they also say Sam has changed his tune. He's talking less about the Apocalypse and more about God's love. Maybe this time he has found the Lord."

"And Margaret?"

Oates's face brightened. "The school board dropped the charges against her. Arthur Layton, who's the new county attorney, decided that she was protected by First Amendment guarantees, but also the movement to have her fired disintegrated. Even Laurel Davis has been quiet."

"Where can I find Margaret now?"

"The school year ended last week and I assume she's at home."

Thomas got up. "Read my article. See what you think. I'll be back later."

He drove down State Street to Houston. The political climate had changed, but the weather hadn't. It was blazing hot. Still, there were kids on the street who had just started their summer vacations.

As he approached Margaret Masters's house he saw the car in its port and that the side window in the study was still shattered. She answered the door herself, her dark eyes lighting with surprise.

"Hello, Quijote." She let him in and led him to the study. Schoolwork covered the desk and overflowed onto the floor.

"Still working?" he asked.

"No. Those are final exams, which I've already graded, and the grades have been turned in. I'm done for the year."

She poured him a Coke, and for herself not her usual gin but an orange juice. He studied her face and found her looking less pale, more rested. Her high cheekbones had some some color under them.

They took their customary seats, and lifted their glasses in a toast. "Here's to you and the First Amendment," she said.

"I understand you'll be teaching next year," said Thomas.

"They've told me I can come back. In fact, the chairman of the English Department is retiring and I'm next in line. So I'm going from being a triple murderess to being eligible for promotion. Quite a change of affairs. But first I have to decide if I want to stay at all. My friend Hester Prynne left town and didn't come back until she was old and gray." She sipped her juice. "And yourself? Off on another noble quest?"

"I have an assignment, but nothing heroic," Thomas said. "I have to write a travel piece on Alaska. It's not so much a job as a vacation. How about you?"

She shook her head. "Being at the center of a murder investigation, I totally forgot to make vacation plans. I thought I might be vacationing as a guest of the state. It would be nice to get out of this heat."

She looked out the window into the glaring June sun and then back at Thomas.

"Alaska sounds nice and cool, now, doesn't it?"